THE KILLING FRATERNITY

Stephen J. Prior

Copyright © 2025 Stephen J Prior

All rights reserved

The characters and events portrayed in this book are fictitious. Any similarity to real persons, living or dead, is coincidental and not intended by the author.

No part of this book may be reproduced, or stored in a retrieval system, or transmitted in any form or by any means, electronic, mechanical, photocopying, recording, or otherwise, without express written permission of the publisher.

ISBN-13: 9798303805446
ISBN-10: 1477123456

Cover design by: Art Painter
Library of Congress Control Number: 2018675309
Printed in the United States of America

For Lisa. Thank you for being the most tolerant woman alive. xx

THE KILLING FRATERNITY

ONE

No one sees anything on a crowded beach.

The husbands are too busy devouring young women in their colourful swimsuits and bikinis, desperate for their misremembered youth. The wives are watching their husbands, scoffing at the sucked-in stomachs and middle-age spread. The parents are glued to their children, forming a mental barrier between them and the waves, framing their location and memorising it. While their children aren't glued at all, especially not to the spot where they've promised faithfully to remain.

The bustling cafe owners and entrepreneurs scan the crowd, eager for trade. And the sculpted lifeguards observe nothing but the swell of the spitting churning ocean. Because no one ever drowned in the sand.

So, when a figure emerges from the water in a wet suit mid-afternoon, no one notices. When he undresses to trunks near the water's edge, he goes unseen. When he melts into the crowd, he is nobody. Vanishing with the castles hauled back to the sea, he too evaporates.

Invisible.

An illusion.

A bona fide beach ghost.

And when days later, a healthy young body with a harpoon through its stomach washes up along the shore?

Like all those sandy citadels, it is like our apparition never really existed at all.

TWO

There were two types of agents at Le Troisième, the liars and the fools. Leclerc was a fool. Worse, he was bound by heft to his desk. He would tell you that he had been in the field, but it was only ever to pick the fruit of his youth. Only there at all by luck, a drunken fumble with Marie Foucault anchored Leclerc with the first of their precocious brats and it was Marie's benevolent father who provided our ultimate supervision. Sat somewhere in that grand hierarchy of government responsibility, Monsieur Foucault's oversight was not so effective, however, that he could see through the idiot occupying desk number two in our petty pecking order.

Stood before me, scattering printouts from his email, Leclerc smiled. I don't know why. The images were sent to me four hours before the clown was even out of his lukewarm bed. It was a miracle he didn't suffocate poor Marie.

'What do you think?' He asked as though I had never seen a body with a harpoon through it. He hadn't, of course, because you cannot go swimming from a swivel chair, and his weight would have drowned him anyway.

The ugliest man in all of Christendom, his eyes were a size too small for his over-inflated face, and no razor blade ever fit between his thick lips and bulbous nose, so he declared a moustache and let it frame his crooked teeth. There wasn't a dark grey suit in the world to fit him.

'An accident?' He waved his arm to draw the sting of argument. He knew much better, of course, but we were not really on speaking terms Leclerc and me, not after he dropped me from the Mossad job. A man could tolerate only so many indiscretions, after all. 'Well, Berthier,' he pressed, 'what are you thinking?'

What I was thinking was that the ten thousand Euros he owed me was small change to remove yet another irritating asshole from my life, but the money was not mine to lend. Leclerc now held the keys to my honeymoon suite, and it was a door Gabrielle yearned for me to open.

'It was not an accident,' I told him.

'Pah. How can you be so sure?'

'Because there are no sharks to spearfish in the Golfe de Saint-Tropez.'

This may or may not have been true, I was no expert on marine biology. But I did know the man on my desk with a rod through him worked for the Direction générale de la sécurité extérieure.

And I knew for a fact it was no accident.

Because I knew the killer intimately.

Unlike Leclerc, I was one of the liars. The only honest man on our team of eight desks, one vacant since an almighty fuck-up the previous month, we didn't last long as a rule. Which is why it didn't matter that the overbearing bureaucrat was in charge. None of us lived long enough to complain.

'Well?' he said, again, and this was how he instructed us. No formality, no objectives, no detailed briefing around an electronic table of insight gathered by a network of informants. Just a glance from the pinprick eyes and a nod of the beachball head. For we were the mongrels of French intelligence, and we were only ever fed on scraps.

'Leave it with me,' I reassured him, watching as one of the newer guys fawned pathetically and Leclerc's fat ass disappeared from my orbit and into his. No doubt they had a politician to bug or oligarch to despatch, it was all the same to me. Just so long as I was left alone to fulfil my promise to Gabrielle. Right about then, she was loading the tiny Renault, ahead of a weekend relaxing in the woods–

She greeted me at the door with a rare frown, which pinched her nose and flattened the deep brown eyes to little more than upturned lashes. Sunglasses trapped her dark curls which erupted in any case, coiling down the faded white Levi's t-shirt tied to reveal her tanned stomach. Her denim shorts were barely decent, revealing a tiny heart inked on a bronze thigh. My God, I loved that woman.

'You're late.' She denied me a kiss, concerned her Dali heels would be melting in the little car's trunk.

I wanted to take the convertible, but it remained wilfully unrepaired, Monsieur Grosmond complaining that he could not summon the appropriate parts from 1963. There was a spare carburettor in my lock-up, which he would receive in due course, but I drove the Veloce Spider on my coastal errand, and it was safer on his ramps for a while.

Throwing my battered tan holdall into the back seat of the little blue hatchback, I spied an old favourite - Gabrielle's straw hat. It was the only thing either of us was wearing on the day we met. It was the last thing I noticed.

'Shall I drive?' she asked, knowing that I was exhausted after three days in the buying regions of Burgundy and Reims, where she no doubt imagined my indulgence was not curbed by the cork. Gabrielle would have abhorred the real me, but she adored the wine and art dealer I played. She drank and painted, and I approved wholeheartedly of both.

'Did you bring home samples?' is all she enquired of my trip, and I was pleased to report success, although the champagne was purchased that very morning on my account at *Lavinia* in central Paris. The store was a stones-throw from our ugly office above the pretty parfumier on rue des Capucines. Cornering too fast on purpose, she confirmed the bottles in the trunk, smiling and clutching my thigh. 'This is why you'll make a perfect husband,' she said, and I inferred from this that we were still very much in love.

I enjoyed Gabrielle's driving, and not only when I was tired. Her golden legs pedalled with the assurance of a racing driver, slipping the clutch and changing gear on the redline, drawing every ounce of breath from the throaty little motor which shivered at her expert touch. The brakes, she left mainly well alone.

'Did you miss me?'

Taking her gear-lever hand, I kissed it. 'Always.'

'And will we tell Isabella tonight?'

She meant, would we give her grandmother a date for the wedding, but I wouldn't. I wanted to quit the field first and assume a desk like Leclerc so that I was around to enjoy married life.

'We'll see.' She knew I meant "*no*" but didn't seem to mind, figuring perhaps that I might dispense with the handsome decorator who was making such painful progress on our kitchen if and when we wed.

From the quiet spaghetti strap incline of our approach, the monstrosity appeared. Leering awkwardly over us from its narrow clearing on the tree-covered slopes, Isabella's house was expertly designed for its magnificent views over Fontainebleau. But her late husband, a former Ministre des armées, must have commissioned a blind architect for the building was nothing more than angry angles of concrete and glass. Or perhaps the abject creation was a lasting memorial to his unhappy work. Either way, when Isabella died, no doubt the forest would reclaim the hectare of ugliness.

We stayed an hour, drank sweet wine and discussed the fate of Isabella's waning republic before departing at dusk. Then forty minutes later we arrived at our own hide-away, on the other side of the valley with a view over nothing and nobody, at the end of a wild track that disintegrated to woodland. There were no clues who built the original barn, but it was me who converted it, using a small builder from the regions, under oath and paid in cash. Besieged by firs, the low sun traced the top half of the door, cossetting the wide veranda from where it regularly perfected our immodest tans.

Before our first glass was empty, Gabrielle was throwing back her head as I watched her hair tumble and spill. She was eleven years my junior but didn't know it. Thank God for Le Troisième's quarterly medical and my mother's genes; she was a Californian athlete who married a Frenchman from Reims where she inherited and maintained a small vineyard with the help of my sister. It's why I elected to deal in wine when Gabrielle first asked. Beautiful, sensual, exquisite Gabrielle, whose back arched before she collapsed onto me again, pummelling my chest with her fists, then rolling off me in a cloud of contented sweat. After a minute or two she leaned over to her bedside table. I prayed the day I could no longer go her pace never came.

She rolled back, offering me a cigarette.

'I worry about mamie,' she said, indicating that, thank God, I wouldn't be required to go around a third time. It's not that I didn't want to, but I would hate to have disappointed my goddess. 'She didn't look well. I wonder how long she has left.'

'She'll outlive us both,' I said through a pall of Gitanes. In my case, it was almost certainly true.

She punched me. 'I'm serious. What if she were to die before we wed?'

'And what if the anticipation is the only thing keeping her alive?'

Gabrielle was bright. She was intelligent. She was executive assistant to a man who wielded the biggest sword in all French media, but her life was not dependent on quick wit, whereas I was only alive because mine was.

'I hate arguing with you, I need more practice.'

'That's why you're so keen to marry, then.'

Before she could respond, my telephone was vibrating violently, Gabrielle cursing likewise. 'I will use that damn thing next time, and to hell with you,' she crowed, but that was Colombia talking. Falling out of bed, she threw me the finger en route to the bathroom, and even though I am more French than Napoleon or Voltaire, she delivered her usual coupe de grace with meaning: 'Fucking Americans.'

Withheld number.

I debated answering.

There were several people I did not wish to speak to right then. But perhaps the wine, perhaps the afterglow – 'Berthier? Are you there? *Berthier*. Merde.'

'I'm here, Jean-Christophe. What do you want?'

'Where are you?'

'I'm at home, where else would I be?'

Jean-Christophe was one of the few tolerable fools. He worked the night shift from a fear of human contact, any contact in fact. He was another who was rarely in the field, for the public's safety as much as his own. He killed his demanding landlord - a junior agent at DGSE - in a fit of temper, but the man was a monstrous crook and Leclerc spared Jean-Christophe prison, instead sentencing him with us. He was the boss's poodle, but for some reason he heeled for me too.

'Something has come across the wire,' he said, waiting for me to ask him what. During interrogation training they taught him never to volunteer information, only they didn't distinguish friend from foe. Or maybe they did, and this was the unhappy result.

'Something for me, or something generally?'

He paused, his breath trembling and short.

'Come on JC, it's only me here. No one else.' An errant toilet flushed, and Gabrielle padded back towards me loudly humming the *Star-Spangled Banner*.

'Who's that?' Jean-Christophe barked, as I searched in vain for the mute button, leaping out of bed.

'Calm down, it's just the crazy woman in the apartment next door. She's on her balcony outside my window, but don't panic, the ugly old goat is deaf as a post'. I dodged a pillow and a second, scooting around the bed and out onto the veranda for real, pulling the door behind me. 'Tell me what's up and let me solve it for you.' I heard the lock turn so that both of us now had immovable problems in the middle of the night.

'I tried the boss,' he continued shakily, 'but he's not picking up.'

'It's fine, honestly, what's wrong?'

Another lengthy pause. 'It's Christine.' Jesus, it was like dragging blood from a corpse.

'What about Christine? Is she giving you a tough time again? Should I speak to her for you, or to Leclerc. You know with her it's probably just–'

'No, no, you can't speak to her, that's the whole point.'

'What is?'

He hesitated again, summoning courage from his pitiful reserves to tell me straight out as best he could. Mumbling, he said, 'Christine. She's *dead*, Berthier.'

THREE

The bespectacled pathologist was a heavyset morose man whose intonation made his description of the injuries sound like a whispered commentary on golf. He prodded and probed the body with disdain; autopsy was beneath him, and his laboured explanation was an adjunct to a busy schedule he could well have done without. It did not help that neither Leclerc nor I were introduced, so he peppered his patter with regular references to law enforcement to tease us from the dark into his unforgiving spotlight.

The body lay naked on a cold steel tray.

It was grey and stiff in every sense, legs tight together, arms by the sides, as though he would have preferred them bound behind her back. She was slim and once was healthy, but no longer. She could have been young or middle-aged from our viewpoint, the expert was keen to keep us waiting. He was revealing many secrets, but only to himself. For the two of us knew the corpse well.

'She was between thirty-eight and forty-three years of age,

according to bone and dental analysis,' the pathologist said proudly, neither of us correcting him. 'She hasn't given birth and, apart from the obvious injuries, was in otherwise excellent health. Although, I did notice a repaired hole in the heart which I imagine was corrected shortly after birth. I would be surprised if it troubled her.'

It didn't. The woman had no heart.

'Time of death?' Leclerc asked, and I admonished myself for not asking sooner.

'She had been dead three hours when she was found.'

Leclerc was in a corner then because he did not know when she was found and to admit so would also have revealed something of us. I congratulated myself for not asking about the time of death.

'Of course.' Leclerc nodded in that knowing way of old detectives in black and white movies; in their case it shielded an inspired insight, but in Leclerc's it concealed only the vacant mind. He waved his hand around the woman's missing face. 'And this, how was this done?'

The pathologist looked over the top of his steel-rimmed glasses and after a long pause, smiled. 'Presumably, you are not asking me for *cause of death*?'

Leclerc puffed up his chest and scowled. 'You have identified a calibre at least?'

The pathologist batted this away with all the condescension it deserved.

'Was it close range?' Leclerc pressed home his ignorance.

'My colleagues at the scene believe the murderer was above her, across the street. Most likely an upper window is my guess. Half the apartments in Paris are empty.'

'Appears to be an accurate shot,' I couldn't help myself from saying.

The pathologist scoffed. 'Hardly. With a fifty-calibre round from twenty metres, a blind cockerel couldn't miss.'

Back outside in the thick air of the city, Leclerc leaned on a low wall, puffing from the exertion of the stairs. 'What did you think of him?'

'Arrogant prick.'

He nodded. 'Did she have family?' I had no idea why the man was asking me. He sat in the woman's office at least once almost every day for eighteen months. I only spoke to her on operations, and occasionally in bed. Another secret she had taken on her voyage across the Styx. It was less than five times for sure, and we were drunk for most of them. 'The pussies will have to investigate. They won't let us near it.'

DGSE were housed in the Central Administratif des Tourelles. We didn't need to be creative when the jokes wrote themselves.

'I will insist on a shadow,' he continued, offering me a rare cigarette, 'and a daily update delivered to me personally at the office. It's intolerable to think they would keep us in the dark about something of this magnitude, something that affects us all. Two days, Berthier. Two *whole* days ago she was killed–'

He looked at me with that sense of injustice which served him well with the fools and motivated them. I waited for his question, which I had already anticipated because he was at heart no more than a coward.

'Should we be worried?' he asked finally, drawing on his cigarette.

'About what?'

'Dammit man, the head of Le Troisième is assassinated outside her home? No one is supposed to know who she is, let alone where she lives. She had a high-ranking clerical job in the Ministère de l´Intérieur and went to the palace at least twice every week. Now she's lying dead in the morgue with her face obliterated.'

I placed my hand on his shoulder. 'Don't worry, chief, you're perfectly safe.'

And he was. For as long as it took to pay me back my ten thousand.

'Money troubles?' he asked, and I wondered momentarily whether he could read my mind, before remembering that he was a shallow narcissist who assumed the only ailments which afflicted the population were his own. 'Was she into anything or anybody we should have known about?'

He gazed at me, studied me hard, checking around my face for tell-tale signs, urging me to give up any secrets on Christine, but I had nothing. She had no secrets known to me bar one and giving that up would have meant giving up everything, giving up all of us. Even him. He checked his watch. 'Lunch?'

I knew immediately what was coming.

Leclerc was mean. Some people are careful with money, some are prudent. Some are as tight as a frightened hedgehog. Leclerc was downright mean. Marie had money and he hated it. He could never spoil her the way her father did. He would never ascend to the same pedestal as Frank Foucault, and that was his great pain, one that would likely kill him in the end. It was even rumoured he informed the local Gendarmerie of human bones found on the family small holding near Limoges, to save the cost of hiring a plough and turning over the field himself. At every liar's untimely death we found, mysteriously, that Leclerc had only recently furnished them with some essential costly item, one that must be reclaimed through government expenses without access to the requisite paper trail from the deceased. We liars didn't seem to learn though. Maybe if we had stopped our requisitions, we might have survived a little longer.

In silence, we took the short walk from the morgue to Leclerc's favourite café on Ile St-Louis, leaving me to wonder who would reclaim poor Christine. Her fingerprints, dental records and even DNA drew a blank on the national crime database but were immediately flagged to DGSE and by extension finally, reluctantly to us. She would sleep on a cold steel bed in the basement of Pitié Salpêtrière Hospital, silently waiting until the local cops were disavowed their privileges to investigate. Then, maybe some pathologist from the firm would ask some more questions of her before she was finally returned to her family already neatly disposed of.

The toxicology report was likely clean, save for the usual mix of adrenaline or sleep inducers that kept us all sane in our godforsaken jobs. She was shot. There was nothing else to tell from her body unless certain fluids indicated she left a lover in her vacant bed. He or she might then have remembered Christine taking a telephone call, but they were unlikely to know what was said. We all of us had balconies or dressing rooms or closets. Her operator would have given up records, but the woman was called by a telephone stolen from an international courier company. If they were smart, and some of them were, they'll have suspected she knew the caller, or she would not have come down so easily to the street, but as for worthwhile evidence, the pathologist had found none.

Arriving at the sunny establishment of Leclerc's preference, we took a table on the pavement and watched the massed ranks of faux worshippers spilling from the wreck of Notre Dame. Leclerc ordered an omelette, salad, and small beer, which he drank quickly and went on to order two more. Joining him in the omelette, I declined the beer in favour of sparkling water. Alcohol dulled my senses, and I needed them razor sharp for the conversation that was about to unfold like Leclerc's napkin.

He started by asking about Gabrielle. We were none of us supposed to share such details, but we had history Leclerc and me. Years before, he saved my skin and more than once he had asked me to return the favour. To him, she was just a name anyway. There must have been thirty thousand Gabrielles in France, a tenth of them in Paris, and Leclerc could not find his feet in his own bed. I confirmed she was as lithe and wanton as the best of them and asked about Marie for politeness, although with Leclerc such an enquiry was akin to opening a sluice gate. It was fine to do so, just so long as you were prepared for the flood. Right then, I was satisfied to let the man's repressed rage wash over me to pass his time.

'She works too hard,' he said, which meant he was pissed that she pulled in a bigger salary than he did, and always would while he tethered himself to that wretched desk. 'The au pair is asking for a pay rise,' he bemoaned. So would I if invited to mind the brats. 'Which is why I've been looking at jobs.'

He didn't mean the appointments page in *Le Monde*. He meant the 'green sheet', the weekly list of vacant or new secret service roles that were fashioned from the latest crisis. Our own department only existed because some idiot could not check a ship was empty before detonating the mine placed on its hull. DGSE required oversight, some 1980s politician decreed, to spare the nation's blushes. So, there we were Leclerc and me, babysitters for the finest intelligence agency in the world, still cleaning up for them forty years later because some services never grow up.

'And now–' He cut himself short and looked at me. Lowering his voice to little more than a whisper he said, 'It wasn't my first thought, naturally. But it's an ill wind that blows no good. And what with the state of things. There's benefit in continuity, Berthier, don't you think?'

He talked through the mouthfuls, chewing on his own argument. He wanted Christine's vacant chair. He always had. Men like Leclerc gravitated to seniority like career advancement was a board game. If they could endure the contest long enough, eventually the dice rolled in their favour.

'It's a lot of paperwork and politics,' I reminded him, which was music to his ears. From a seat on the upper floor, he could command a rare view of Paris and, better still, control the entire Le Troisième budget. Begrudgingly, I conceded that such an outcome would also suit me, refraining from saying so. Then, our debts were even.

'It would be good for you too. No promises on my role, but the right word in the correct ear…' His voice trailed off. We both knew to whom he referred, but Foucault took advice from no-one except the barrage of lobbyists.

'Spare me such a fate,' I said, and meant it.

'But if asked, you would not be averse to seeing your old pal in the hot seat, right?'

I confessed I would not. Better a fool than another liar.

'Will they give it to you?' Intra-departmental promotions were rare in our world. To progress, it was usually necessary to move from one pool of shade to another, lest the rising sun should shrink our shadows and expose us all. 'It has never happened before–'

'Dammit man, the boss has never been shot before!' he said bluntly, verging on desperation.

'Then perhaps we should consider you a suspect?'

He stopped, his fork in mid-air and examined my face again, scanning for sincerity. I held his gaze just long enough to stop him eating before he shook his head. We both knew he was innocent, but he had no idea I knew it.

'What do you think about it all?' He waved his loaded fork towards the cathedral, the river, the south bank, maybe the whole of France. It was like he was asking me to crack the universe. He found mystery in everything. 'That body, I mean. What was all that? Did anything come of that body on the beach?'

'Complete dead end, I'm afraid.'

He departed before we finished to attend an urgent call he had neglected far too long. Just long enough to avoid paying, but it was no matter to me. I used our dead colleague's mistress fund for such occasions, reassured Thierry would have approved. Leclerc was my little dalliance, after all. The proprietor cheered the rise in trade since the fire. It had breathed new life into the old lady, he said from behind a counter full of matchbooks. I snatched one in case I needed to apply a little heat of my own.

Rodrigo was not the stout Colombian's real name. The records department computer which we accessed when they were off duty could have confirmed it, but the truth was I cared less for his moniker than even he did. What concerned me was his business, a rare coffee shop just off Avenue George V, secreted within the walls of our city's untraceable wealth.

Selling by the milligram not the cup, he allowed tastings in a secure room out the back, behind four inches of solid steel and a biometric lock. The sharpest safe crackers in Paris had tried and failed to relieve Rodrigo of his stock, two paying the ultimate price. None had been reported to authorities, the shopkeeper preferring to exact his justice the South American way, while the French police preferred to look the other way. Could you imagine the fate of the poor Gendarme who came between the elite of France and their favourite flavours?

'Ciao, Berthier,' he greeted me with his wicked Latin smile. What he lacked in height he more than compensated for in menace. With a warm welcome appended to the most unwelcoming pockmarked face, if he used French at all it was by accident. Instead, we navigated my usual order in a mix of English, Spanish and Italian. The latter because so much of Rodrigo's merchandise seemed to make its merry way to Sicily in due course, and those Sicilians were suckers for their mother tongue.

'How's business?'

He winced. 'The economy has turned to shit, and that is always good for me. Everyone needs a little pick-me-up right now. Must be tough in the art market, though?'

I nodded.

'But the wine is still going down strongly?'

'Everyone needs a little pick-me-up.' We agreed that some businesses were ever recession-proof.

'How is your beautiful wife?' he asked, ghosting behind the

wooden counter, fussing with the straps of his black apron. He never met Gabrielle, but he was introduced to Christine halfway through an old job. I didn't have the heart to tell him her head exploded.

'She left me.'

He nodded. A great deal of wives left their husbands in Rodrigo's line of work. A great many more husbands left their wives. 'Pity. She had the most beautiful eyes.'

She did. It was a great shame to see them closed permanently.

'Your usual?' He didn't await confirmation, instead disappearing and leaving me alone to admire the crowded shelves. There were neat brown bags full of Kenyan, Honduran, Indonesian, and of course Brazilian. There were percolators and presses, Moka pots and cafetieres. There was even a cabinet eleven shelves high, stacked with porcelain from large cappuccino bowls at the floor to fine espresso cups accessible only with the use of a stepladder sitting idle in the corner. The inventory never seemed to change, unless an item found its way into the hands of a passing tourist, confused that the coffee-shop branding did not extend to sales of steaming black liquid in regular, large, or grandiose. Rodrigo's was a traditional Dutch coffee-shop in the contemporary Colombian style.

Presently, he returned, handing me a branded bag. The brand was Hermes. 'Your loyalty discount applies, but I'm afraid prices reflect recent demand.' He passed me a small piece of paper with a number on it. Reaching inside my leather blouson, I removed a plain envelope, taking out a couple of bills and handing over the remainder. He examined the bundle before placing it into an immaculate automated note-counter.

'Can you believe,' he said, 'that this infernal machine must be configured to allow for the additional weight of cocaine?'

'Shocking.' But it wasn't. Experts in DGSE once gave a presentation to the European Central Bank advising that all the fine powder on the Euro notes in circulation amounted to over ten tonnes of cocaine, once refined of everything from talcum powder to asbestos.

'Perfect,' Rodrigo exclaimed finally. 'Always a pleasure doing business with you.' He gestured to the packets of beans on the bottom shelf, from which I selected two and deposited them in the bag, before removing a dusty bottle of *Chateau Marguax* from my brown leather satchel.

'And a little something for you, Rodrigo.' Because margins were always under pressure. Fair weather or foul.

'You are a good man, Berthier, she was a fool to leave you.'

She was. But she was also a liar. And liars, as we knew, were never long for this world.

FOUR

Tennis Club Henri Moreau was buried between modern office blocks in the commercial centre at Issy-les-Moulineaux, to lure the testosterone from their boardrooms. Unlike the Club de Paris or Racing Club, Henri Moreau had no strict entrance criteria conferred at birth, nor via some intimate and inexplicable membership network. There were no fat millionaires hogging courts, berating teenage coaches. No, Henri Moreau existed purely for players, and its dusty red surfaces were a pleasure to play on. I did not enjoy them half as much as the club's immaculate senior captain, however, who treated me to a royal thrashing, six handsome games to my ugly two.

Shaking hands at the net he proceeded to slap my shoulder, his white smile beaming from within the year-round tan. You would not have known it from the black hair, willowy body and complete absence of any trace of age upon his smile, but the man was seventy-three years of age with barely a line to follow. 'Cheer up,' he said. 'You've played much worse and won.'

In the musky changing room amid the fug of deodorant and cologne he asked about business, telling me over the shower stall that he had invested in several cases of *Talbot en primeur* in the expectation of another vintage year. He could well have been right, my mind was elsewhere, but I made a mental note to investigate and report back before our next match.

In the bustling bar, I bagged a banquette beneath a faded portrait of *Roland Garros* in goggles and scarf and ordered two cold beers while awaiting the captain's arrival. Entering in a dark blue linen suit, he shook hands like he was appealing for re-election. A word in an ear here, a denial there. A request for a rematch accepted with a handsome wager no doubt. A clutch of elderly female members followed his path eagerly, but none with the confidence to confess. He reached me as our refreshment arrived.

We raised glasses, and in unison swallowed a large mouthful of pure joy.

'My favourite moment of every week,' I said.

'My favourite moment of every *day*.' He laughed, taking another longer pull. Pascal was retired and could do as he pleased, as often as he pleased. 'And how is my number one girl?' he asked, for Pascal was also Gabrielle's father.

'She is a credit to you.'

'And to herself, of course.'

We both nodded.

'She works too hard, but she seems to love it and who am I to come between a woman and her first love?' I said to Pascal's obvious delight. He knew her mind was not for turning by anyone, least of all him or me.

Over the best club sandwiches in Paris, we discussed the

economy because like any father, he cared that his daughter was well maintained. He had been to the apartment only once, and it was two months before it was furnished with a selection of minor works by major names. If only he had been more recently. I am convinced he thought his daughter had fallen for a kind but penniless above average tennis player. Yet, never once had he said a bad word about me to the woman who we both adored, and from that I was assured he was a decent man. The very best.

'You were in Reims last week?'

Reaching into my sports holdall, I removed a bottle of my sister's champagne, a premier cru that retailed for seventy or even eighty euros a throw.

'You shouldn't have.' He beamed and slapped my leg. 'But I'm glad you did. Now I know what Gabi sees in you, Berthier. Special occasion, perhaps?'

He guffawed. He knew that Gabrielle and I planned to marry but had rebutted my request for her hand. *She is her own woman, as well you have learned*, he had told me. *She's no more mine to give than she is yours to take*. Nevertheless, he pronounced himself content in his daughter's happiness and, in pity, offered me fifty thousand towards a ceremony. It was refused most politely, for Gabrielle had nothing quite so grand in mind.

'What do you think about this body which washed up in St. Tropez?' I asked him nonchalantly.

'What body?' He raised those pencil thin eyebrows, and I knew at once the former chief of police was lying.

'It was on one of those scandal sites. They claim he was shot with a harpoon–'

'*Pah*. Harpoon my ass. You really must stop believing everything you read online. You kids have been fed such a diet of fake news and propaganda, that you find it impossible to tell real from imagined.'

'There's nothing to it then?'

If there was, Pascal would be unable to hide it. He was the last of the great Paris crime fighters before the world abandoned its analogue heroes and villains. Even when they didn't consult with him officially, he was the most avid consumer of locker-room talk, a shoulder to many in authority. He had no idea I knew more about him than about his daughter. Nor that I spent two years training in telling lies, my own and everyone else's. Misinformation and misdirection were the weapon of choice for most of us.

Leaning forward, he placed a firm hand on my thigh. 'Bodies wash up along the coast all the time.' He paused. 'Drowning is the third biggest cause of death in coastal towns. Did you know that? What makes this one special?'

He was teasing out how much information was available on the internet, so I shrugged, having exhausted my only insight in my opening gambit.

'The bigger question regards this government of ours,' he continued, assured that the irritating body had been returned safely to the morgue. 'It's their absolute inability to kick-start our slovenly economy, I fear. That's where a businessman like yourself should be directing his curiosity if you'll permit me a little piece of *fatherly* advice. It's time for change, Berthier, don't you think?' He smiled, raising his glass again.

He was flattered when asked about police matters and, even when he had next to nothing to say or no wisdom to impart, could maintain a conversation on criminality for hours. Rejecting an opportunity to discuss this case, he told me all I needed to know. The Préfecture de police were aware that their local citizen, former member and late DGSE rising star was dead. In good time, Christine Montgolfier, a claimed descendant of the two aeronauts, may steer them in the direction of the guilty man. But right then, her and my silence remained paramount.

Two days later, Leclerc had good and bad news. He had been granted the role of Acting Director of Le Troisième. The obvious candidate for the position from DGSE was going on maternity leave in a month; not long enough to complete an induction, nor to conclude activities in her current role. But the implication was clear. She was next for the job long-term unless Leclerc could pull off the sting of the century. And then came the good news.

'I have put you forward as shadow on the investigation into Christine's assassination,' he said. 'I made it a stipulation of accepting the role.'

I smiled. Stipulation was some claim. He would have accepted the role if it required the sacrifice of his first and second born.

He handed me a small handwritten note. 'You're to report here at fourteen hundred tomorrow. They'll brief you on progress to date. And in turn I expect a full update immediately afterwards. You understand? *Immediately*.'

Leclerc knew my schedule was my own. My briefings were researched and prepared in the finest detail, to provide genuine analysis and insights for the team. Anything less might as well have been rumour, especially when the information originated from DGSE. A more unscrupulous bunch of liars did not exist. Apart from us. His request was of no consequence, however, since the contents of my first report were already written. The wonderful advantage of shadowing was that only the two shadows were the conduit between our respective agencies. 'Naturally.'

'Oh, and one other thing,' he said, scratching at his temple. 'That body. Word reaches me he was a policeman from Paris. Apparently, he was banging the wife of the local mayor. The husband is in custody, picked up yesterday. What the hell was he thinking putting a spear through his wife's lover?'

'Really? The things some people will do.'

If shadows were playing cards, you could not have been dealt a finer hand than Nicole McQueen. The pin-up girl of DGSE, she headlined recruitment campaigns across our shrivelling empire. Diversity delivered us the Senegalese beauty whose real name was likely far less glamourous, but whose glamour it was quite impossible to counterfeit. Her notoriety from posters and the internet was the perfect cover for her modus operandi – she was the diva of the division, not for the corps de ballet was our Nicole.

'How's your butt for love-bites, Berthier?' She welcomed me to the quiet bookstore by the Seine, moving with all the grace of a gazelle. If I had been made to select an executioner, I could have thought of no finer finale. She was bound from head to toe by *Saint-Laurent*, sketching lines where none should exist. Her deep brown eyes were the most defiant of any woman I had ever met, directing me elsewhere within the store. Leather boots wrapped her thighs and kept her feet in check, her plaid skirt no more than fifteen centimetres from hip to hem. Legend had it she had killed a man between her knees. I had never felt more suicidal.

'I like your jacket,' she said. 'I didn't know you rode a motorbike.'

'I don't. I just like the way it looks.'

She smiled, coveting my garments rather than the man inside them. 'It's a great shame about Christine,' she continued, stretching to retrieve a copy of *Little Women* from an upper shelf, even though she was as tall as our most famous landmark. 'I really did like her very much.'

We were none of us supposed to form strong attachments in the service. It wasn't the sex but the security they feared because we could be compromised so readily; a hostage would sooner surrender their love of country than sacrifice their lover. Nicole fingered a dozen more spines, before tilting a copy of Bronte's *Villette*, letting it fall back into its berth under the watchful gaze of a diligent bookish assistant.

'What can you tell me about her?' she asked, skirting from the layers of female fiction to more familiar terroir, the wine guides and gastronomy.

'Not much. She was a typical professional administrator. Prepared, punctual, precise. You know how those bureaucratic types are.'

'Not the type to open her door in a negligee at three in the morning, then.'

'We all of us have *secrets*.' I smiled.

Nicole looked away, letting a long scarlet nail scrape along a shelf, examining the result between her thumb and index finger, a thousand tiny worlds dancing in the dust. She flicked it to the floor. 'Dirty little secrets, mostly.' She grinned like we were flirting over cocktails and not the corpse of our dear departed colleague. I hesitated. She knew that women were my singular weakness, and she was the smartest of them all.

'She was good at her job, Nicole. Beyond that is a mystery, I'm afraid.'

'Bullshit,' she said loudly enough to draw a frown from the five ladies crowded around the delicate lettering of *Louisa May Alcott*, while our bookworm remained stubbornly unmoved. 'Tell me you didn't fuck her.'

My smile broadened. She didn't know. All she knew was my reputation. Locker-room talk. Two or three of her colleagues maybe. I heard they had a rating system, those ladies in Tourelles and that, for my sins, I was nearer the summit than the foot. 'If I only owned half the charges levelled against me.'

We circled the island of new releases, her thighs brushing the polished wood, pulling a volume momentarily out of shape from the towers of unsold best-sellers. Stopping, she waited for my gaze to alight on her face. 'Well?'

I shrugged.

'Buy me a drink, and then let's agree a plan of action,' she tempted.

The bookworm charged me twenty Euros for a tale Nicole could recite by heart. She had a Masters in English, a post-graduate diploma in political studies and five years inside of government. The only diminutive women she knew ported stilettos. Most often in their shoes.

Across the river, we picked out a shaded table in front of my favourite restaurant on Place de l'Opéra where my father would never eat because the owners nourished Nazis in the war. Such was the history of our complicit city.

There, I was invisible once again. Not a man alive would have seen me in the shadow of my companion, and only the most determined of women. She pawed at a menu from which her reputation vetoed her, before ordering a large glass of Meursault, which I quickly made a bottle.

She laughed. 'Are you planning to get me drunk?'

'Would it help?'

Scoffing, she fished a metallic blue cigar from her tote bag, flicking it, then sucking to release an abhorrent stream of pungent faux raspberry or blueberry. 'I will have you horizontal one of these days, Berthier.'

I smiled.

'But only on a cold grey slab.'

The sommelier with his pained expression arrived, encouraging me to distinguish the flaked almond, vanilla and butter, amid the rampant fog of fruity nicotine which consumed us both. I invited him to leave the bottle chilling in its bucket for when the gas had cleared.

'How's life at DGSE?' I asked, hoping that those contraptions provided the same quick fix as a Gauloises or Gitanes.

'Pretty shitty if you must know. We had our budget cut again because we no longer need an infantry to fight the war on terror. Why secure the streets when you can scan them from above?' She gestured to the battalion of unseen watchers, devouring us from their desks. 'Analysts, that's all we seem to talk about these days. More hard drives, fewer hard-ons, that's the current thinking.'

Plus, ça change. There would be an algorithm to do my job too soon enough.

Studying her was an exercise fraught with contradiction. She was at once both confident and cold, bewitching and bellicose, impossible to ignore while resistant to every overture or compliment imaginable. *Impervious*, was that the word? Enigma, for certain. 'Tell me. Did you really like Christine?'

She paused, blew a final mouthful of smoke in a seductive ring and poked her finger through the hole, snapping it in two with a callous click. 'There were too few of us already. She was kind to me.'

I forgot that Christine spent three years across the city before she came to us. It was just possible that the woman recruited Nicole. Perhaps too she mentored her. 'Was she a confidant?'

Standing, Nicole slid effortlessly behind me, retrieved the ice bucket and claimed it for herself. Taking out the bottle, she filled her glass, ignoring mine, and took a long, slow mouthful. Swirling like it was mouthwash and not the finest product of our valleys, she finally washed away the taste of fruit.

'If I tell you this and it leaks, I swear I will kill you. Understand?' Removing her sunglasses, she stared at me with eyes so naked I knew at once she was about to tell the truth. 'We were lovers.'

Fuck. I nodded as though the idea was one that I was fighting to clear, not to savour.

'Pah, you are pathetic. Is there a man in your department who is not a misogynist?'

Sadly, I don't believe there was. But at least the ploy seemed to work. It's hard to fake disgust. 'I'm sorry, Nicole, but you know how it is. I'm just another of the hard-ons they're looking to cull.'

She took another mouthful, this time with feeling.

Filtering through the bottle, the sunlight strobed her hand, catching angles of her brilliant white diamond and its intricate latticework of clasp. The slim rope of platinum on which it sat were two conjoined hands wrapped around her finger.

A sudden stab of rising guilt disappeared again quickly at the memory of Christine's actions. 'I'm genuinely sorry for your loss. You know this job. It makes us all immune to death.'

She smiled. 'It's fine. I know what blunt instruments they employ over there.'

There was nothing so sharp as a liar at Le Troisième. 'Did she have family?'

She shook her head. 'She was orphaned by an avalanche in the Pyrenees at nine. On a skiing holiday. At least, that was her story.'

'And you believed it?'

Closing her eyes, she nodded.

'Checked it?'

She looked away, down the street, where all of Paris looked back and longed for her.

'What was she into? I hardly even spoke to her, apart from operationally.'

'Art and horses, mainly,' Nicole said, from a pit of stoicism that she had clearly nurtured for her paymasters. I wondered why she had revealed her secret to me. 'She loved Géricault and Delacroix, you know? She used to ride when she was young, at boarding school.'

I pictured the apartment with its rich teal walls and fine gilt frames, the prancing stallions hanging by golden threads from a high picture rail; old masters and new artists Christine favoured, arranged with precision around her enormous sleigh bed. 'Did she gamble?'

Nicole looked suddenly back to me. 'You think this was over money?'

'Why are people normally murdered?'

'She wasn't murdered, Berthier, she was *assassinated*.'

'Of course. But you know our business, debts can often be passed on–'

Raising a delicate hand, Nicole then lowered it to grip the neck of the bottle again, her veins throbbing. I resolved to say no more about possible motive, preferring to promote my ignorance through silence. Finally, she filled my glass before topping up her own. 'Do you have anyone?'

I nodded.

'Serious?'

The best liars always understood when to rely on the truth. 'As any of us dare.'

She shrugged and smiled. 'Take care of her. You never know how long you have.'

We both knew the pain of loss was one that we ourselves inflicted without mercy. Treating our enemies as disposable, we rarely thought of those we left abandoned, staring into the abyss. Yet here she was before me, a woman rendered widow by the service she loved. I raised my glass to her. I was sorry only for Nicole, not a shred of sympathy for the cold hard bitch she mourned.

I got as far as 'where should we start,' when I saw him.

He sat outside a bar on the corner opposite, behind a newspaper he could not possibly have read. Because he was young with a hipster beard, and designer sunglasses and clothed in the denim of liberalism, and *Le Figaro* was none of those things. And this is how we earned our trade. He stirred, tossing ten euros onto his table, folded the pages of incongruity and walked away. Only when he removed his glasses and looked back over his shoulder at Nicole did I realise–

Too late.

Reaching out for her, we were wrenched apart.

With a sudden dull whump, it thumped me.

Punching my back and left side like blows from a giant boxing glove, it swiped and then tossed me from the chair, smashing me through the spiralling umbrella like a rag doll discarded in a hurricane. Like a paper bag, blown by wind. I was as nothing. A soon to be statistic in an angry news bulletin.

My arms and legs were numb as they twisted around me, folding and flailing of their own free will. Through the crash of air my eardrums burst again and again, until the echo of death reached me. The shattering carnage. Rolling and reverberating like a thunderous wave of noxious noise.

For an age, I seemed to fly.

Hanging in the sky, flipping, flopping, neither alive nor dead. Until suddenly it stopped. The ground or the stationary car, I don't know which, hit me. And it hurt. By Christ it hurt. From travelling to stopping, all the chaotic momentum met a catastrophic wall of weight. My soul screamed at the agony.

For a short while, the clanking carried on around me.

Seeping through the smoke, it seeped between the sting of cordite and the stench of burning flesh. It smelled like a human hog roast. *It reeked of instant death.*

Slumped against the fender, the image of the café probed me.

Through the darkness and fuzz of sound, I pictured it.

How many were sat around us? Six or eight? How powerful was the explosive? Not very, or I could not have been doing those calculations, always assuming I was still alive.

It was not intended for me. Or I would not have been alive.

I was only able to think at all because Nicole was the target, and she was almost certainly dead because we were both sloppy, because *I* was sloppy.

I spotted him far too late.

Shit.

The smoke still drifted ahead of the sound, which caught it. Then I heard them: the screams, the cries, the pain; the destruction; the distant echo of sirens; and worse than all of those, the *silence*.

I had to move. To get away.

I reached for my legs.

My pants were wet from blood, and wine, but mainly blood, I was sure. Mine, Nicole's, the spill of anyone in my path between the table and the car. Wet or not, both legs, thank God, remained intact. Broken bones inside them, maybe.

I crawled. And then I stopped. Then I retched as the pain crippled me, wrapping me like razor wire, hauling my head from its perch to the pit of my stomach, then tossing it angrily back again. Falling onto my knees, I vomited. And again. And again. There was blood amid the bile and sputum. I coughed up every milligram of sympathy and pain.

I tried to stand, but the feeling would not come. The messages left my brain but faltered on their journey. React, damn you. *React.*

Upright, I lasted but seconds and fell again to the tarmac.

The pain. *Jesus*, the pain.

Maybe I should have died? Just lay down there and died.

Who would really have cared? I could have joined Nicole. Maybe I owed her that.

My last remaining act was to reach inside my shredded leather jacket, also soaked in blood, to pull out a syringe.

Flicking off the top, I lifted it as high as my will allowed, and with my final breath, I plunged it into me.

FIVE

There were faint intermittent sounds.

The sweet notes of birdsong. The soft echo of car doors closing. The urgent growl of a motorcycle. The clank of garbage cans spewing up breakfast. Laughter. All pieces of some audio jigsaw which the mind assembled, slowly, deliberately, presenting them gently to the frontal lobes alongside the smell of mould and body odour. Like a nurse might nudge awake her patient, so the dormant brain awakened, easing me back to consciousness. But it was fleeting, and before long, disgusted I was still alive, it preferred to keep me dead.

The adrenaline was gone.

Only the pain remained.

Darkness swallowed me once more.

Finally, but barely conscious I checked my cell phone. There were six missed calls, all from Gabrielle. Three voicemails, the first left eighteen hours previously. A soft reminder: papa's birthday drinks. Then the SMS messages, from simple 'where are you?' to more serious 'what the fuck are you playing at?'

Then the second voicemail: 'B, I'm worried now. If you're messing around or busy, text me. Anything to let me know you are safe, ok? Ciao, baby'.

Then the third: 'Berthier? B? There's been an explosion. At Café Centurion. Call me. I love you.'

I ran through the timing in my head. It was two days since the bomb. *Two whole days.* I must have slept for twenty hours straight. I looked around the tired room, with its faded yellow wallpaper torn and stripped back to plaster. I was naked. There was blood on the white sheets. Clothes on the rough floorboards, soaked. But the sheets weren't. Just spattered with random stains. I must have washed. There was a glass of water on a wooden box beside the bed. A line of coke. It started to come back–

Slowly.

Nicole. *Jesus.*

Poor, poor Nicole.

Gabrielle.

She must have been out of her mind. I had to text. To let her know–

No.

Wait, Berthier. Think like a liar, not a fool.

Gabrielle had a direct line to the enquiry. She must have called Pascal. Pascal would have called his locker-room buddies. A quiet word. The coroner's office. By now, any bodies that were unknown would likely have been identified. Apart from the one that was not unknown. She was a black female not a white male. It may have been some time before any tourists were named officially, but the delays of television news channels were mostly for the benefit of kin, not for lack of information. This was a small explosion. Designed to kill one. Two at the very most. Anything more was bad fortune. He had not expected me to be so close, but neither had he cared. Most likely, it was inside that damned electronic cigarette.

Gabrielle must surely have known I was alive.

Because Pascal will have known for sure I was not dead.

Right then, though, my love had to wait on my wellbeing for both our safeties.

Surveying my surroundings, my location began to solidify. A safe house. Off the Bois de Boulogne. Near the autoroute. It was coming back. Climbing off the bed, the pain punched me once more. As well as the coke, beside the bed there was Vicodin. Grabbing the glass, I sloshed the water and swallowed a handful. Enough to knock me out in half an hour, just long enough to take a leak and check the news reports on my phone. The place stank of abandonment. I still smelled like death.

They blamed extremists, of course.

Christ, three dead.

There was camera footage. From across the street. Further down than the culprit. Filming what? Nicole perhaps? It panned away. Not Nicole, then. We were both hidden by a parked car. The very one that broke my fall. Only our open umbrella was visible. Then came the drama and excitement. The dull thud of explosion so unlike its Hollywood counterfeit: an off-screen flash; the resultant jolt; the roll of shockwaves; and only then the noise, the terrible noise, racing to catch its cause.

The camera span around, seeing nothing but the veil of dust. It held. The carnage looked worse than three dead. Sounded worse too. The echoes continued. The rain of metal and fabric and, now we knew for sure, the red mist of three defeated bodies. The smoke swirled and eddied in a kind of comic danse macabre, masking everything and everyone, before a shrill voice cried out for the emergency services, the cameraman urging his wife or girlfriend to call. But she was already doing so, screaming her desperate demands. They were unnecessary. There was a police car down the street. I clocked it as we walked.

Through the smoke, he zoomed to see a murky head. Above a car. *My* head. Obscured by the swirling debris. It was there for a fraction and then gone. Dropped from view.

Then came the news anchor again. No remorse. No disgust. No regret. Just speculation. And the imagery of Syria, or Libya, Afghanistan, or Iraq, Gaza, even Iran. I no longer cared. I no longer watched. Because the bombing was no act of foreign terrorism, it was an act of savage home-grown murder.

And before the drugs hit me again, I visualised the callous face of the liberal.

And I remembered again the solitary police car.

Waking a second time, at least my fully conscious second time, another six hours had passed.

In the bathroom, the water bit my wounds.

Thank God, I saw him and thank God I was already moving away. My side was scarred and bloody from the shrapnel which pierced the leather. My back likewise. There were two or three pieces still in me, for sure, but there's a reason thick leather jackets are so favoured by bikers. They may not always save your life, but they sure as hell do a fantastic job of providing a barrier between soft flesh and solid asphalt.

In the mottled mirror, a man's tattered and torn face greeted me.

Flying glass had drawn a deep gash across the left cheek, where the skin was held together with six butterfly stitches applied inaccurately by a comatose hand. The cut was three centimetres long and would mark the poor fellow for life. When he eventually returned to Gabrielle, it would take some serious explaining. His right cheek was grazed and severely bruised from an abrupt meeting with the steel and fiberglass, but that would heal in days. Thank God for wind tunnels and pedestrian safety regulations. There may have been one or two cracked ribs, but twenty years previously, such a collision with a stationary car would have proven fatal.

The barren kitchen was well stocked, like a space capsule or nuclear bunker: dried milk, dried eggs, instant coffee, vacuum-sealed meals of every flavour, bottles of whisky and wine. There was no refrigerator or microwave, no electricity at all because there must be no bill, for the same reason there was nothing but bottled water to drink, to wash in, to flush. To the outside world, the old renaissance building was abandoned. Boarded up. Locked. A sign on the dilapidated fence indicated the property was soon for renovation and had been for more than three years. Such planning delays were not uncommon in Paris.

Reaching for the whisky, I looked at my wrist to check the time, but where the hour should have been I found only a thick band of fairer skin. The watch, meanwhile, lay strewn on the floor, its face smashed, and the hands stuck on fragments of the remaining glass. It had survived my father's war, unscathed and was closest to Nicole. The bracelet was dented like an old tin bath. It likely saved my hand from being severed. I drank the whisky, morning, noon or night, quickly realising it was not night, because bright sunlight leeched in over the top of the rotting window boards.

As the liquid burned my throat, Gabrielle whispered into view.

Pulling open a drawer in an old oak chest tucked in the corner revealed a dozen burner phones, all pre-GPS, all off but fully charged. I powered one up to find three bars of life. She answered on the fourth ring.

'Hullo?'

'Baby it's me.'

A long pause. 'Oh my God, thank fuck you're alive.' Some tears perhaps.

'Baby? Is something the matter?' This was asked as casually as a man caught in the delicate arms of a fragile mistress.

'Where are you? Where have you been? *Jesus*, Berthier.'

'I'm with Oleg. My cell phone fell in the sea. You know what he's like. Spur of the moment trip–'

'Christ Berthier, the news! Have you seen the *news*? I thought...' her voice trailed off.

'What news?'

She laughed. The little nervous laugh when I brought up ex-boyfriends who were mysteriously back in town. 'My God, you are a self-centred *bastard*. I'm sat here scared out of my mind and you're out on some playboy's yacht fucking his Eastern European girlfriends.'

Oleg was my best customer. A Russian oligarch with a superyacht and harem of, I had explained, mainly former glamour models. I may have dabbled, but not often. Gabrielle had a love hate relationship with Oleg. She hated that he dragged me away without notice and often for days or weeks at a time. She loved that the price he paid for above average wine and dubious art furnished our apartment, funded our hide-away and secured the enormous diamond which hung around her neck. He had no manners and treated women and men with equal disdain. He was a vagabond and dinosaur, whisking me away and spoiling me rotten in return for some prize picks at auction and an insight into the new harvest. Oleg was a gambler, a drunk and likely friend to the Russian mafia. But for some reason, he adored me. Most likely because Oleg was a figment of my imagination and known only to the two of us, and Gabrielle vicariously.

I would rather have accepted the cold shoulder for a week of drinking and carousing with the former Soviet, than relay how the blood oozes from a carotid artery slit with my own fair hand. We each of us had our little red lies.

'You bastard,' she said. 'You could have called.'

'The fat old crook threw my phone overboard the very first evening as I was about to call you. Can you believe that?' The silence told me she couldn't. 'Seriously, I'm on the sat phone from the bridge. The captain allowed me to call. Oleg has no idea. Cherie, I'm fine. Trust me. How are you, my baby–'

'Are you using?' she asked, thanks be to God.

'A little, but it's under control. Honestly, Gabrielle–'

'Three days without contact and it's "under control"? Berthier, for fuck's sake be careful.' She paused a beat. *'Please.'*

Perfect. Oleg and his penchant for crack cocaine had bought me another few days, maybe even a week.

'Where are you?' she asked.

Covering the microphone, her question was relayed with deep

sincerity, before telling her, 'Off Portugal, south of Lisbon.' Of course we were. Where else would we be to stock up than the coast of Morocco? Probably out at sea, a handover took place under the cover of darkness. Money going one way, merchandise the other.

'Be careful,' she said again, a rarity for her.

'I will cherie, I will. Ciao.' I hung up before she could respond, slinking back to the bed with the mother of all headaches. Pouring another tumbler full of whisky, I slung it back and allowed myself a restless, dreamless sleep.

I had been awake three hours, the last of those sketching out the liberal bomber. My memory was far from photographic, but a skill acquired at school, and which served me well in business and pleasure came to the fore. Sketching. A work or two adorned the walls of the apartment. I even sold a couple in my youth. Naked wives for wealthy husbands, who paid me handsomely, but not so pleasurably as the subjects.

The face was near perfect. Late twenties or early thirties, slim and angular, with a classic roman nose. The hipster beard might have been easily removed, but the solid jaw and hairline were unmistakable. His height, I pitched at a little under one metre seventy and weight around eighty kilos, five kilos ether way. There was no point telling anyone where he was sat, the table must have been sanitized twenty times since. A few more strokes of biro, and I appended the name 'lost uncle' to the top of the page.

Taking fresh jeans and plain white t-shirt from the closet, I fingered my shredded jacket one final time. It likely saved my life. I hadn't worn Kevlar since Kabul but reaching for a black cotton blouson left me suddenly naked. Exposed. Reminded of the frailty of human flesh, I folded the picture into a back pocket and ventured out into the dusk for the first time since the explosion.

The worst available internet café turned out to be a half hour walk away. Thirty minutes in which I dodged attention and flinched twice from the bangs of industry and transport, peering through the gloom and taking the least predictable route a tired mind allows. Inside the café with its peeling paint and small collection of Paris's least employable but most pungent, a shitty scanner delivered a medium quality version of my sketched photo fit. I sent it from a Hotmail account to Leclerc's personal email. There were times when a debt of ten thousand Euros was helpful.

Although they would need to have been watching every internet café and library in Paris to find me, it was best not to hang around. Even if, as Nicole had bemoaned, locating me was half as likely as before the cull of my ilk.

Back in the house, I pulled out another of the burners and dialled Leclerc at home.

One of the brats answered and insisted on repeating a new curse she had overheard at school before her father finally interrupted her fun.

'Leclerc,' he barked, in that pompous manner of a man completely uncomfortable with his station.

'Did you check your emails?'

He hesitated before explaining to the irritated Marie that he must take the call alone in his study. A minute or two passed. 'Where the hell did you get this number –'

'Did you check your emails?'

'I'm opening them now. It's a Sunday evening, for Christ's sake–'

'Is it?' I asked from genuine ignorance.

There was another pause before, 'Christ, Berthier, is this who I think it is?'

'Yes, that's him. As close as I can,'

'I'll run it through the database–'

'No, Leclerc, *listen to me*. He's one of theirs, I'd swear it.'

'One of theirs?'

'DGSE, he's one of–'

'I know precisely who *they* are. But you cannot seriously expect me to believe the Pussies have murdered innocent tourists on the streets of Paris. Have you lost your fucking mind, Berthier?'

I took a deep breath. 'They killed McQueen.'

There was silence while he assimilated the news. Firstly, that our grand pin-up was no more, but more importantly that several days ago he was not informed that the most notorious member of DGSE was blown to smithereens outside a café in the centre of the city, and that no one had yet seen fit to tell him.

'You're sure?' he asked, to spare his own blushes.

'I was sat next to her. They damn-near killed me too.'

More silence while he processed. What to do, what to say, what to ask, to ensure that his hands remained clean; the ever-bloodless Leclerc. 'Where are you now?'

'Alive, and thanks for your concern.'

'You should come in. We'll take this straight to the top.'

The top? What did he mean 'the top'? Did he mean the pinnacle of that greasy pole to which he was so artfully affixed? 'Find the name of that man,' I urged him. 'But for your own sake do it carefully. If they were happy to jettison their carnival queen, they won't waste a second on your fat ass.'

'Why, you insolent fuck–'

'Carefully,' I repeated, before cutting the call.

With some people, warnings to act with caution are a complete waste of time. Racing drivers and jockeys, for example, can be given all the safety instructions in the world, but the second the flag falls, they are at the mercy of their impulses. The red mist, the will to win at all costs, trumps even their very basest instincts for survival. Not Leclerc. Leclerc was a cockroach of risk and would likely outlive us all. He would handle the identification from arm's length, many anonymous hands between his and the intended investigator, which introduced the one factor beyond both of our control. *Time.* I resolved to give him a full day before calling again. And in the meantime, I needed to establish whether whoever killed Nicole was prompted by the death of her secret lover.

SIX

It's possible that Leclerc could have tracked me down, but the necessary resources would create attention neither he nor I desired. No doubt he checked the agency's own safe houses. Tended by unprepossessing housekeepers and mute caretakers, they were scattered the breadth of France, fifteen in Paris alone. Home to recovering spies and hidden informants, they were staffed, served and sanitized by our central resources. My own hideaways on the other hand, of which Bois de Boulogne was but one, were funded and owned by the deceased or the never truly born. But what all our illicit little domiciles shared was a complete absence of connectivity. There is no easier way to track a man than a cell phone or the internet. Hence my only personal phone was registered to a corpse, a fellow who ran his checking account with all the certainty of the tides. Money in, money out, and never a question but fictitious mother's maiden name to despatch. The benefit of on-line banking.

Even so, research with care was paramount. Too many hits on Google for monitored phrases and the gendarmes would be at the door before the queries were returned. Instead, skating around the required information, and disguising intent, was the order of the day. There is a difference in the bunkers between browsing and looking. As any married man will attest.

The late Jules Martin's telephone was tethered to an old laptop. It was painful to replace the batteries so regularly, but much less painful than the searing heat of a bullet narrowly missing a vital organ, or the slow seep of water through a cloth stretched across a gaping mouth.

Finding details of Nicole was easy. She was twenty-eight or twenty-six, but Senegalese for sure. Recruited from college, she was described everywhere as nothing more sinister than *analyst*, the veneer for a multitude of mortal sins. There were pictures galore and all of them flattering. Hers was the face that launched a thousand bombs. *How can the same government which so values beauty be so supposedly merciless?* they asked, and her duty was thereby done. She was the available, the unattainable, the unmistakable totem for all of France's favourite sons. Its soldiers, sailors, pilots and policemen adored this vision of a woman they could never know, instead adorning their lockers in full repose, while what's left of her rested in a refrigerated locker of her own. I wondered when and how they would share the news.

There was nothing about her family, real or adopted.

Nothing about her real life.

No interviews from former friends or lovers, so favoured by our media. No revelations of any kind, in fact.

She was the perfect spy.

If only I hadn't let her die.

Christine on the other hand, had a history. And plenty of it.

She was educated and graduated from the finest establishments in France, before the ubiquitous spells in government administration, and a ranking role with the Ministère de L' Europe et des affaires Étrangères. Her appearances before committees were recorded verbatim, apart from those given behind closed doors or denied altogether. Our former ambassador for Belarus, she was withdrawn to Paris in the wake of rising Russian aggression, which it is always safest to combat from inside a steel front door, rather than at a flimsy garden gate.

Her time with DGSE was legendary.

As second in command, she oversaw the expulsion of five diplomats for spying, all of them gorging on the false information they were so expertly fed. Their ringmaster, however, remained elusive, one of any number of names. She strode the middle did our Christine, nemesis of all those at the extremis. Left or right, black or white, she was egalitarian in her retribution.

All of which fair legend blew Christine to us.

Eighteen months beforehand, her Chanel suits first graced the ugly offices above the parfumier, on the very same day she was appointed Oficier du renseignement en Chef, France's top spy with a direct line to the President. No surprise there. They had known each other since their aristocratic boarding school.

She walked into my office during her second week, thrusting her wrist towards me. 'Tell me what you think of this,' she commanded.

I took a deep sniff of lavender and jasmine, citrus and sandalwood, before pronouncing, 'Novichok?'

'What are you doing tonight?'

I shrugged.

'An escort is needed for a most important function. Do you own a dinner jacket?'

'*Naturally*, what kind of spy would I be without one?'

'Good,' she said as though she didn't mean it. 'The car will collect you here at eight. Not a minute earlier or later.' She handed me a note with an address near Montmartre. Of course, where else.

I watched her derriere depart my office, to be replaced by the enormous asshole that is Leclerc. Squeezing the door closed, he approached the desk like a penitent parishioner facing his priest, rubbing his hands together before leaning both knuckles on the desk, swamping me in the waft of stale cigarettes and the food trapped between his stained teeth. I preferred the Novichok.

'What did she want?' he asked.

'A date.'

He raised his eyebrows.

'I'm serious. She has some function and needs eye-candy.'

'Why you?'

I smiled at him. 'If you mean why not *you*, may I recommend an optician?'

'Oh, fuck off,' he said, exiting the office more loudly than he entered.

At the time, I guessed the car collected me around half a mile from her home. Sliding in beside her, she was revealed from the slim waist to the strapless sequined dress, her blonde hair up and guard lightly down.

'What should I call you?' she said.

'Berthier.'

'No first name?'

I paused. 'You may concoct one if you prefer.'

'Tell me then, *Berthier*, is it true what they say about you at DGSE?'

'If it is good, most likely. If it is bad, most definitely.'

She smiled. 'And thirteen kills, correct?'

'If that's what it says in the record.' It said thirteen in the record, each approved or admonished by Leclerc and his predecessors. There were and ever would be many more that would go forever unclaimed.

'You're not ambitious?' she said, turning to me. Her high cheeks and pinched nose suited her air of calm authority, the cold headmistress of the school for wayward boys. Steel eyes revealed no emotion despite the rank enquiry. Were there others in the service at the time whose record superseded my own? Unlikely. There were Legionnaires of twenty years with less illustrious achievements. The only difference being that they received a chest full of ribbons, whereas our modest recognition consisted of nothing more than a continuing heartbeat. We were only blunt instruments because they so rarely oiled or polished us.

'I have an ambition to stay alive. You are aware of some higher calling perhaps?'

'The Russian ambassador will pinpoint a member of staff to me tonight,' she said, unmoved, talking instead to the back of the driver's discreet head, all eyes no ears. 'In turn, I will indicate him or her to you. Take them alive if you can, but either way, we need that individual to return with us tonight. Do you have your firearm?'

'I didn't realise it was more than a social engagement.'

She paused and smiled. 'There is a Glock in the glove compartment.'

'We won't need it, and besides, it won't make it past the metal detectors.'

Twice before I had extracted information from the imposing concrete and smoked glass obelisk on Avenue Chantemesse. The first time, during a simple exchange in the children's playground opposite the building. A mis-directed football, a quick apology. A smile, a joke, and the entry code to a naval base exchanged in chosen syllables. The second time, a cleaning contractor found themselves one short of the required complement, and I was only too happy to wipe down files for minimum wage.

This was to be my first visit by invitation.

I chaperoned the new boss for as long as was decent, before excusing myself for a comfort and cigarette break at the appointed hour. By then, the target was already relaxing in the formal garden at the back of the building, where she stared impassively at the forest across the street, only too happy to share a light. Fifteen minutes of small talk later, she took the offered drink, laced with Mexican Valium. Then all I had to do was accompany my very drunk new girlfriend out through the front door of the embassy, apologising profusely in my best Slavic Russian for my foul-mouthed companion. By the time Christine joined us, the girl was asleep in a cheap motel room five kilometres away.

She was no target, no apprentice *spy*.

Just an accounts clerk in way over her head who could have been detained at any railway station or boarding a plane. Even picked up in the morning on a routine traffic stop. She had done nothing more serious than falling for her DGSE handler, making promises she could never hope to fulfil: threatening to expose 'Kremlin' secrets; maintaining a list of internal meetings and their attendees; downloading the payments ledger; keeping copies of embassy bank statements. It was like listening to amateur spy craft from a tawdry holiday paperback. At twenty-two years of age, she was expelled back to Moscow and the brutish hands of the *Kuznetsky Most Street* crew. God knows whether the poor kid survived the suspicion.

But I did know one thing, right there and then.

I knew I could never trust Christine Montgolfier.

SEVEN

Leclerc moved slowly. He knew no other way, and even if he did, it was elusive. He swayed like a bridge in a gale, foot to foot, a trailing leg heaved to keep up, his shoes dragging at the toe. Crowds parted as he approached, to avoid the flattening they feared, squashed beneath the burden of the bureaucrat. He could be nothing else. In that dark grey suit, square black briefcase and unpolished shoes, at best he might have aspired to accountant. More likely he was the gargantuan government administrator who eulogised our emphatic employment laws. Sack Maurice? he would cry incredulously because incompetence was no excuse for termination. Faces flashed from fear to pity as he passed, and some from apathy to scorn. Fat was as unfashionable as ever in Paris.

Hunting him was easy, the tide was visible for blocks. Like an enormous zipper, he snaked his way along the sidewalk, opening and closing the brigades of tired tourists and solemn shoppers without a cent to their name. Moving close enough to be heard but not seen was not so simple. I waited until he paused at a crossing, ghosting into the melee behind him.

Halfway across the street, directly in his shadow. 'Anything?'

The ears twitched. '*Café Splendide*. Upstairs.'

He walked on and I drifted away through his wake, turning left as he pitched right, causing yet another ripple of silent complaints.

With my back to the café's brick and plastered wall, I watched his giant head emerge through the parquet, hatching from the spiral iron staircase into the empty first-floor. It had taken all his meagre energy to ascend, and panting he examined me during the dance between the staircase and my seat. The hard wooden chairs did not fear his approach the same way people do, the stubborn among them brushed aside by those enormous thighs.

'You look a mess,' he said.

'Mine is temporary.'

He smiled. 'Didn't blow your sense of humour off course, then.' Picking up the menu, he studied it, concerned that the hobo-like appearance of his agent may extend to an absence of cash. 'Are you ok?' he asked, squinting. 'Physically, I mean.'

I nodded. 'No thanks to Nicole. Or Christine.'

He looked up suddenly. Blew out hard. 'Do I want to hear this?'

Summoning the waiter over, I ordered a croque monsieur which gave Leclerc the confidence to do likewise. He looked at his watch. It was just before midday. So, we also ordered coffee. 'What are they saying?' I asked him.

'What can they say? They'll claim extremists, of course. They've got a third name ready, just in case.'

I looked at him.

'The bomb exploded prematurely, or it was a suicide attack,' he said, almost casually.

'You can't be serious?'

He shrugged. 'They can hardly admit to losing their only non-secret agent, can they?'

'There will be CCTV footage.'

He stared at me. 'You'd better fucking hope not.'

The returning waiter brought our lovers' tiff to a dramatic interlude, preferring like me that any killing should be quiet and clean. As soon as he departed, Leclerc leaned in. 'Nothing on the face,' he said, adding enough sugar to his coffee that I expected it to overflow. 'Not a thing anywhere. It came back negative so quickly it was almost like they were waiting to be asked.'

'There was a police car.'

'Where?'

'Along the street from *Centurion*, a hundred metres, give or take.'

Leclerc stopped adding and started stirring. His action mirrored the cogs that whirred inside his giant head. There was a smart thinker buried beneath the fool's slovenly exterior. His stomach was not his only gigantic organ. He sometimes fed his brain too. 'Did they clock you?'

'I don't think so. It was late afternoon, either they had just come on or were going off. Either way, not at full observation pace.'

'Christine,' he said, almost cutting across me, raising his eyebrows.

'Nicole was the shadow.'

He whistled. 'And gone before you'd had the opportunity to have your evil way.'

Ignoring his childishness, I waited for the cogs again,

watching them roll and grind without the oil of nicotine or alcohol to lubricate them. He examined the coffee which whirled like a dim brown galaxy with a small nucleus of bubbles at its core. He tilted the cup, slowly, delicately, but still rattled the spoon with his enormous little-finger; for Leclerc had no *little* fingers, only large fingers that were marginally smaller than the rest of his bear paws. 'They killed them both,' he said.

I shook my head.

Undeterred he carried on, 'They killed McQueen to stop her finding Christine's killer. She was onto someone, or something. She knew the old lady better than anyone, I hear.'

'It wasn't the same killer,' I assured him.

'How can you be so damn certain?'

I didn't want to have to tell him. 'Because I know who shot Christine.'

If he had a gun, I swear he would have pulled it. His face floated in that hinterland between astonishment and horror. If I were a written confession, he would have rejected and shredded it, clearing the very idea from his mind. He motioned to say something.

'Don't. I will answer when I can.'

The waiter's timing was impeccable since Leclerc's mouth was then so wide that the plate and its entire contents could have been tipped in. But that cavernous black hole might also have pulled in the restaurant and everything else within a kilometre radius. The offer of mayonnaise was despatched by my brisk nod.

Even as I loaded my fork, still the silence.

'Give me one good reason I shouldn't have you arrested?' he said, finally regaining control of his lower jaw. 'Or better still, hanged or shot.'

'For one thing, I might have a taste for killing the head of Le Troisième.'

He shook his head.

'And for another, they'll come for you.'

His big left paw scratched behind his ear as he shook his head again, quickly this time like a dog with fleas, blinking and yawning. He hadn't slept as much as I had those past few days. 'What's your next move?' he said, and for once I believed he cared.

'You don't want to know.'

He was annoyed more than angry. He could not conceive that I would act without authority, that it was, in our clandestine world, even possible to possess a single autonomous thought. And even if he could, his choices were impossible, and he knew it. Shopping his subordinate for the murder of his former boss would have signalled the end of the man's career. If they didn't assume he was complicit, they would smell his rank incompetence. He could end up alongside me in the cell. Or worse.

'What do you need from me?'

Thank God the man was so predictable. The grip on that temporary chair, and the notion that I must have some higher paymaster flipped me from irritant to insider. He was wary, perhaps even disbelieving, but he was also searching, clinging to the buoy of my confession while he contemplated his own new course.

'Keep going on the liberal,' I said, causing him to look up. 'The bomber, I mean. We must identify him to piece together who was behind this. And one other thing.' He raised his eyebrows. 'I need to know what *Eric Bernard* was working on.'

His face searched mine, lines skipping from his temples across his brow and back again. 'Bernard? That scurrilous rogue. How the hell is he mixed up in this? Don't tell me he had something on our new Napolean? Has Macron employed his wife on a million Euros too? And after making such a fuss about political corruption–'

'Just find out,' I said before Leclerc began another of his weary political monologues.

Eric was my father's sister's son. With a degree from Oxford, he was European Political Correspondent for the *London Standard*, with a rare talent for caustic observation on the machinations of the Union. A pure anglophile, he despised populism while remaining the most popular of our generation, the world-changer my father always wished I would be. He was destined for greatness in print before a catastrophic court-case curtailed his career. The moral of his most memorable story? Never investigate and be sued by the billionaire proprietor of your own newspaper.

Hence Eric found himself back in his homeland and, for a while, living with the former black sheep of the family. The hardest party animal of them all, Eric was to blame for my Colombian predilection, but also an introduction to my sweet little lamb. She was his former colleague, and possibly more, and when he delivered Gabrielle to me, she repaid him with an interview with her boss. It was a no brainer. What media mogul does not delight to employ a man with the inside track on an opposing titan? But you don't draft a fox into the henhouse without a muzzle, and so Eric found himself far from the front-line politics he loved, digging trenches from where colleagues could infiltrate their prey, raising his periscope and providing battlefield reconnaissance, exposing the hypocrites, the real liars and fools. He'd acquired a reputation for unveiling dirty secrets. Mostly at the behest of his boss. Sometimes corruption, and often men thinking with their least thoughtful organ, especially online, and especially with technology-literate paramours of an indeterminate age. Politicians and celebrities blackmailed for millions or favours – lest their infamy swell beyond the size of their former reputations. When last we spoke, Eric laughed about the stories they buried for the favourable tax treatment and laissez faire attitudes to media regulation.

The press, Bertie, are the real political power in France today, he told me.

And then he died.

A car accident just north of Grenoble, on one of those rubber bands of asphalt that twist around the mountains balanced on picturesque views, where bends can snap a car in two. The kind of road you always dreamed to drive, shitting yourself when the opportunity knocks, suddenly aware of the millimetric difference between postcard and post-mortem.

I read the report.

It was the most thorough of any I have seen: the length and timing of the skid; the terminal velocity and Newton Metres of force; the decomposition rates of ferrous metals, and the lacklustre attitude to barrier maintenance; and the angle of the incline and accelerating speed of descent. I read it all. The gorgeous Drophead Aston Martin stood no chance. Less still its less than vintage driver. If he wasn't killed on impact, he was burned alive in the wreckage of his rare English beauty.

It wasn't how he planned to make headlines. The outpouring of sympathy for the beautiful car, splashed across a centrespread, dwarfed any modest grief for the ugly journalist behind the wheel.

Eric was like a brother to me.

We fought like two cats.

We stole one another's clothes, girlfriends, even dreams growing up in the most beguiling region of France, where the chateaux still dominate and employment flows in and out as brut or demi-sec. It's where we two first discovered our mutual taste and distaste for money. The old guard who came in their battered Citroëns and dishevelment, to purchase a case or two for summer, and their fat new financiers in oversized off-roaders whose gales of waved banknotes flattened smaller growers.

When he first went to England, it was as though I had lost him for good.

Thirteen desolate months of injurious college education passed, pecking at my confidence, before the conquering hero returned. And boy had he conquered, if there was a shred of truth in the stories he was telling even then.

'Come back with me,' he begged. 'At least for a week, or two. I promise you, Bertie, you will not regret it. Not for a second.'

I eyed him suspiciously. He was always the clever one, the thinker, practiced in the skill of manipulation and art of false desire. He could lure you in with a look, make his wishes yours, then carefully withdraw to fan the flames. The innocent arsonist.

'Honestly, Bertie. You will have the time of your life.'

Who was I, at eighteen, to disbelieve the stardust in his eyes? And my God, for once was he being honest.

I crossed *Le Manche* a child and returned a man. Never have I been more grateful for my mother tongue, and the curriculum of lessons in its use. If ever again we go to war with the English, we can be assured their women will surrender gladly on our first word. *Say something,* they pleaded, *anything, so long as it's in French.* Never has the language lulled so many horizontal. Who cares about the meaning? Just say it. Over and over, and over –

Yet, despite all Eric's pleas, I knew I must come home and study harder to avoid the fate of only ever riding on his shadow. I yearned for that same spotlight for myself. But for twenty years he had retained it, while I plied my trade in the darkness. Then came the news I dreaded.

The brightest light I ever knew had been extinguished.

The man who helped to make me was broken. They claimed by his own stupidity, producing the forty-eight-page report to spare the blushes of the highways department, further blackening the reputation of the tarnished reporter.

Gabrielle cried for days, each tear more buoyancy for my anger, drowning the grief and flooding me with vengeance. Because they had made one fatal mistake.

Eric had stopped driving.

He called it *'retinitis pigmentosa'*. Tunnel vision, loss of night-sight, the world becoming a chaotic blur under stress or tiredness. It had been affecting him on and off for weeks. He was in Grenoble to see the foremost specialist in the field of degenerative eye diseases in the whole of France, where he had been reassured some kind of visual prosthesis might yet save his sight, or at least prolong it for the sake of his career. Instructed under no circumstances to drive, and certainly not a vintage classic in concours condition, Eric had hired a part-time driver. A driver who died suddenly of cardiac arrest. On the very same day his newest customer vaporised in the valley of death.

There was no post-mortem on the dust of Eric. There was a post-mortem on the body of his new chauffeur.

And there was also a coroner with a young family. A family which, once threatened, provided sufficient motivation for the medical examiner to reveal the original toxicology report, providing a full description of the government official who arranged its replacement. His little girl offered so much encouragement, in fact, that our shaking hero handed over his signed copy of the Document officiel des secrets d'État, its ink as wet as the crotch of his pants.

And there it was, at the bottom of the page, a claim as much as an admission, the signature and title of the recently murdered *Paul Baudelaire, DGSE*. And that is why Le Troisième existed, because our primary secret service could not do a single thing without leaving their filthy dirty fingerprints all over it.

I watched him for six weeks.

It was enough.

The twice-weekly trysts with the married girlfriend on the coast and the meetings with Christine in Parc de Buttes Chaumont where lack of tradecraft had been the demise of so many in our game. It was simply my good fortune that Baudelaire liked to fish alone after assignations at the pretty bijou cottage on the quay. He had caught nothing but his own guilt by the time I located him. All I had to do was call his name and wait for him to turn around. My eighteenth kill, he was by far the least satisfying, crying like a baby while he bled out. Who was I to correct his assertion that he was killed by the cuckolded husband? At least this way, he died for love.

Remote recording equipment had already confirmed who gave him his final orders.

SEVEN

Leclerc was agitated, his hobbling gait increasingly lop-sided as he sped from the parfumier to the river, fumbling at the ticket office for a billet abord the midday sailing. The fierce sun bringing out his handkerchief as he waddled down the gangway, he took a seat in the tight rear bench. The pleasure cruiser listed as he shifted, and a family in front swapped sides.

Untying the aft rope unseen, I jumped aboard and entered via the staff access, sliding in to trap him.

'Aren't you getting bored with all this time off you're taking?'

With a mess of facial hair and dark glasses I was barely recognisable, but no tourist would occupy this seat by choice. He looked out towards the grand lady, whose skirt billowed in the breeze revealing a latticework of steel that still supported her roof. The stonework gleamed. 'Was I followed?' he asked.

'Only by me.'

He smiled. 'Then you have another day, two days maximum,' he said, removing a crushed cigarette packet from his jacket pocket.

'*Hey, no smoking!*' one of the small children shouted from the opposite bench over the droning mechanical introduction of our host. Leclerc nodded and when the child looked back to his mother, tossed the box and its contents overboard.

'What do you mean two days?'

He shifted again as the boat peeled further from the bank and into the procession of craft that circumnavigated Paris until we seemed like fixtures in a Canaletto painting, seen but unobserved by the massed ranks of extras on the banks.

'That police car. They took your picture.'

'Merde.'

'Foucault is sitting on it until I deliver you or your explanation. I told him you were working for a higher cause, but since he thinks he's God, that story doesn't really wash. If he doesn't have a satisfactory answer by tomorrow lunchtime, you become suspect number one in the death of three tourists and a blow to our tourism industry.' He waved his arm towards the packed seats at the front of the craft.

'Three *tourists*?'

'It seems Nicole lives.'

I was stunned. It was not possible. Not with the force of an explosion that hurled me twenty metres, confirmed again by the shaky footage. 'How–'

'Oh, don't fret, she's dead alright. The third was a hobo who died conveniently the night before the attack. So, it seems–'

'It won't go down as a suicide attack. Because they can't come hunting the ghost of the bomber. *Fuck.*'

'Quite my hairy friend.' Leclerc was enjoying the situation far too much. A welcome distraction from the drudgery, and an opportunity to write off one of his many unpaid debts. 'There is good news, though.' He turned to study me. 'Found out what the filthy little hack was up to.'

He waited for me to award some form of recognition. I gave a desultory nod.

'He was doing a puff piece on *Fraternité*.'

For a moment I was confused. Why would Eric write about brotherhood, did he mean to expose me? How would that have been possible when he had no clue that I was anything more than a buyer and seller of amateur art and professional wine?

'Fraternité,' Leclerc repeated, 'the *new force for the future of France*.'

Of course, politics. Eric's first love. The new political party that was sweeping the nation's centre-ground and hauling the rest of us with them.

'His editor thought he might have something brewing on the side, though. Had that faraway look in his eye last time they spoke, he said. Wasn't at all surprised by the crash. Apparently, he'd been drinking much more recently. Kept walking into things in the office. Hangovers most likely, the editor said. Anyway, what's your interest in him?' Leclerc turned his gaze out again towards the bank, and I heard the echo of Foucault in his question, picturing the two of them shrugging shoulders as they discussed my fate over cognac in one of the many bars beside *Tourelles*.

'I heard a rumour. He was looking to blackmail one of ours.'

Leclerc stiffened, turned back to look sideways at me, barely containing his smile. He adored gossip, did Leclerc.

'Christine,' I said, holding him dangling for a moment. 'Apparently, she was protecting that body which washed up on the beach.'

Leclerc broke into a broad grin, before choking on laughter. 'Christ, don't tell me you offed him too, Berthier?'

'Don't be so ridiculous.'

Even entering a coffeeshop, she created a stir, and a bittersweet stab of jealous pride bubbled under my cracked ribs as two handsome men appraised her. One had the courage to engage and, laughing, she responded to whatever practiced line was served, returning it with venom.

Her head turned as they left, and there was that flash of white and red, that most beautiful pillar box smile. Her eyes skipped around to see which way her admirers went, rejected or otherwise. She was a sucker for a funny pick-up line as I knew to my great gratitude.

The archetypal Parisienne, she wore the city like a fine chemise, wrapping her from head to toe, reflected in the way she threw her head, checked her watch, tapped her feet one after the other. With her legs crossed, she oozed desire. She positively screamed seduction. Or perhaps I was simply missing her too much after so many lonely nights on the stiff bed with its wafer of mattress. Those places were never intended to be used for more than one day, two at most.

I realised I had never seen her like this before.

This was the working Gabrielle, the organised Gabrielle, the professional Gabrielle. It was a side of her I liked instantly. She was more confident than ever. An inch taller at least. I had always known I lived in her shadow, but only right then did I see how far it stretched.

She collected a regular order, more than enough for her, something for the mogul too no doubt, then tapped a quick message on her phone. She was studying the screen as I darted between the cars, crossed the street and stepped into her path. She looked up partly, apologised and returned to business. As she started to slide around me, I gripped her arm.

Astonished, she looked up again and I feared the wrath of the legionnaire who taught her self-defence before faint recognition flashed in her face.

'B?'

I lifted my other hand delicately under her chin, to close her mouth. 'Don't say anything. Just walk.'

'What do you mean?' She instantly ignored me. 'What the hell happened to you? Have you been in a fight? Jesus, B, your face–'

Spinning her lightly around, away from her route, I directed her into a quiet cul-de-sac of tall townhouses where only clothes on empty balconies would overhear us, where even the sun was made unwelcome.

'Berthier, you're scaring me,' she said, which I felt in the goosebumps of her arm.

'Gabrielle, listen to me.'

She pulled herself free. 'Have you been using again? Berthier? That fucking Oleg. I knew this would–'

'Listen. This is important.' Taking both arms again, I relieved her of lunch, setting it on a doorstep, shoeing away a ginger cat who eyed the bag eagerly.

'Gabrielle. There is no Oleg.'

'What? I don't understand. Where the hell have you been?' Her eyes reached into mine, and then the scar. The gash. She lifted her hand and ran a light finger down my cheek, tracing away the last remaining ache.

'Who the hell did this to you?'

Taking both her hands into mine, I pulled them to my chest, and closed my eyes. 'Baby, I am not an art and wine dealer–'

'What do you mean?' She motioned to move away. 'Is this some kind of sick joke? Did that fucking Russian put you up to this? Is this his idea of fun. *Well*, is it?'

I hesitated. 'It's no joke. Please, believe me. It's deadly serious.'

She stared, said nothing. I had never lied to this woman before. Never. Not about anything. What passed between us unsaid were only secrets, never lies. She studied me. 'I don't–'

'I'm a *spy*. The wine and art, it's just a cover. It's what I do. It's what I know–'

'Bullshit.' She shook her head, and the hair tossed like it did when we made love. Then the head turned in ecstasy, not disbelief.

'In the next few days, you will come to know it. Pascal will confirm it.'

She stopped and thought about Papa. Papa would know what to do, of course he would. He would know how to fix Berthier, what to do about him, where to find help for the drug-taking drinking womaniser who had finally lost his battle with every vice known to man.

'I was there,' I implored her to believe me, 'at *Centurion*. This,' I ran my finger roughly down my cheek, wiping the soft memory of her healing touch, 'was the result. As was this.' Pulling up my shirt revealed the cuts and bruising, and the amateurish bandages wrapped below my chest to help protect the broken ribs.

Her mouth dropped open, horror sweeping in as suspicion

slipped away. 'Jesus, B, you need a doctor.'

I didn't. Any attempt to visit a hospital, and the next medical professional to assess my broken body would have been the golf commentator.

'Were you close by?' Touching me tenderly again, she welcomed me home.

'I need to go away. For a couple of days, maybe even a few weeks. I will call you I promise. But listen to me, baby. What I am about to ask of you now, may save my life.' I could not bring myself to tell her it might also save hers.

She nodded. 'Anything.'

I relayed a list of items which she needed to memorise. And I knew she would. Because even in the revelation that she did not know the man with whom she shared her bed, she remained the most professional woman of any I had ever met. She disappeared without her lunch, which I shared with the grateful cat.

Ninety minutes later, Gabrielle was back, handing me what I had requested. As I let her go back to life before my brutal confession, she stopped.

'Will we still marry?'

'The second it's safe. I promise.'

His home was only half a house. A beautiful square of art deco style sliced at the first floor to create accommodation for two families in the aftermath of the war, Vichy downstairs, resistance above them, as ever. Eric lived upstairs, of course, alone with his political conscience. I examined Gabrielle's key in the lock, not for its first time I imagined.

Inside there was a small pile of mail. Confirmations from the utility companies that the deceased was no longer required to pay his bills, but that they wished him all the best with his new provider. Eric spurned the heat of cremation in favour of burial, keeping his gas costs to a minimum until the very last. There were two condolence cards for my aunt, which I folded open and stood on a shelf. Their flowered faces were the only living things in the place.

A cap and shooting stick lay on the same set of shelves that also housed Eric's dark green 'Wellington' boots, dusted with mud. And he wondered why the French establishment detested him so.

Opposite hung an enormous photograph of Scotland; two misty peaks, one purple the other a greyish yellow, and in the distance, on the crest, the faint outline of a giant stag. It looked like some prehistoric lion of the glens, king of all it surveyed. It now surveyed Eric's lounge from the far wall where its head nodded mournfully above his desk. 'Congratulations,' it seemed to say, 'I didn't see you coming.'

Eric's laptop was gone.

The neatness of the paperwork could only have been achieved by someone who turned the place completely upside down. A search for anything was pointless. Not even Eric's fingerprints remained among the dust that gathered first after his passing, and then again since the clean-up team under the direction of Christine. The books, of which there were many, hundreds of them in English, stretched across the wall adjacent to his rich brown desk. There were stories of Churchill, biographies alongside portfolios of the statesman's amateur art. An entire shelf was dedicated to the history of the Union, arranged chronologically, and then by author. The stag could have recited the writers as they slept. At the end away from me, nearest the window which warmed the dusty air, were the volumes of Eric's own works, analyses of the 'European Project', its foundation, machinations and much forecast demise.

There was a faded antique globe which warned that kraken claim emboldened sailors; a world shaped in the image of our empire with all its craven misgivings. It opened to reveal enough malt to sink a tall ship; Jonnie Walker Red, Green and Black were all near full, while The Macallan was all but gone. Pouring myself the final dram in one of Eric's cut glass crystal tumblers, I raised a toast to my long-lost brother. *Salut, mon brave.*

Collapsing into his old leather winged chair, I saw it.

Buried amid the ranks of political tedium. *Stiff Upper Lip, Jeeves.* Wodehouse. Eric's favourite author, to whom another half shelf was devoted elsewhere. But not there. Definitely not there. Pulling the volume eagerly from incongruity, it was obvious that I was not the first to check it. There was not a single speck of dust across its pages, which had been shaken for hidden gems, for sure.

Like so many others among his collection, it contained a personal dedication. Only this one, despite its claim, was not written by the author: *'My dear Bertie, what fun we had. To the memory of the dreaming spires where we did everything but sleep. Eternally, yours.'*

All, in his most favoured tongue. English.

Oh Eric. You were ever the most intelligent among us. Right until the end.

Downing The Macallan, I deposited the empty bottle back in the globe; the glass, rinsed and dried on my sleeve, was also returned from whence it came. The book, minus its note to me, was slid back to entertain its dour neighbours. Then I collected the two cards which I would send to my aunt, took the bills and, closing the door, posted them back through to land where I found them.

Anyone who looked closely would know there had been a visitor, but most often such observations were farmed out to the local gendarmerie, where the task of checking on the wellbeing of the dead fell to the most dispensable among their number. In any event, the only information worth having was folded neatly in my pocket and of the two men who might have understood it, I was the only one still alive. But for how long?

EIGHT

The English and French navies had not been so threadbare since Churchill's attack on Darlan, the one wartime victory over which we still held a grudge. At least Wellesley had the decency to be on the opposing side. Now, our respective meagre fleets were trapped together in a circular crusade, turning the tide of migrants in the Mediterranean, sending missiles into the Middle East so ever more set sail. As a result, the few frigates which remained rarely policed the real villains in The Channel, and it was aboard one of their boats that I had secured my passage. Just one illegal cargo among the billionaire's many.

We moored in Southampton, shielded inside our black windows and behind the gleaming chrome. As the captain disembarked to register with port authorities, his human contraband slipped ashore unchecked and, in my case, into the bar of the glamorous Marina Hotel. A smart concierge welcomed me, well used to wealth disguised as old seadogs.

The bar extended the length of one wall, sleek and spartan

with a mirror behind and stocked with a stellar cast of colourful spirits. Staffed by a pair of identical close-shaved twins, they greeted me in unison.

'Take a seat,' the one on the left directed me.

'Someone will come across to take your order,' said his brother.

The chair was less comfortable than my former berth, seemingly designed only to keep me thirsty. There were tubs and sofas, green velvet and ochre cloth, all collected like a boutique furniture store around footstools and side-tables just big enough for olives. The view out over the harbour was spoiled by the rows of gin palaces which dwarfed the rare beauty of the sailing yachts.

'What can I get you?' The waitress dropped a paper-mat beside my seat, on which she perched an array of South America: Macadamia, Brazil and walnut. Blonde and petite, and educated-looking, I guessed she was a student on break.

'*Parlez vous Francais?*' I asked, watching her coal eyes turn diamond. She flushed.

'*Une petit peu. Je l'ai étudié à l'école.*'

I smiled. And released her from the torture of the classroom. 'It's ok, we'll manage in my *little* English.' Rose ivy crept from her chest towards her face. 'What's your name?'

She looked at her badge to remind herself. 'Justine,' she said, nervously.

'Very well then, Justine, what would you recommend?'

'Do you like whisky, only the barman does an excellent old fashioned.'

Looking across, I noted his traditional displeasure at my flirtation. They were an item before I had arrived unannounced. 'I like the sound of that. Why don't you take one for yourself too?'

Her pale face all but pink, she retreated with a nod, afraid the next word may be her last. I watched as she relayed my shame-faced order, nodding at her former beau whose bitter smile went unacknowledged by me. He looked a stylish fellow and would lure her back from this fantasy with that famous British pluck, for sure.

As Justine returned with my drink, I noticed she had a cross tucked into her blouse.

'Tell me,' I said, 'do you know the Church of St Aloysius Gonzaga in Oxford?'

She started. 'The Oratory?' Those diamonds were now worth a million each.

'Yes, you know it?'

'I do, I'm studying at Somerville College.'

I knew she was too clever for the model at the bar. 'And what do you study there?'

She eyed me suspiciously. Could I have stalked her through social media on a phone I clearly didn't possess, else it would have been enthralling me like all the other lonely drinkers? 'Applied Physics,' she admitted, caught between curiosity and concern.

I smiled. 'Then you're very smart. So, tell me, *Miss Einstein*, what's the easiest way for a simple Frenchman to get there?'

For a second, she was thrown, before she laughed a little nervous exhale. 'It's around an hour and twenty minutes on the train,' she said, regaining her composure. 'But be sure to catch the direct connection, otherwise–' She remembered I was French. '*Much too long*'.

'And the station, it's near here?' I remembered that English was my second language.

She pointed. 'About a twenty-minute walk, but it is uphill'. She waved her arm upwards in case my vocabulary did not stretch as far as her cotton blouse.

'Ah, *inclinaison*,' I said, and we both laughed.

But despite the flirting, neither of us was really inclined to spoil the dream, and before too long my drink was drunk, *l'addition* was settled with a handsome tip to remember the roguish Frenchman, and the frog departed unprinced by Justine's kiss.

She was right.

The walk was all uphill, apart from a short downward sprint to catch the ten thirty-four to Oxford. It was not a busy service. But neither did it deliver its promised eighty-one minutes, instead affording me a lazy tourist's view of Southern England which, together with its transport network, appeared significantly unchanged in two decades. Only this time, the seat opposite was empty, and not filled with the promise of Eric. And no young girls were hanging on our every word, urging us not to improve our English but to maintain their aural pleasure.

I sighed. And noticed an old lady further down the carriage who smiled back. She looked a little like my mother, that same melancholic air of widowhood.

I thought of maman and Edith, one losing a son, one a nephew, and prayed it stayed that way for the sake of them both. And mainly, of course, for me.

◆ ◆ ◆

On the doorstep, the ruddy faced buxom don greeted me mournfully, removing her glasses and willing a smile that would not come for a man she never hoped to see again. It was twenty years since the one weekend I slept on her uncomfortable couch for little more than three hours, and everything had changed. Yet still, the cloud of floral colour and wild hair wafted aside with the scents of summer to usher me within.

'He came to me six weeks ago,' she said, pouring tea from a proud pot, offering me biscuits from between roses and thistles. They also bloomed on my cup and saucer, and on the sugar bowl. 'It was a shock to see him like that I can tell you.' She settled back into the bouquet of a sofa and raised her cup to me.

'How have you been, Agnes,' I asked for politeness, when all I really wanted to know was *where is it, what is it, and what did he tell you about it.*

There were almost as many books there as at Eric's. Either side of a real fireplace, they were assembled and jumbled on narrow shelves which followed the uncertain path of ancient walls. They were nowhere near as neat, because they hadn't been arranged by French intelligence, but by good old English literature.

'I've retired, now, of course. Do a little writing, editing for one of the glossies, and crosswords for *The Standard.* Always nice to be busy.'

Agnes Berry was Eric's favourite professor. So much so, that for the last two years of his studies, he occupied the bedroom at the back of her bronze-age cottage a stones-throw from his former college.

'However did you find me?' she asked, from inside the craziest sandy walls in Oxford, bedecked with a wisteria that felt like an extension of her wild and greying hair. With its neat thatch and lead windows, Agnes' home was on more postcards than the Bodleian.

'The church.' I nodded out through lace curtains towards *The Oratory*, a few backstreets away. 'I remember it so well.' I also drew her tiny hobbit-like home from across the street, sketched into the city walls to imprint the memory of that fine weekend. The finest of my early adult life. My whole life even.

'And are you a journalist now too?'

'I am, but I fear never so successful as Eric.'

She smiled. 'He was my proudest achievement.' I believed she meant it.

'Did he talk to you ever, about his work?' It was impossible to know whether Eric maintained relationships with any of his past conquests or landladies. They were too numerous to keep tabs, his amiability earning passion and friendships everywhere.

'He did because I'm afraid we were on opposite sides.'

I raised my eyebrows.

'The great divide,' she encouraged me. And then, when it was clear her clues must leave the cryptic and settle upon the simple, she directed my gaze to the window. There in its uppermost pane was a Brexit sticker, the glass beneath it cracked from shame. 'I'm afraid I'm not a believer in size,' she said with a wry smile, 'or safety in numbers. Rather the hare than the herd.'

'Small is sometimes beautiful.' I remembered the waitress.

'Not your Eric, though. He was a true disciple. A follower 'til the bitter end.'

We both fell silent, thinking of the apostle in his crown of thorns. 'When did the two of you last speak?' I said finally, when the ticking of an old grandfather clock reminded me that there was perhaps a solitary day before my notoriety would overtake my cousin's.

'Just before he died. Most heated I ever heard him. Outraged about your new political party, he was. So strange, really, because he was such a staunch liberal. Never more at home than on the tolerant middle-ground. *Live and let live*, that was Eric's motto. And yet there he sat, right where you are now, proclaiming his love of France – *Liberté, égalité, fraternité* – as though his very life depended on his loyalty. Or rather, on France's loyalty to him.' Taking a mouthful of tea, she nudged the plate closer to me. 'Go on, there's a Viennese whirl with your name on it, just to show there's no hard feelings. I can't abide all this division.'

It was several days since my last proper meal, and I was no longer hungry only for justice. A man cannot survive on adrenaline and alcohol alone. 'He was never a patriot,' I said, between mouthfuls. 'He loved you English far too much.'

She laughed and her ample bosom joined in. 'He was spoiled here, really. I think we gave him a taste of milk and honey from which he never recovered.' She laughed again and I could imagine how easily Eric fell for her and for England, how he was so quickly won over by the charm of both. Then she sighed and a soft silence fell between us once more. 'Anyway,' she said drily, rising and reaching for a book on the shelf behind her chair, 'you didn't come all this way simply to sample the delights of English breakfast tea.' She chuckled to herself, before handing me the volume. *Madame Bovary*. 'He gave me this to keep,' she said, the sadness back from the doorstep. She didn't let it go immediately, retaining her last gentle grip on the student she and I both adored before he gently slipped away. 'He told me someone would come for it. And that I would recognise them when they did.'

I too held the book awhile, a battered hardback that was likely studied no more here than at home. There was no dedication this time, but the inner cover had been repaired more than once, the last time recently.

'He said it would mean something to you.' She nodded towards it.

'It does.'

'Doesn't look your type of thing?' She smiled at the rough mess of a man sat in her pretty parlour with its unkempt blossoms and lace, where even the clutter of magazines was immaculate by comparison to me.

'It belonged to my aunt, Eric's mother. They had a falling out.' It was true. Eric's mother did not approve of airing dirty laundry at all, let alone from the public scrutiny of the front page. I sometimes wondered whether his father's prosecution for embezzlement drove his motivation.

'Would you tell her how sorry I am,' Agnes urged. 'His mother, I mean.'

I nodded. 'Of course.'

At the door, some of the mournfulness was gone, but not the regret. 'We may have disagreed on politics and even literature, but Eric was a decent man, an *honest* man. It's always the honourable ones he takes too young.' She looked skyward.

'It is.'

And right then this liar vowed to serve vengeance in full on those dishonest bastards who really took my cousin.

NINE

The foppish kid eyed me suspiciously. His blue branded t-shirt was a size too small, even for his skeletal frame, and his machine swung like a shackle around his neck. The astonishment had passed, replaced by mild panic.

'You want to pay in cash?' he said, again.

'Yes.'

'But it's *seventeen hundred pounds*.'

'I know. Also, I will need a continental power lead, and a case. You have those too?'

'In cash?'

There seemed to be some confusion about the sale of goods in Oxford. 'Yes, in cash.'

Shaking his blonde head, he walked away, most likely to lie down in a darkened room until the shock subsided. Instead, he returned with a glaring supervisor.

'Good afternoon,' she moaned, from beneath geek glasses and above another swinging terminal that was not large enough to contain the price, nor even the small amount of my anticipated change. 'My colleague tells me you'd like to pay in cash, is that correct?'

'No flies on you.' She looked at me quizzically, revealing that she was neither real nor programmed for sarcasm, so I returned to the script. 'Yes, that is correct.'

'Well, this is very rare,' she said, like she'd unearthed a Roman coin while digging a new border to plant geraniums.

Withdrawing two thousand from my pocket, I offered it all to bring the transaction to a hasty conclusion, uncaring whether it looked like the proceeds of crime. In a way, of course, it was. Just like all of it. 'Please, I'm in something of a hurry. I'm working to a tight deadline and my current machine has blown up.' They both stared at me. 'Crashed,' I corrected quickly. 'Beyond saving. And I have a story to file–'

Their faces lit up. 'Story?' the skeleton repeated.

'I'm a foreign news correspondent, and my office always send me away with cash.'

'Expenses,' the supervisor said, relieved, but also concerned. She wouldn't have wanted to find their franchise on the front page for obstructing a member of the press in the execution of his duties. 'Of course, expenses.'

'Tight deadline?' Confirming my urgency, finally they took the cash away to the back of the store where a long bar served no alcohol. Seven excruciating minutes later I was finally free of the flimsy brand promises and making my way to the nearest genuine bar.

I chose the corner of an old English pub. Smelling of oak and wood-shavings, cracked leather and bad food, it was dark and suitably discreet. Before me, meanwhile, my new screen clucked like a freshly hatched duckling, doing everything possible to ingratiate itself with its new owner. I had no desire to form some emotional bond with a hunk of tin and wafers of silicon, despite its best endeavours and adopted female name. Slipping the tiny flash card into the slot, I held my breath.

The very first file bore my name:

How are you, Bertie?

All cried out by now, I hope. The bastards got to me, then? I guessed they might, which is why I left all this for you. Everything you need to know is here, chronologically. Work your way through and reach your own conclusions. Tell Gabi she was the one that got away. Tell mama, I'm sorry for everything.

Love as always, Eric.

PS: I never believed you traded art or wine.

I hope I was right?

I studied my shaking hands before progressing down the list of other files. The fists were clenched so tight the knuckles rippled red and white. Bright blue veins in the wrists throbbed, just as they did while reviewing those forty-eight pages of pure fiction. All the closure I felt in watching Christine's head explode was gone. It seemed someone else pulled the strings of Eric's death.

The barmaid delivered another beer unrequested, bringing me back from the brink. 'On the house,' she said, nodding at the laptop. 'Doesn't look like good news.'

I thanked her, thinking about my dishevelled appearance. There was no point fictionalising an explanation, she would have heard them all before. 'You're too kind.'

The files were unencrypted.

But there were also hundreds of them.

They were mainly scanned newspaper clippings, with sentences and paragraphs highlighted, the first from *Le Monde* on the latest protest movement sweeping our nation, the rise of the 'gilet jaunes'. So too the next, which criticized failings in immigration and integration, a breakdown in our social fabric – no news there. Next came a story from Eric's own rag, on yet another oligarch with his hands on the tiller of power; donations made to parties across the union, in the countless countries he called 'home'. More Russian-sounding villains followed – do-gooders and charity-flunkies lauded for their generosity, in London especially. That wealthy crooks buy innocence, however, was a tale as old as time.

I scrolled to the end and a 'Bibliography' that was nothing beyond an endless list of URLs, like Eric's entire browser history was downloaded to pdf. I had no idea whether I was meant to visit each of his hundreds of links, but if I was, that required something all liars know to avoid. *The world wide web.* Instead, a quick search of the folders and files revealed nothing of Christine Montgolfier or Baudelaire. Nothing at all. Neither was there any mention of DGSE or my own merry band of fools and fabricators.

In Eric's head, this may all have made perfect sense, but how I could have done with his famed insight. Even a précis. For a journalist who wrote six books, he had been agonisingly scant in his written assistance. That's the problem with intelligent people. They too often overestimate the rest of us. *What the hell were you onto Eric? And why was any of it worth dying for?*

◆ ◆ ◆

The service from London's St. Pancras station to Paris takes a little over two hours, and thanks to an agreement between the respective governments, officially the train also embarks from France - a rare piece of détente that survived the big breakaway. With border formalities on departure, all I needed was to buy a ticket, present a passport and board the service. Then, on arrival I could slip quietly into Paris among the crowd at Garde du Nord. Once back, a proper assessment of Eric's intel could be undertaken, perhaps with help of someone who knew him and understood a journalist's modus operandi a little better than me.

It was around an hour into the journey, when there was a message from that very someone, on one of the twin phones she purchased for us.

We had only just emerged from the tunnel, accelerating through rural France, finally reaching top speed when my pocket vibrated. It coincided with a gentle chime from the train which elicited some modest clapping from the tourists, since it indicated we had reached three hundred kilometres per hour. That was nothing to my heart rate when Gabrielle's message opened in my palm.

It was a photograph.

Of the late *Julian Martin*.

Without a smile or facial hair. Without the scar that now blighted him. It was the photograph that was used to board that very train. The photograph from all eight of my passports, in fact. Because it was my official service photograph.

The message was simple.

Without a word that could be traced, she had told me all I needed to know.

They were looking for me.

So much for Leclerc's promised two days.

It also meant they would implement *'Article Soixante-Sept'* if they had not done so already.

At any moment, a security officer in London would have their dreary day disrupted by an alert from central Paris requesting a check of the passenger manifests for every inbound and outbound service. A maximum of twelve minutes later, a secure message would be sent to the unsuspecting driver of my train. As soon as it was received, he or she would make an announcement to the train manager using a recognised code. Then, that manager would walk calmly to the rear of the service where they would find the leader of a well-drilled armed security detail, dressed in the most conspicuous plain-clothes. Other members of that team of four would be secreted throughout the remaining coaches. Not the one I was travelling in, thankfully. I had already checked.

From the moment that message was received at the rear of the train, I had around ninety seconds before being detained at gunpoint. I knew that, for sure. Because I reviewed the protocol for Christine, after a Brussels-bound service was derailed by some fanatical suicide bomber. Right then, however, there were three things in my favour.

One, their suspect looked like a hobo, not their image.

Two, I knew they were coming for me.

And three, most importantly of all, they had not yet received their alert.

Because there had been no public address from the driver.

Unfortunately, *they* also had one major advantage that could not be overcome.

We were travelling at three hundred and twenty kilometres

per hour, galloping along in a pressurised metal tube, hurtling through rural France with nothing but agricultural farmland between the train and the horizon in all directions. It would take over three and a half kilometres from applying the emergency brake for the train to reach a dead stop - a minimum of forty-nine seconds - and a further twenty before the coach doors could be opened manually. And then, assuming I had somehow evaded identification, where the *hell* would I go? Even running as fast as a mistral, I could be visible for hours.

There were no hopeful options.

It was time to improvise.

As casually as possible, I smiled at the gaunt grey business face opposite, excusing myself for the bathroom. Half a minute later, returning briskly to my seat, I engaged him: 'Don't be alarmed, but there's a guy acting suspiciously in the next compartment along, I'm going to find the train manager to check up on him, would you mind my bag for me?'

Perking up, the charcoal-suited executive examined me. 'Suspicious, how?'

I shrugged. 'Furtive, carrying a rucksack. He looks extremely nervous and muttering to himself. He's *agitated*, you know?'

The businessman shivered. 'Should I... go and see for myself. Maybe–'

'No.' I placed a firm hand on his shoulder. 'I'll find the train manager and send them this way. If you see somebody sooner, tell them to check on the passenger in Coach G seat forty-eight. Ok?'

He nodded, complicit in this exciting new venture, the highlight of his week, for sure. 'Seat forty-eight', he repeated, and then again for good measure.

As I rose, he gripped my arm above the wrist. 'How can you tell such things?'

'*Pardon.*' In a hush, 'Excuse this rough appearance. I'm an undercover cop.'

He grinned widely. 'Fantastic', he crowed, thinking about how he would relay this to his wife over spaghetti in their loft apartment, before they made love for the first time in months, the climax of his new heroic status. He hesitated. 'Is it safe… sitting *here*?'

'Yes, yes, the doors are blast proof and the train weighs over nine hundred tonnes. You're quite safe, my friend, trust me. And anyway, he's probably just a pickpocket or thief.' I smiled broadly as I gave his shoulder a hearty squeeze.

Maybe he would remember Brussels and the fourteen tragic deaths. Hopefully, he wouldn't recall that most were caused by the derailment, rather than the device. One thing was certain, if my new accomplice was going anywhere, it would be away from the direction in which I was headed.

I squeezed his shoulder again. 'See you shortly.'

Making my way swiftly back through Coach G, any member of crew was elusive. I was nearly into coach K before she appeared. Tending her trolley of unhealthy snacks, the dark-haired urchin was rearranging miniature bottles of undrinkable wine in the airless clanking gap between carriages. Sliding around the cart, I gripped her arm.

'I'm sorry, but there's a guy down there, Coach F, grey suit, grey hair, grey face. He doesn't seem at all well. Sweating, shaking, his head lolling forward. I'm no doctor but I think maybe you should go and check on him?' I shuddered. 'It's just that… well, he seems exactly like my partner before he… before he had his *heart attack.*' My eyes filled. '*Please.*'

She dropped the final bottle into place without looking. 'Of course,' she said, rising. 'Do you know which seat?'

I winced and nodded, stifling a sob. 'About halfway down, left hand-side–'

She forced a smile. 'Leave it with me, I'm sure he will be fine.'

Thanking her, I reached awkwardly for the toilet door and stumbled inside.

Ten seconds later, I exited to find her gone, and reaching for the bright red emergency handle on a panel above my head, I yanked it with all my might.

Instantly, an alarm began to wail like a strangled cat. It set my teeth on edge.

Heaving open the door to the next coach, I plunged awkwardly inside, pitching left, then right, roaring *La Marseillaise*, and belching and groaning between bars. Heads turned as names were barked at random, to the left and to the right, as the rich smell of a recently served boeuf bourguignon filled me with confidence.

'*Hey, Maurice, Antoine, Frederic, how are you?*' I zeroed in on my target, head down over his rare beef wishing himself invisible. A retired lawyer or banker, he drizzled his dauphinoise with jus. Dark blue blazer, salmon shirt, a tan from years of practice and enough gold to weigh anchor, he dined alone inside an exclusion zone of his own choosing looking everywhere but up.

Leaning in, I slapped his back. '*Marcel. You old goat. You never stop being ugly.*' Roaring with laughter, I poured myself some wine.

'Please, I'm not your friend,' he said, recoiling as though poverty was contagious.

The other faces mainly looked away too. Apart from the solitary child. The little blonde was enthralled by this unfettered clown, without a red nose or curly orange hair to adorn him. She earned a wink from me.

I leaned back, swaying. 'Ha! You're right, you're even *uglier* than Marcel.' I bellowed again, spinning around a full three hundred and sixty degrees, before crashing across his table with an almighty clatter of glass and steel. 'Oh, look at me, what an idiot,' I crowed, as Marcel rolled back his head in despair.

As the clown stumbled onward, his memory was wiped away with a despairing napkin. The other passengers flinched and winced, fearing they may be next.

'*Vivre le revolution,*' I yelled at the top of my voice, as the deceleration became more obvious, the wailing of the siren now a frustrated lament. Irritated and despairing faces looked skyward, resigned to stopping for no apparent reason. This is why they all detested the train so much. A complete lack of control. Over their journey, or who they shared it with. Then from the heavens, came a lone impassioned voice: '*Ladies and gentlemen, this is your train manager speaking. We apologise for the slowing of this service. It appears there is a serious incident aboard the train. It's nothing to worry about, and hopefully we will be underway and back up to full speed again very soon. I will come back to you shortly with more information. Thank you.*' The metallic automaton clicked off.

The faces stared at me. Was I *the incident*? Or was it the heart attack? Or the would-be suicide bomber?

At the end of the coach, I belched a grand farewell and the doors closed upon me like the end of a Jacobean tragedy. I didn't hang around for the encore. Diving into the next toilet,

I removed my jacket, transferring the contents quickly into my jeans. Throwing water on my hair, I styled it with the help of soap, untucked my shirt, rolled the sleeves, undid a button, damped my beard. Checked the mirror: ageing computer guy, west coast, probably a seller of addictive mobile apps.

Exiting, I walked casually but quickly to the very back of the train.

There, the doors of the final car heaved apart to reveal him. Sitting near the rear of the half-filled carriage, his tall bulky frame sported black pants and a blue lightweight jacket thick enough to hide his holstered weapon, but not so heavy it would restrict his ability to run and fire. His attempts at nonchalance in the echo of the alarm were pitiful. Fists flexing and feet tapping, his beady vigilant black eyes stared from the shaven head like two dead flies on a pancake.

Approaching him, I whispered in my mother's American accent, 'Are you an undercover security agent?'

He eyed me cautiously, pulling one hand from his knee to his waist, closer to the source of his power. His face remained unmoved.

I swayed as the train jolted to walking pace with an irritated hiss. 'The train manager told me I would find one in this coach.' He said nothing. But his eyes confirmed it. 'The alarm was pulled by a guy with a beard in Coach F,' I continued, now loud enough to be heard elsewhere. 'He abandoned his bag and looks like he's trying to get off the train. The stewardess is searching for him now. She sent me to you for help.'

The agent stood. 'Stay here,' he commanded, reaching inside his blouson, before moving off the way I'd come. The other passengers craned their eager necks to follow him. And while they did, I slipped quickly and quietly out of the rear doors.

As the smoked glass whispered closed behind me, the siren cried its last and the service rumbled to a quiet disgruntled halt. Hurriedly pulling two forks from my waistband, I slid them into the panel next to the rear cab and cursing angled them to find the lock. They were not ideal tools. Small and delicate, they were designed for aesthetics not for leverage. They barely skewered the tender cow and slipped in my sweaty palms. Through the doors, I could hear muted conversations begin. Irritated chat. No one looked my way but that was going to change quickly if the damned cover didn't open to allow me into the cab. There was no need of any extraneous driver or guard back there. At least, there wasn't when Christine approved the protocols.

Finally, a metallic click signalled success and the little hatch swung open. I threw the manual switch and heaved the heavy door. Light flooded the frosted glass framing me. Thankfully, not long enough for anyone to raise the alarm. I slipped inside, slammed the door and breathed again at last.

Immediately to my right, there was a triangular window with 'Issue de Secours' emblazoned on its glass. The instant I pulled the emergency lever, it fell crashing onto the ballast below. Swinging around, I threw my feet out and dropped to the stones, crouching alongside the train's yellow and blue nose. The stench from the overheated brakes was not unlike the whiff of cordite, while above my head, cables buzzed like they meant to scorch me too.

Four pairs of tracks were trapped within an escarpment that stretched forever, and either side the two banks wore nothing more than knee-high grass. There were no welcome clumps of trees or shrubs in which to disappear, no obstacles to shield me at all. Just the clean, well-maintained boundaries of the SNCF. *Fuck.*

There was no option but to run.

Back towards London.

Directly down the centre of our track where I knew for certain I would be safe from any immediate flattening, unseen until they checked from the rear cab. With luck, the people sent to look were still occupied elsewhere.

Sprinting for what seemed an eternity, lungs searing, limbs bursting, each sleeper was like a take-off board, as I leapt and ran. After two hundred metres, there was silence but for my hard breath, racing heart, and the rush of blood clogging up my ears. I raced another ten seconds before tossing a coin in my head.

Right.

Veering across the other rails, I hurdled them like a stag, reaching the far bank only milliseconds before I heard it. The bellowing rage of the TGV horn. It nearly deafened me, blaring my name in vain, before a blurred wall of reds and greys flashed by. The squealing bogeys shrieked at the missed opportunity to slay me, before the warm tailwind whipped me horizontal, throwing me headfirst into the grass. It felt like a punishment for escaping the metal monster, which thundered on in search of other prey.

Chalking off one more life, I started the climb to learn my fate. Hand over fist I scrambled, gripping and pushing off the tufted matted grass which clawed agonisingly at my feet. Gravity was slow to relent her hold, as I slipped, fumbled and crawled, hauling myself towards the greasy summit.

At the top, sat a two-metre chain-link fence, laced with jagged razor wire, an answer to the question of migration posed in

Eric's notes. But beyond the wire there is sometimes hope, and the Gods it seemed were on my side that day, delivering up the outskirts of a small forgotten town. Directly ahead of me, I could see a builder's yard flanked by rough painted walls and strewn with old materials. There were pallets of worn red bricks, many still sporting their mortar, and piles of uneven stones – yellows, sandstones and greys of all shades – and behind the rubble, two enormous rusting doors opened into a vast corrugated hangar. It was as though the very walls had fallen off the building. And leering over everything, an angled spire pointed to an elusive freedom far beyond the town.

As the noise of the TGV evaporated, came the distant angry shouts.

One glance was all it took. Three of them. Two with pistols drawn, and the senior security agent who I'd waylaid once already who was bellowing my name. No more than a hundred and fifty metres away, they crossed the tracks with a caution I could not afford. If only I'd still had my leather jacket to smother the legion of head-height barbs. I didn't. Tough shit, Berthier. Gripping the wire, I threw my feet sideways, ran up the fence and launched, pivoting like a pole-vaulter before hitting the ground with a crunch as the first warning shots rang out.

Ducking out of sight, I sprinted like hell towards the open shed.

Inside, I skipped around more stacks of ragged stones and statues, dodging a spitting gargoyle, only to collide head-on with an old man in overalls. He looked at me agog. Maybe he was a retired priest, and the contents were his pension – a stolen church to sell off piece by piece. I bowed a quick apology, before darting around him and out through another gaping doorway.

Once back outside on the quiet suburban street, I slowed to a walk and looped nonchalantly back in the direction of the Eurostar.

Behavioural science says a quarry will run as fast and as far away from the course of its hunter, the result of millennia of genetics. My pursuers knew this too, but they had no intimate knowledge of their prey. They knew only that I was a man who fled a train, because his name appeared on a manifest in London. Long may they continue to chase the late investment banker Julian Martin, while the very present Berthier eluded them.

Crossing the street, I cast my eyes back over my shoulder a final time, before threading through a small parade of boutique stores, and towards a crossroads and some clue as to my locale.

The houses were all a muddy brick, with steps up their rooflines and patterned yellow stonework marking each storey like cross-stitching in the walls. Former commercial properties, the work had obviously dried up and the buildings converted cheaply to homes. Same occupants, different lives.

At the next intersection, my situation screamed at me from a large digital display. *Bois-Grenier* was advertising its 'town festival' in four days' time. Opposite the sign, a former hotel in which a man could hide for days had been lost to a new apartment block, its plastic windows graced by boxes of well-tended blooms. So instead, I took a right at the junction, heading back towards the railway line. But the quiet pitted road was one of those where buildings thinned to fields and would soon expose me completely from a lack of suitable cover. Up ahead, the road veered further right, and I prayed for civilisation, somewhere to conceal myself among the locals. A rare surviving bar perhaps, or a tabac where elderly men sat drinking Calvados, smoking cigars while they lamented the fall of their rugby or soccer teams.

Rounding the bend revealed nothing so obliging.

Instead, there was a small pharmacy with angular windows, and outside, parked nose in, a boxy white Mercedes van from one of the big drug companies with its stinking diesel engine idling. Looking both ways, I split the logo on the rear and climbed aboard.

Inside, there were a dozen branded boxes, but beyond them, immediately behind the seats, there was a slither of space occupied by nothing more than a rough blanket and faded green tarpaulin. Climbing in, I closed the door, clambering through to secrete myself.

I hoped desperately the driver was one of those rare ones who kept his attention mainly on the road. A full five-minutes passed, before the door opened with a cheery whistle, followed by the clunk of seatbelt, crunch of gears, and the dirty growling motor spinning faster. He reversed out and we were away.

By my estimation we were around a kilometre from the railway tracks, which was confirmed as the van climbed and then dipped over the high-speed line which bisects the whole of Northern France. Minutes later, the radio went on and I smelled a cigarette burning on the lighter, a waft of sour menthol nearly causing me to cough.

'I didn't expect to find you there,' he said.

My heart missed two beats.

Until he laughed. 'How long have you been working the afternoon shift?'

I breathed a sigh of relief.

The conversation carried on while he discussed his remaining visits. They meant nothing to me, just a list of local pharmacies and not a national chain among them. Even the town or village names could have been newly discovered stars. Recognition only came at the conclusion to their call. 'No clue what time,' he said. 'You know Lille traffic.' Perfect. The kind of migrant-filled industrial city where a man could disappear for weeks on end. Probably forever. Just so long as he didn't find me sooner.

For his next three stops, I was in luck. But at the fourth–

Footsteps leapt into the rear of the van and boxes were tossed out noisily to waiting hands, my dimmed vision increasing with every shuffle. 'Make more space up front,' a gruff voice grumbled, and I prepared for him to arrange my misshapen heap of material into something more organised. But far from folding properly, he aimed a lazy kick narrowly missing my feet, before shoving my legs and the tarpaulin tight into the seat. My head and body, already squeezed as narrow as a pencil, were left alone, thank God.

The daylight all but disappeared as the chassis sank under the weight of our new cargo, which I prayed was well secured lest it ended my career under sackcloth in a van. Although I wouldn't have been the first or last liar to depart this way. With an endorsement for the new national football coach, and cheery whistle, we were on our way again.

An hour later we slowed, and the driver reported his details to a bored security guard before parking up to the sound of clanking metal and the whine of a forklift truck. He stepped out and a conversation began. It was finally time for me to make my move.

Clambering quietly over the cargo, I squeezed through to the rear doors and threw them wide with a flourish.

Two men looked at me in horror and surprise.

'Where the fuck are we?' I bellowed at them both.

The faces, the balding driver and a weedy red-haired colleague with a clipboard and high-visibility vest, stumbled for a second, staggered that their freight had come to life.

'Well?' I leapt from the rear of the van into a wide-open logistics yard where trucks were backed up to warehouse loading bays, and vans like mine were lined against a dirty soot-stained wall.

'Who the *hell* are you?' The driver said dumbfounded. 'How–'

Rushing towards him, I jabbed my finger in his flabby chest. 'Did you abduct me from that bar? Were you there? With that Greek fellow I refused to fellate?'

The supervisor was no longer looking at me.

The driver shook from head to toe. 'No, no, no – What bar, what do you mean?'

'Oh sure, *what bar*? Like you don't fall to your knees outside that shitty waterhole every Friday night.' I spat just beyond his feet. 'I want the cops. Call the cops! You closet types are all the fucking same.' I waved my fist and shook it at his cowering colleague.

Immediately, we were the centre of a crowd. Small, but perfectly formed. They were around five metres away in a stunned high-visibility arc. No previous cargo had ever accosted a driver before.

'I don't know what… what the hell you're talking about,' the driver stammered, but not to me, to the clipboard wielding tyrant who already owned his working soul.

'Like hell you don't. Did you know this man abducts other gay men?' I asked the supervisor loud enough for the gang to hear. 'Is this a regular thing? Are you covering for him? What is this place? Some kind of kidnap operation.' My eye of suspicion swept over all of them with their shifting feet and hidden knowing smirks.

I began working my way sideways towards the entrance gate with its simple red and white pole that could be hurdled in an instant, slid under in less. Hell, the gap between it and the fence was negotiable by nothing more than breathing in. I gestured towards the security hut. 'You have a telephone in there?'

'Wait,' the driver said. 'There's been some mistake. I had no idea you were in there I swear. I'm sorry–'

'Stuff your apology.' I said, shaking my head furiously and growling like a caged panther. Three of the assembled audience were now peering into the open Sprinter, wondering how it was even possible to secrete a stowaway. One scratched his chin as though a long-held suspicion might just have proven true. Another grinned like he had landed an unexpected monster gamble on an outsider at Longchamp. The third, meanwhile, studied me and weighed me up for honesty or motive. It's not like I could have hidden a palette of branded paracetamol in my pocket. 'We'll see whether you thought I was in there or not.' I began to walk away.

The driver followed while the others returned to discussing their opinions of the man. 'Please,' he urged. 'You must believe me. My shift only started at eleven. I wasn't even working last night. You can ask my *wife*.' He threw her in loudly for his colleagues.

Approaching, I prodded him one more time. 'Then I suggest you check your rotas in preparation for a call from my lawyer.' And with this idle threat ringing loud, I left them standing bemused as I ducked under the security barrier, past the entrance hut and away down the street to seek my non-existent legal recourse.

TEN

A change of clothes was the immediate priority. Two streets into a Lille shopping district, my greatest hopes were fulfilled. A camping and outdoor store boasted rack upon rack of camouflage and khaki, as well as a phalanx of hunting knives. I selected a pair of dark green trousers with a matching military shirt and chose two blades – one small and one large. Then, to ensure the owner did not report some loner terrorist, I also picked up a fishing rod and net, some tackle and provisions, joking with the guy behind the counter about my friend's stag party and the perils of a mid-life crisis. He took my cash without complaint.

A hundred metres down the street, I slipped into an alleyway and changed, dumping my old clothes and the fishing gear in a garbage cart beside a dilapidated Cantonese restaurant. It was a little after six and as I turned to go, a hand in the window swung its sign to 'open'. I figured I may as well eat since the chance had presented itself, and the diminutive owner's delight at my unexpected custom was more than adequate to satisfy any curiosity about my recently dispensed trash.

Entering through the narrow-panelled lobby with its dated décor, a beautiful heart-shaped face behind a recessed bar welcomed me. But before I could acknowledge her coquettish smile, I was stopped by a more familiar expression on a television screen above her head. It was a man who looked a lot like the old me. That he continued to do so was testament to the continuing tacit support from Leclerc. When a photo-fit appeared with beard and scar, then I would know our fraught relationship was finally over.

The petite Asian waitress from the bar attended to me, while the owner returned to the door in anticipation of a slew of fellow diners. He could not hide his disappointment that his solitary customer preferred a seat in the shadows to the glare of low sun in his window. My best side was already promoting his bar, what more did the old man need?

'What's your name?' I asked the waitress, who flushed at the request. Her coy smile and dark eyes told me she rarely offered up such secrets. 'Chenguang,' she smiled.

'That's a beautiful name, so tell me, *Chenguang*, what would *you* recommend?' I gestured to the faded menu with its multitude of choices. She looked at me askew, in the way a puppy might, head tilted a little to the left, so her coal black hair fell over one eye, before she blew it back, brushing the lose strands behind her ear.

'What is your chef's speciality?' I repeated softly, which brought the proprietor back from the window. Berating the girl in Canton, he sent her away to the bar to fetch me a complimentary rice wine, before yelling barked orders after her. She fumbled with her notepad. 'Banquet for you, sir,' he said, turning to me with a customary nod.

And a banquet it was.

Duck, chicken, lamb, beef, enough vegetables to fill a market stall and noodles for a family of five. I wolfed the lot. It was my first proper meal since that fateful weekend with Gabrielle. *Poor Gabrielle*. I had to reassure her I was fine. But not at home where the line would be bugged. Or even her cell phone. No, in her office. That was the only remotely safe option, and even that was risky. Likewise, my mother and sister needed to hear from me, before they alerted the cops that the picture doing the rounds of a wanted Paris bomber bore a startling resemblance to their son and sibling. Thankfully, there was no television set in Reims.

Just as I began to feel satiated for the first time in weeks, four boisterous men in their early- to mid-twenties filed in laughing and cursing, jostling one another like a small herd of wildebeest. Shown to the table directly next to mine, their unruly behaviour threatened to extend to Chenguang. The biggest of the group placed his hand on her arm and stroked it despite her flinch. The dark overweight one accidentally brushed her thigh as she dodged between them removing wine glasses and opening menus. Her father sighed and winced.

Resolving to keep a closer eye, I ordered another beer and a *lychee* that I really could not stand. No matter. The repugnant taste and tropical smell ensured it would take me at least another two hours to eat. And besides, I had no obvious bed for the night. As the old man took my dessert order, I nodded towards the group and raised my eyebrows. His shrug told me all there was to know. He needed the custom more than the girl's modesty. It was an unholy trade, but one repeated the world over.

While they remained sober, there was no genuine trouble from the rowdy colleagues, although the sly remarks and innuendo proliferated, increasing the more they drank. There were bawdy jokes and sexist slurs, but only when an arm extended around Chenguang's waist and rested there too long, did I finally intervene.

The old man frowned as I rose.

Taking a firm hold of the back of the two chairs nearest me, I surveyed the group, making eye-contact with each in turn. Opposite me, the freshest of the faces grunted and sneered. He had the looks to be their leader; young, handsome, bright blue eyes. A fop of overly coiffured blonde hair. To his left, an overweight prop-forward flexed muscles in his thick neck, assessing me with beady eyes that pounded within a pink-red bowling ball. While beneath me, one black and one Asian athletic type pretended I didn't exist, pulling in unison at their beers.

'Gentlemen, how would you prefer this wonderful evening to conclude?'

'What is it to you?' said the leader, from the safety of a round table which he imagined could not be breached. The young buck had no idea that if I stamped on my side, it would break the beautiful square jaw on his.

'I am the customer satisfaction manager of this fine establishment, and it is my solemn duty to ensure you all enjoy yourselves tonight.'

They laughed and scoffed, and the far arrogant fool could not help himself. 'Fuck off,' he said, grinning. He was the ringleader no doubt.

Placing my hands on the shoulders of the two athletes and

squeezing, I leaned a little closer. Close enough to smell their cheap designer cologne. 'Please. Eat and drink as much as you like tonight, but if any of you so much as lays a finger on the waitress again, I will snap every single digit. And yours, my friend,' I stared into the blonde's empty soul to ensure he heard me, 'will be the first.'

They stopped laughing.

Straightening up, I ordered them a round of drinks on my account and returned to my seat from where they slowly let their gaze escape, resuming a stilted version of their previous conversation. Chenguang smiled at me and blushed. The old man looked away. They may come back again when their new nemesis was long gone, but for that night at least the girl was safe.

I waited until they left before paying my bill and doing likewise.

They were loitering on the street outside. Of course they were. Leaning on a rail that ran around a quiet park opposite, the ringleader at their centre flanked by his comrades, they smoked and joked beneath an amber streetlight. There was no hiding for them, they wanted to be seen. But as I exited, they looked away. So, not by me. Turning sharply, I walked two hundred metres at brisk pace, feeling their glare on my back. They watched me go. Not to follow, but to ensure I was gone.

They weren't waiting there for me.

Behind a large white panel truck, I stopped and out of sight dropped to my haunches, sliding sideways and underneath the cab. Crawling forward on my belly, I could just about make them out beyond the tip of a regiment of stationary cars which halted just short of the restaurant. In the evening breeze, they laughed and swore goading and cajoling one another. They were shit scared of me for sure, so they were waiting to take revenge on the restaurateur. I hoped he lived over the shop.

A light went on above the closed door. Good.

But then the door opened, and Chenguang stepped out.

Fuck.

She wasn't the old man's daughter.

And she didn't live safely inside.

Noticing her tormentors, she looked down, pulled her dark coat around her neck and walked swiftly away. Predictably, they followed. Less predictably, I slipped across to the far sidewalk and trailed them from behind the row of cars, picking up speed in case I needed to intervene and quickly. The street was reasonably well lit, and there were cameras outside of almost every establishment no matter how delipidated they looked. But at the end of the parade, where the road curved and slipped beneath a railway line, where the light didn't penetrate the trees and the sightlines were all but obscured, *there* was the danger zone.

Chenguang accelerated and the gang and me likewise. She skipped along just short of a run. Poor kid, she must have been absolutely petrified.

As she rounded the corner into the shadows I heard her muffled scream.

Sprinting like hell to the mouth of the tunnel, I could just make out their outline in the shadows. The ringleader had her pinned to the wall. Little more than two amorphous shapes, from the quiet anguished sobs I imagined him squeezing her or worse.

'Get the fuck away from her. *Now!*'

He didn't, and his three lieutenants emerged from the darkness, forming up to create a swaying barrier between him and her, *and me*. The black athlete on the right was fat, his Asian counterpart too slight. Like Goldilocks, though, the one in the centre spelled trouble. He was stocky and heavy and athletic, with years of education in the scrum.

I accelerated and hit them all hard.

Throwing all ninety-five kilos headlong towards the man in the middle, I roared like hell and tackled him to the floor. He stared at me with pupils wide as I crashed my elbow into the very breach of his ugly nose. A crunch and scream followed. Broken. Snapped like the breadsticks with our meals. Levering off the idiot, I grabbed hold of his balls twisting hard and shoving like a karate jab. No one ever got up from that. His agonising groan set the other two back a metre but didn't scare them off. They were drunk, bouncing on the balls of their feet like a cross between amateur boxers and overweight ballet dancers. Hearing a muffled cry from the wall, I rushed the pair of clowns, my arms outstretched like Jesus, crashing hard into their midriffs.

The black one on the left collapsed to the concrete, but the Asian dodged right, so that he was only caught sideways on, enough to unbalance but not to floor him. Crouching, I swung my leg like a Russian Cossack dancer, taking him out at the ankles. They were both down now and struggling to rise, sunk by the alcohol and surprise. Theirs was not a good idea. Springing up from my haunches, I kicked the black guy in the balls as he was rising so that he yelped like a strangled dog. I knew, although I could not see it, that his eyes were also wet with agony. His companion scrabbled backwards and sideways like a crab, desperate to get away. No doubt he had an ovulating wife at home. A hard stamped foot was enough to terrify the pathetic idiot. He turned and ran, revealing the limp cowardice that had always plagued him.

Which left their organ grinder.

And me.

'Fuck off now, or I'll hurt her bad, man,' he promised from the safety of the shadows. It was too dark to know, but perhaps he held a knife to Chenguang's throat.

Against the rough wall there was only enough dim orange glow to make out the two silhouettes, which merged into one just above the waist. Three legs, one arm, likely his, the other wrapped around her, at best pinning her to the wall, at worst holding a sharp blade to that fragile slender neck. A curve of shadow may have been his head, but they were standing on the apex of a bend pressed into a triangle of darkness. If only he had been half a metre closer.

'Come out where I can see you. Your argument is with me, not her.' I hoped she might be able to ease him towards me if she could only grasp my hint.

In the event, she didn't get the chance. The broken-nosed lieutenant groaned suddenly from the asphalt, gurgling and spluttering through the bloody sinew that once adorned his face so confidently.

In an instant, his captain's head turned, moving fractionally away from Chenguang and momentarily into the tiny slither of light. Right into my target zone.

I launched.

Right arm, flat palm, sudden and straight. Heel of the palm thudding into the very bottom of his jaw. It was enough to throw him back only half a step, but fully into the light, eyes glaring, nostrils flaring, spittle collecting on his bottom lip. Retracting my arm, I hit him again like a flailing catapult. Only this time, it was with my fist, side on as his head turned back towards me. *Crunch*. I loved the sound of breaking bone.

He was out cold, dropping like a demolished tower-block into his foundations, crumpling in a heap of cheap designer cloth. His head went crashing towards the ground, until I threw out my leg and caught him on my ankle. I had no desire to kill the idiot, just to teach him a lesson he wouldn't forget. Once the pain and amnesia subsided.

Levering out my foot, his head lolled onto the hard pillow where he would sleep awhile before waking with the mother of all headaches. Before then, I decided to leave a more permanent reminder that you never *ever* abuse a woman. Reaching for the downed-man's waist, I began to undo his belt.

'Look away,' I whispered, but Chenguang didn't. Instead, she moved into the streetlight, her wide eyes trailing my every move like a hawk. She had been silent throughout and remained so. The only sound, the relief of her shallow breathing.

Taking the belt, I joined the clown's hands together and secured them, before gripping his pants and ripping them at the waist. I took out the smaller of my knives. And on the silent abuser's groin, I carved a tiny but visible cross, so that when his wife or girlfriend asked the memory would haunt him ever more. Chenguang finally turned away, before twisting slowly back and nodding. Thank you, her eyes seemed to say, but she also blamed me for inciting the fools. Perhaps a touch in the restaurant would have been enough to satiate their drunken lust. Perhaps my protection only made her more desirable.

That's the risk we take on behalf of our fellow men. Men, of whom that night I was deeply and rightly ashamed.

'Come, let me walk you back home.'

Fifteen minutes later, at the door to her tidy modern apartment building she stopped and looked up at me. 'Come inside?'

Taking a quivering hand, I kissed it to make it stop only for it to tremble even more. She was indeed a beautiful prize. Rich black velvety eyes stared at me, unblinking.

'Go upstairs,' I said to her, still holding the hand that fizzed. 'And go to bed. You would make the finest reward of any in France. But not tonight. Tonight, I saved you only to redeem myself.'

Was she disappointed? No, only relieved.

'Chenguang?' I said, absent-mindedly. 'That's a very pretty name.'

'It means morning glory.'

I bit my knuckle. She and I both lived to fight some other glorious day.

ELEVEN

In the dilapidated hostel shared with mainly immigrant workers, my need to plan at first awakened and then consumed me. Lying on the threadbare sagging mattress, the pain of the past few days accelerated and almost overwhelmed my senses. For a week I had been at the mercy of one primal instinct. Survival. Yet all the while my mind, my subconscious mind at least and not the one on formal defensive duty, had been churning in the shadows. Rousing from its silent state, it finally started to speak.

First, we weighed the advantages, as always.

France was a big place. A man could stay hidden there forever, and many do. And unlike all of them, I knew my hunters' methods inside out. I was one of them. *Used to be* one of them. I knew their drills and decision-making framework. I knew how they thought, or rather how they didn't. My pursuers were methodical, practical and constrained by governance. We, by contrast, were bound by nothing and no one since it was our job to oversee with a lack of ritual known only to us. There was no handbook at Le Troisième. There were no books at all, in fact. Everything at Le Troisième was off the books. I was no arrogant fool, but I did know where they would look and how.

But then there was the bureaucrat.

He would be wearing the pressure of our secret like chainmail, and it wouldn't be long before the sound of rattling gave us both away. He was onside when I arrived back in France, but how long he would remain so was a mystery known only to the man's gluttonous ambition. I had to reach and feed him quickly before his hunger for power consumed us both.

In the miserable shower stall, I pined for Gabrielle.

Pascal would have learned my real trade, it was unavoidable. Whether he would have shared as much with my darling fiancée we would soon find out.

Ten minutes from waking, I was up, away and out the door in my new disguise. An army veteran on the slide and looking for work. If the following few days didn't kill me, that's exactly what I would be anyway. I put my chances of unemployment at less than fifty-fifty.

With a new burner phone, I called the office of *MediaCors* and asked to be put through to the only colleague of Gabrielle's whose name she had mentioned.

'Claudette Monfils.' She had a pretty voice.

'Claudette, you don't know me, it's Gabrielle's fiancé–'

There came a frisson of excitement. 'The mysterious *Monsieur B*?'

There was now a balance. Too much frivolity would waste time and initiate an unwelcome relationship – for her sake as much as for my own. Too much haste and it would draw the inevitable questions Gabrielle would have to fend. 'The very same. Would you mind asking her to come to your phone for me?'

'I can transfer you—'

'I'd rather you called her to your telephone. I need her out of her office for a moment.' I didn't explain why. I couldn't. Claudette might have assumed perhaps that there was some wild romantic gesture planned. Maybe that *Monsieur B* was, at that very moment, calling from the window cleaning cradle en route to make a surprise proposal. From her cheery demeanour this was exactly what she had envisaged.

'Of course.' She placed me on hold.

A day or more seemed to pass.

Eventually, Gabrielle spoke in a barely audible whisper, her hand clearly cupping the mouthpiece. 'B, what's happening? You're all over the news.'

'It's ok, I'm fine. Has anyone spoken with you?'

There was a pause. 'Only papa. He came to see me last night. He wants me to let him know the moment I hear from you. He says you're in trouble, *serious* trouble. He says you're in way over your head. I'm scared, B, what the fuck is going on here?'

Pascal may have been my way back in. 'Honey, please listen to me. I am the man you met. And the one you love. I swear I have never killed an innocent soul my whole life. Whatever they say, whatever they tell you, you *must* believe me. I am no terrorist, Gabrielle. Go to see Pascal today. Ask him about Le Troisième. Ask him for the truth. Say that I will speak again with you tonight. Tell him that if what you tell me is accurate, I will contact him directly. Remember, *Le Troisième*.'

This time there was a real fear, and alarm. Her normally confident voice trembled. 'What are you talking about? What do you mean, you will contact papa? What is this *Le Troisième*? There are three dead tourists, for fuck's sake. They won't reveal your name. It's like they don't know it. Like they're asking for someone to come forward and tell them who you are, and *where* you are–'

'I know, I know. But don't fret, baby. They're familiar enough with me. They have a desk and pension waiting. As for my location, I hope to God they don't find out. Not yet at least–'

'Where *are* you?' she asked without meaning to, purely through love and instinct.

'Safe, cherie. Believe me.'

'Your mobile phone–'

'Gabrielle, listen *carefully*. Don't look for me. Don't try to contact me. Don't speak to anyone but Pascal about me. I am away on business, that's all you know. They will be bugging your telephones, maybe the apartment too. They may even follow you. Pascal *will* confirm it.'

If he did, I would know for sure that he trusted me.

'The cabin,' she said. 'Should I go there for a while?'

I thought about seeing her, holding her, even for the second before they shot me dead. 'Soon, we'll find a way, I promise you. But not yet. Don't go anywhere or do anything out of the ordinary until I tell you it's completely safe. Understand?'

'Jesus, B, you're really scaring me now. How will you call me later?' she asked, and I imagined her forewarning Claudette to await some future contact, picturing her staying in the office glued to this very telephone all night.

'Trust me. You'll know, but not at work.'

She waited. 'Ok,' she said, a timid mouse and not the lioness I loved.

'Gabrielle, *trust me.*' I hung up. And set off to find the nondescript transport required for my journey back to Paris.

The best place to steal a car is the middle of a busy railway station car park. These owners did not arrive for the early shift, starting in the soulless darker hours. Nor are they using the train for a short appointment or interview like those at the rear or spread around the sparse periphery. No. It is the centre ground which plays host to the vast swathes of dour executives pasted to their mediocre commuter existence. Nine to six, every working day of every weary week.

There it was. The dull grey Citroën sedan of a bank manager or accountant at a middling ordinary firm. It was parked inside that triangle of freedom from the battalion of cameras, placed where they assumed the eagle eyes of fellow passengers would keep it safe.

They didn't.

Inside of three minutes I was on the exit ramp with half a tank of fuel, sufficient for my assault upon the capital. Driving below the speed-limit in the city and then just over on the auto-route, it was two hours before I was parking in a quiet Paris side-street where a lack of resident permit would reunite the homogenous shape with its unambitious owner. Only I would ever have stolen it, anyway.

Taking a battered old rucksack, I set off to find Leclerc.

As in almost every European city, there was nothing so anonymous as the homeless. Heads turned as if repelled by some magnetic force, eyes dwelling only for the nano-second required for recognition. Alone on the bench in the parc Vincennes, I imagined how it felt to be Chernobyl, impervious to all but the extremes of curiosity and bravado. A small child kicked her ball inadvertently beneath my seat and left it there, until I gently rolled it back. She studied me, before turning and running to the sanctuary of her mother's outstretched hand.

Meanwhile, Leclerc entered the park via the southern gate amid a crowd of tourists, the only one among them in a stiff grey business suit. He checked his watch to signal he was alone and walked the curved path like the hapless clerical officer on his ill-deserved lunch break. He perched ungainly on the far end of the bench, pulling his trousers at the knee.

'You said two days.'

He smirked. 'Like I am the controller of such things.'

'Give me your phone.'

Smiling, he shook his head, reached into his jacket, and removed his cigarettes. Sliding his mobile phone beneath the packet, he checked over his right shoulder and offered both to me. I took them, pulling out a cigarette while discreetly turning off the phone, and slipping it into my bag.

'What's the latest,' I asked him while he surveyed the myriad of city workers in their momentary escape.

'It's not good. They know you killed Christine.'

I didn't bother to ask how. I knew Leclerc wasn't their informant, and anything he told me now was intended for my ears, or they would not have told him.

'Any more news on that body by the sea?'

He shook his head. 'Not a word. Probably a lover's tiff.'

'Some lovers.' I mulled over that they did not know, or maybe did not care who killed Baudelaire. He was, after all, nothing more than a junior foot-soldier in the war on our enemies, at home or abroad. Perhaps despite his potential he was nothing more than one of Nicole's lamented hard-ons, shortly for castration.

'So, what's your master plan?' Leclerc shuffled uncomfortably. For some this would be a clue to their disposition, but not the hefty bureaucrat. Discomfort was his middle name.

'I will prove my innocence and then come back.' Said so boldly it sounded almost as easy as the humdrum jobs of the unhappy administrators we surveyed from the dark green wooden bench with its splintered paint and tarnished dedication.

'And face the firing squad for treason?' Leclerc frowned.

'She was the traitor. I'll prove that first.'

'Judge, jury *and* executioner, now?'

'Only executioner. You don't pay me for the other two.' While I would not have trusted the man to negotiate his exit from the park, he knew it helped to have me free in case he had a little dirty work of his own to commission. Anything to remove the word *Acting* from his title, like exposing his sainted predecessor, would keep Leclerc dutifully honest with me. 'Well, if there's nothing else, I'll be in touch again. Just keep going on the liberal. But be careful–'

'You seem to forget I was a field agent once,' he said, grumpily. 'I chose the desk.'

'It chose you, and now you're tethered to the damned thing. Just be careful, that's all I'm saying. This goes to the very top.'

He laughed. 'Your concern is admirable.'

'Fuck my concern, I'm relying on that money for my wedding.'

He stood suddenly and reached into his jacket pocket removing a light brown government envelope and handing it to me. 'Consider this the first instalment. It's four thousand, no need to count it.'

I was stunned.

'Thought you might need it, from my experience *in the field.*' He smiled, nodding as though satisfied some minor proof of his resolution had been delivered.

I dropped the money into the rucksack and retrieved his phone, handing it to him before turning and heading for the furthest exit. I didn't look back.

But I did look every other way.

And after fifty metres, in the farthest corner of the park to my right, there he was.

Unmistakable.

The Liberal.

Leaning on the wall of the public toilets, almost hidden by the rollcall of tourists rotating through the pissoir, he could not have been more conspicuous. Wearing a dark blue service-issue suit, with his hands in his pockets, he was gazing straight ahead and not at me.

Merde. They followed the fat fool.

Picking up pace, I veered and circled back towards the main entrance of the park. They would have that covered too, of course. But it was a busy place the entrance to the Paris Zoo. These animals might have stopped me there, they might even have trapped me. What they would not do, however, was pull a gun and fire it into a crowd, which gave me my only advantage however marginal. There were also several hectares of thick Bois de Vincennes Forest adjacent to the park in which to disappear.

Speeding up, I dodged between a pair of tourists to create a fuss and from the safety of the glaring eyes behind me, I started to hurry. Bumping into as many walkers as I dared, I sparked a swell of antagonism. Mostly they were angry that I had forced my existence upon them, made them see me, watch me, follow me. Even in camouflage I was not yet invisible. And this offended them as much as any bumping, barging or lack of manners.

Behind the wall of angry faces, only two masks remained unmoved.

The liberal tracked me from the grass on my left, and a colleague began to follow from the right. The new assailant was my main concern. He was a big Nordic looking fellow in black trousers and a brown suede jacket. Maybe two metres tall or more, he was also wide and built like a brick shithouse, all barrel chest and beard. He was a proper heavyweight, not wiry like the liberal. Walking the treeline, he was cutting off my escape route to the forest of ochres and browns which would conceal me. Smart move, but not necessarily deliberate. Somehow, I had to pull him further into the open and into the madding crowd.

Startling him, I sprinted forward, crashing through a pair of office workers flattening one and leaving the other floundering and cursing. I hurdled the child with the ball, dodged her mother, and for shame grabbed hold of a providential wheelchair spinning it hard. The surprised carer careered after it in my wake. Angry shouts and curses followed, arousing the attention of a smart young gendarme up ahead. He stopped his conversation with a tourist to look my way. He was cautious. They had history with the homeless and phones were already pointing at me which was good. But also, very bad.

The liberal, meanwhile, had maintained a steady track inside the park and was much closer, while his Scandinavian colleague was maybe fifteen metres back. The big man may have been slower than both of us, but he was also cutting a direction which blocked my access to the minimal safety of the treeline.

The gendarme reached for his radio, before a woman in a black suit stopped him. A quiet word in his ear from the slender dark-haired patriot sent him away to the gate and the safety of the direction-seeking visitors asking after the conveniences which played host to the liberal.

So that was the team.

Three of them.

Their code now made them predictable. They would operate like an arrow; the point and two feathers, designed to squeeze me towards her like flankers agitating a bull towards the matador. She would be more skilled than the other two. Far more dangerous. That she was a woman was a trick as old as time, designed to lull me into a false sense of security. I was supposed to believe she would crumble under the weight of my first punch. I had no desire to find out. The bull rarely lives to tell the tale despite his bulk and horns.

Skating the crowd, I found exactly what I needed.

A group of schoolgirls. Twenty-five or more.

Sitting on the shallow grass incline up ahead, they were eating their packed lunches, laughing and joking while sketching the fine stalks of grass and the wildflowers that escaped between them. Theirs was a carpet of mottled green and blue gingham. Perfect.

I feigned left and forced the liberal to drop back, before making my real move.

Slipping off the rucksack and holding it before me, I sprinted towards the schoolgirls. They had all seen the news. They took one look at my beard, my clothing, but above all the bag, and they reacted. Like a flock of scattered pigeons, they hurtled backwards falling over one another slipping on the grass. Screaming. Cowering. Paints and paper erupted alongside flailing hair, pigtails snapping back and forth like bullwhips. Instinctively, they coalesced to form a giant terrified arc between me and the Norse.

It wouldn't hold him up for long, but every second counted, and I was into the woods before either of my pursuers reacted, stealing a precious twenty metres. Fighting every sinew in my neck not to look back, I ran.

Thick, gnarled trunks came at me left and right as I dodged and weaved like an over-excited boxer high on acid. Small saplings snapped, but the giant French oaks and elms would finish me in a heartbeat unless my concentration was absolute. I hurdled the lower branches, ducking under those that yearned to decapitate me. Focus, Berthier. *Focus.*

There was a stumble and yell from behind. The Norse. He could no more dart his way through there than one of the camels from the nearby zoo could pierce the eye of a needle. He would fall back, double down and flank me to the right. Not good. Already the woman would be flanking from the left. From memory there was a path which cut through to the clearing up ahead. She would make double my pace without the trunks and foliage to deter her. Dead ahead, a tree shed bark suddenly. And then I heard the silenced 'phut'.

Fuck. They meant business.

My heart raced from the fear more than the pace. I could have run full pelt for another kilometre or more, and even then, drop down for another five to outrun the fuckers easily. It was beyond even me, however, to outrun a bullet from a Beretta or

G36. There was no option but to sprint in a crouch, which made avoiding ankle height branches almost impossible. It slowed me down. Too damn slow.

Another piece of tree splintered centimetres from my left ear.

I took a chance. I needed to. I hated the stench of cordite.

Switching left, I bolted for the freedom of the path. It made aiming a revolver almost impossible as my frame disappeared behind one bole and reappeared after the next. He would only hit me with the most outrageous luck. Thankfully, it was not his lucky day.

Hurtling onto the path, I looked left. Nothing. I knew I couldn't go back that way. If not because of the woman, then because she would have called her back-up team. Instead, I went right and towards the chateau of *Vincennes* with its equestrian and sporting facilities, hoping to God they were busy down there.

Sprinting down the edge of the single-track, my camouflage masked me like a green and brown tiger, but that alone was not enough. Once the shooter was out and in the clear and closing, I would be dead inside a minute. The liberal was no amateur with a revolver based on those near misses in the woods.

I got as far as calculating how much longer to stay on the path when my mind was made up for me. An angry buzz and high-pitched whine could only mean one thing. A *drone*. Worse, it was a racing one. Small and nimble, with a good pilot it could track me through the trees if not at head-height then from above the canopy.

I leapt into the nearest gap in the undergrowth, but it dropped and followed me in. *Shit*.

The pilot *was* one of the good ones.

Lurching right and left then right again, I searched for the clearest course. There wasn't one. So, I sprinted and dodged all over again, only this time my pursuer followed me like an angry wasp gnawing relentlessly at my resolve. While it could do no more than trail me, that alone was a death sentence all the time it was relaying my exact location. They would be assembling up ahead, my captors. Or rather murderers. Those shots from the silenced Beretta were not intended to miss.

Taking a chance, I threw myself into a shallow hollow. Full of dead leaves and fallen branches, it was half a metre deep no more, but low enough to drop me momentarily out of sight. The drone raced by then stopped, hovering and spinning as the camera panned. He knew I was down there, but with the camouflage and mottled light, the picture wasn't as clear as when following my ghostly frame through trees. Edging to my right, I found a decent branch a metre long, and gripping my hand around it, I waited for the irritating insect to take a closer look. The moment he dropped to within reach, I struck–

Leaping to my feet, I swung with all my might. And missed, by millimetres.

Fuck.

I swung again. And missed again.

Calling on all my skills honed on the clay, I leapt a final time, aiming a fierce forehand smash. This time it would have been a direct hit, but the drone veered up and right. Straight into an unseen branch which killed one rotor. It dropped back into reach. I volleyed it down the line, sending startled screaming pieces flying.

No time to celebrate, I chased the chassis to find the processor, the tiny brain that even then was still relaying my position. It was nestling in the crook of a V-shaped beech tree, a single red power light flickering, its camera detached and broken. Retrieving the tangle of wire and plastic, I ran like hell for fifteen metres, then dropped it, before returning all the way back to the hollow. Lying there, face down, my rucksack buried beneath the ferns, I hauled as many leaves across my back as made me invisible from distance. And I waited.

I heard him before I saw him.

My liberal assassin.

He was on the radio, tapping involuntarily at his ear, complaining about the big man. He thought the Norse let me get away. He did. But it could hardly be deemed the agent's fault. There wasn't one among them who had been fully briefed on who or what they were chasing.

At ten metres out he stopped.

His path would bring him directly over me. He was talking again, this time to the man himself telling him to hurry, to cut off my exit route by the dressage enclosure. I imagined the Norse's puffs and pants between answers as he ran. The liberal turned his back, and I thought fleetingly about rushing him, but the rustle of leaves might have given me away. He could swivel and fire before I had made half distance. So, I waited again. Among the stench of fungi and freshly stirred earth.

And the waiting paid.

He walked across to a tree right before me and looking down unzipped his fly, fished out his manhood and started to piss. It was all I could do to stop myself roaring with laughter. Instead, taking this golden gift I launched from the leaves. His face was one of abject failure as he fought to determine whether to put away his cock or pull and cock his gun. In the end he aimed a weak jet at me as his left arm was bludgeoned by the branch before I lamped him hard in the gut with a wet hand.

He crumpled in shock.

As he fell, I jerked my left knee up to his chin and knocked him out cold. Still unzipped, his limp dick twitched as it spilled its final uncontrolled excretion.

It took five seconds to find his revolver and another five his spare magazine. Ripping out his radio, I also took brief pity on the poor bastard and rolled him over to protect his modesty for when the woman found him. To make sure she did, I retrieved the drone and dropped it on my assailant's prostrate body.

Through the earpiece, she barked her orders: 'Thor, Leo, drive him left. Bring him out near the circle.'

After the panted reply of the Norse, came my own muffled affirmation.

'And where's that fucking drone?' she cried.

She switched channels to address the operator – he would be a simple gendarme and not privy to her shoot to kill demands. She snapped back. 'The drone is down, repeat the drone is down. Leo, do you have eyes on the target?'

I did. The bull had doubled back towards the city, far away from the team of murdering matadors converging on the wrong exit to the woods and luring their illusory quarry to his final fight. Scurrying down the centre of the trees, I kept alert for any sign of the big man, or any back-up team. Leo was most likely the sole hunter who pursued me directly through the wood on foot, but caution remained the order of the day.

'Leo? Leo? Confirm *eyes on*,' she yelled into my ear.

Putting my hand over the microphone, I whispered in panted breaths as though running at full tilt: '*Eyes on. Heading north. Repeat. NORTH. Heading–*'

I released the button and let the news sink in. She guessed correctly. Her forces were amassing near the Chateau which oversaw that sprawl of nature in the middle of our city. She would spread them wide to drive me out. She would be there any second.

Dropping the headset, I headed due south, towards the river and temporary freedom.

Now they had seen me, I needed another urgent change of clothes.

TWELVE

There is another type of camouflage for a city. A uniform that is so noticeable as to render its wearer completely invisible, night or day. Replete with tool bag, hard hat and high visibility vest I was at once both humble workman and gilet jaunes, slipping through the streets entirely unseen.

By eight in the evening, I was also ready and bracing myself for the night ahead.

At the end of rue Jean-Baptiste-Say, I leaned and watched. The left-hand side of the road, behind which sat the shallow apartment block, was awash with cars. Residents were parked fender-to-fender in those narrow streets, each berth a golden ticket in a lottery with barely space to squeeze the winning slip between the trunk of one car and hood of the next. Meanwhile, the right side of the road was almost entirely clear. Apart from one inconspicuous Renault Clio, whose cute rear end bore a tell-tale Marseilles licence plate. It was one of theirs, procured directly from the factory with major engine and suspension upgrades designed for fast pursuit through the hair's-width city streets. They were almost as agile as motorcycles, of which there were also two. Sitting at the farthest junction, their riders laughed and joked through open visors ever poised to pounce. Above them, a sour man leant over his balcony, dragging slowly while he surveyed the dusky scene. Maybe one of theirs, maybe just a guy in need of nicotine. Either way, the front entrance to the building was a predictable no go. So too, the rear of the block.

A plumber's van was angled two wheels upon the kerb, with a perfect view both up and down the street. Its owner was apparently attending an emergency so urgent that he was afforded the luxury of several minutes to squeeze adroitly into the narrow space.

At least there were no foot-soldiers. Perhaps they learned their lesson in the woods.

Doubling back, I arrived at the far end of the street behind the motorcyclists, hidden from their view by cars and potted shrubbery, the latter a token gesture from our mayor to bless that stretch of town. For a whole ten minutes I stretched out on a hard wooden bench in front of a closed jewellery store and watched them sitting there near motionless. They had no interest in me. No interest in anything but the door to the apartment building. My guess? They were waiting for someone to leave, not for them to arrive. No ordinary wanted man would be so reckless as to go there. But then, they were not hunting any ordinary wanted man.

At twenty thirty precisely, my grand entrance arrived.

The rattle, clank and hydraulic moan of the garbage truck could be heard two blocks away, sailing through the city like a ghostly pirate ship seen but unnoticed by all who crossed its path. These are the city's apparitions who keep us on an even keel.

Slipping off the bench, I left my hat collected my bag and hurried in the direction of my ignorant accomplices.

Four rugged operatives accompanied the truck, working in rotation like a tag-team. One bin on, lifted and emptied, one bin taken away as another took its place. It was a thing of synchronised beauty. Both sides of the truck's rear completed this routine continuously for as many blocks as it took before the weight of disposable Paris returned the crew to base, launching another empty vessel.

Strolling casually alongside the passenger side, I took a hold of the handgrip, jumped up, opened the door and slid in.

The craggy-looking driver started. 'Hey, the fuck you think you're doing –'

I pulled out one hundred of Leclerc's mint-fresh Euros and slapped them on the dash. 'I need a ride.'

From inside his bushy moustache, he smiled. 'Where to, monsieur?'

'Just keep driving, but there's another hundred if you stop where I say so.'

He whistled, before confirming he was happy to take as long a break as needed. Thinking fast, I also asked about insurance. That cost me double again.

For the next block we crawled along, my eyes as alert as the driver's, the four operatives continuing in harmony oblivious to my presence in the mirror or the seat. They knew these streets so well they barely looked up at all. The great machine kept churning, lifting, tipping, lowering, compacting. So many lives crushed so easily out of existence.

'You know,' the driver said amiably, 'we all share responsibility for any accidents. They have this great big digital board embarrassing all of us alike, not just the man behind the wheel –' He already had four hundred Euros secreted in the glove compartment. 'And there are five of us,' he continued, and I could smell his bullshit above the reek of middle-class trash. 'And maths was never my strong point at school, or I would not be sat here now. I would be in banking.' He laughed and slapped the wheel. 'You don't think five hundred is just a little easier for this poor brain of mine to divide?'

Removing another hundred, I held it up. 'For this, give me your hat too.'

He removed the old green cloth cap like it was on fire and plonked it on my head, holding out his hand. 'Pleasure doing business with you.'

'You might have trouble with division, but you have no such issues with negotiation.'

He roared and slapped the wheel again. With both hands this time.

'Up here, the black Clio.' I pointed it out to him, sitting there like a lame duckling detached from its siblings. The occupants were unmoved by our impending passage, one face down the other scanning the street towards the doorway opposite. It was a view which my new colleague was soon to obscure.

'How hard?' he asked.

'Five hundred Euros worth of damage.'

'These days, that's nothing more than a cracked fender!' He rolled in his seat. Pulling down the cap, I braced for impact, which when it came was barely audible or felt. But the sudden braking jolted me into action, yanking the door handle and preparing to disappear.

'Bon chance,' he said as I tipped his cap farewell.

Looking neither left nor right, I crossed the street between the parked cars, my bag held low and out of sight heading straight for the archway dead ahead. Behind me there was much hissing and groaning, both metallic and organic as the ship continued its chomping and chafing, drowning out the sounds of argument. I vaguely heard my new friend accuse the Clio's occupants of parking naively in a street which was too narrow by half for three vehicles abreast. He had a valid point.

The grey wooden door swung inwards at my shove, closing with a reassuring thud. Reaching up and down, I slid the rusty bolts for extra comfort. In the centre of the stonework lobby was a crude elevator with nothing more than black scissor gates, inside of which a square steel cage was raised and lowered like a bucket from a well on two thick iron ropes. It had a habit of stopping between floors, so I took the stairs which wound around it.

Three storeys up, the steps spilled me into a dark hallway with a lonely window through which light barely penetrated. There was a rich red wool carpet with an antique pattern fraying here and there like an unloved boudoir. It hid the dirt in winter, revealing it again each spring. In the near-darkness I pulled down the cap to hide my face before ringing the bell of apartment 14B.

There was no chain nor spyhole.

'Who is it?'

'Caretaker, here to take a look at your boiler.'

Such maintenance complaints were commonplace in our edifices to the renaissance.

'Just a moment, I'm not decent,' came the muffled reply.

The footsteps departed, before returning a moment later. At the click of the latch, I turned away, so my face was hidden, then as the door opened I rolled with it, placing my right hand across her gaping mouth and forcing her hard body back against the wall. I slid my left hand delicately behind her head to stop it meeting with the fine new plaster. Her eyes startled in fear and then closed, her breath sharp and raspy. Removing my left hand slowly, I took off my cap and threw it before dropping my bag and putting a finger to my lips. Drawing away my right hand, I brushed her ashen face. Then kissing her deeply, I tasted the sanctuary of love, drinking in her scent; oranges, jasmine, rose. *Coco Mademoiselle*. Unmistakable.

With a silken leg she kicked the door closed. Eventually, I eased a hand between our entwined tongues, before whispering into her delicate ear. 'Show me to the boiler in the kitchen and then don't say another word.'

I let go her mouth and took her hand in mine, leading her through the apartment while she performed exactly as asked, leaning on the modest table. I span up the coffee machine, both for cloaking and because it was now seven days since I last savoured the taste of real coffee.

'See him out and then run a bath,' I whispered to her.

She was neither scared nor stoic. She was curious, and from her deep breathing and the way those dark brown eyes never left me she was also angry. She knew about me now.

'That should do it,' I said in a loud gruff voice. 'Sorry to have troubled you.'

'It's no bother,' she replied, as I followed her back through the apartment. 'Take good care now.' She opened and then closed the door with an apathetic thump.

Nodding towards the bathroom, I watched her pad away with her white silk robe flowing, trailing her like a bridal gown. Catching sight of those golden legs as she walked on arched feet, I remembered how we met. And then I thought of everything that had passed between us since. If ever she was lost to me, I would most surely lose the will to live.

I waited until the rush of water, before crossing the apartment and stopping at the foot of our bed. Crisp white sheets looked taut as though unslept in, my pillows sitting slightly higher than hers. My bedside table hosted the antique telephone that never rang, while hers had the clock that she was always on, the notepad for thoughts that plagued her in the night, and the tiny jewellery tree with its one bare branch awaiting the simple band of gold she craved. Sighing and hoping, I entered the emerald bathroom.

Sitting on the corner of the white slipper bath, she eyed me like a cat watching an unknown dog. Steam shrouded her, curling up and away like our secrets. I closed the door and leant on it.

'Tell me the truth,' she said.

'Always.'

'How many people have you killed?' She stared at me, finally revealing her fury.

I shook my head.

'The *truth* Berthier.'

'What does it matter? How many make me a monster?'

She looked up at me. 'Was any of it true?'

'Yes. My love for you.'

She looked away, aiming her hand beneath the running water to test the temperature. It would never be hot enough to thaw the icy front which I had wrought upon us.

'I trusted you,' she said, tightening the belt on her robe, still watching the tap spill its truth as I would inevitably mine. A drop of water fell from her hand and ran down her calf, like she was shedding tears for me. For what had become of us.

'I never lied to you Gabrielle.'

She turned and shook her head. 'Even now?' she said mournfully.

'It's my job. Someone has to do it.' I regretted the words before they left my mouth. Gabrielle's grandmother had wept as her eldest son departed on a train. A single ticket among the thousands who left from Drancy to his fate in Dachau. Following orders was never an excuse. *Never.* 'I keep our country safe.' I wasn't even sure it convinced me.

'From whom or what?' Full of pity, Gabrielle's eyes searched mine; probing, assessing, condemning. Her hands gripped each other for fear that touching me would somehow stain us both. Her legs were not just crossed, they were entwined. There was no mistaking or breaching her defences.

'I was a soldier before we met.' I hoped to reveal something of myself she did not already know. 'Special Forces in the end. I signed up after my father died because, what else was there to do? I thought back then it was to honour his memory, now I realise I was only ever trying to forget.'

Her eyes dropped, as my crown sank with them. I was not the rebel she so wished I was.

'They recruited me after our operations in Afghanistan when... It was all so barbarous back then. They murdered my friends, Gabi. In *cold blood*, not even the heat of battle. They hauled them through the streets, hung them naked from lampposts and then celebrated while they torched their rigid bodies. I had to watch them all die twice. I smelled their fear. I carry their pain. The indignity of death. Every gram of sympathy I ever possessed died with those men. I serve now to stop it ever happening again. So, what does that make me?'

She looked up. 'A psychopath.'

'There will always be a need for men like me, so the people can sleep safely.'

'Why? You think you protect us? Keep us safe? You *don't*. Men like you stoke fires and fan flames, just so your ilk can march in with your petty uniforms and guns like some heroic saviours. And all it's ever for is pride. Or greed. Or both. You *lied* to me, Berthier. How could you?' She stopped the taps. She meant to speak again, to be heard by all their microphones. She meant to lecture us. *Me. Them.* She did not distinguish between her villains. 'How many?' she asked again.

'Twenty or thirty in the caves and mountains. Another eighteen since.'

Her head dropped forward as if the sinews in her neck had snapped. As if I alone had cut them. There was nothing more to say. Nothing that would justify my livelihood. Not to Gabrielle. I wished I shared her certainty. I never had. I wished I knew right from wrong. I always thought I did. Now, all I really knew was duty.

'Why did they turn on you?' she asked, betraying that streak of empathy she so wished she did not possess for me.

'They killed Eric.'

Her eyes narrowed. 'Who killed Eric?'

'*My* people.'

She shook her head. Now we would learn how much Pascal had revealed. 'Eric died in a car crash. We both read the report–'

The mask would never slip from the man she idolised. To claim murder was to sully the reputation of one she loved, maybe even more than me. So, I stayed silent and signalled my inability to disclose for both our sakes.

She reached and reopened the hot tap. Steaming, scalding water flowed. 'Papa says you've gone rogue.'

It was true.

'He told me to be careful, to be wary of you. He says you can't be trusted and that you will lie and cheat and say anything to save yourself. He told me not to tell you any of this, only to beseech you to turn yourself in. He says he can help if you do.'

'Do you believe him?'

She stared unblinking, shrugged. 'I don't know what to think any more.'

I moved towards her, but she shied away. It was all I desired to hold her again, comfort her, make love to her. I hungered for this woman as nothing else on earth. I had betrayed her trust, and somehow had to earn it back. But I knew in my heart there would be more bloodshed. And she would not countenance that. Not then. Not ever.

'I'm sorry.' Apology is all I could offer her.

'I'd like you to leave,' she said.

THIRTEEN

The rain was falling horizontally, whipped by an icy wind that pulled collars tight and left the nearby saplings cowering. The sky was a kind of dark grey reserved for battleships, while the clouds billowed like the underside of a giant monstrous duvet, punctured here and there by shards of harsh white light.

Pascal sat in the centre of an otherwise deserted piazza, his back to the line of bending trees, facing the Metro where fugitives from the storm watched questioning his sanity. At my insistence, he had no umbrella just a fawn raincoat staining brown by the rain's onslaught. It had also dyed his hair from dark to even blacker. He checked his Rolex watch. I knew it would be another five minutes before he gave up completely. Then, he would take the Metro the two short stops back to Pigalle.

Dropping the telescopic sight into my bag, I took out another burner phone and from the multi-storey car park opposite the square, I watched him answer my call.

'You're late,' he said curtly. 'And it's pissing down.'

'I'm afraid I changed my mind.'

He paused a beat. 'I'll give you one more chance. After that, you're on your own.'

'Same time and place tomorrow?'

'If the weather improves, perhaps. If not, you blew your opportunity today.'

I hung up.

He would return the following day even if the rain necessitated arrival by boat. Another few hours of the downpour and the streets would quickly resemble Venice. Perhaps he would come back by Gondola.

Keeping a tight hold of his phone, he talked only long enough to exchange his one simple message. As he ended the call, a hulking four-wheel drive peeled away from the corner of the square, and directly below me a green utility company van started up and completed a three-point turn before sailing away in the direction of the rain. In a high window behind Pascal a curtain was redrawn, and two floors above that a balcony was vacated.

I calculated at least ten. So much for the promise to come alone. Not that I blamed Pascal. He was no more than a retired cop and well out of his depth with the sharks of DGSE. They had fed him full and strung him out as bait, and unlike me they had no care whether he lived or drowned.

As he departed for the subway, I dropped down the fire escape and onto a little yellow Vespa stolen from the ranks outside the Metro. It started up like an angry hornet on my kick and flashed me through the downpour dodging overflowing drains and hidden potholes that lurked beneath the torrents of water boiling with rage. An idiot in an old green camper van swerved to avoid soaking a pedestrian and narrowly missed me too. Such was the unexpected ferocity of the rain I didn't even have the confidence to raise a single finger in anger. It was falling harder than ever it had in Paris. Shop awnings danced a Pasodoble with abandon, while streetlights and traffic signs swung to their own unfettered rhythms. A blizzard of water lashed the city with total contempt, the deluge cascading as though the very sky was torn asunder.

Up ahead at the intersection, a bright red hatchback had crashed into the rear of a long white single-decker bus so that they now resembled a burning cigarette. No one dared to exit their dry seats to extinguish it. Instead, they simply stopped and stared bringing six converging lanes of traffic to a grinding halt where everyone would remain until the clouds and smoke dispersed. I had no option but to mount the pavement and ease between pedestrians not yet swallowed by the storefronts, while the warm dry Metro hurtled Pascal beneath my soaking feet.

Finally, I reached the junction, navigating my way carefully between the morass of parked cars and vans with engines fuming and drivers likewise. The one small mercy was that the collision had emptied the roads leading away from the intersection. And as the raindrops shrunk momentarily from bowling balls to pearls, I opened the throttle to utilise all fifty meagre cubic centilitres of engine. Speed, as Einstein theorised, is relative and the tiny Vespa was relatively slow as fuck. If I had a whip, I would have thwacked the thing down the neck to match my desperate urgings.

No matter.

At the bottom of rue Clementine, there was Pascal climbing

the incline in his sodden coat, hair swept by the wind and water, collar tight like a neck brace on a whiplash victim. I passed him and turned a sharp left at the top of the rise, dismounting and dumping the scooter in a bay reserved for motorcycles. Then, head down, I ran across the street past Pascal's home and along the arrow-straight narrow path to the side of his imposing property. He lived alone, having deserted Gabrielle's mother fifteen years since for his mistress. She left him immediately after taking the mantle of second wife. No woman so adored should ever marry and throw all that lavished love away so carelessly.

The house was a large white grand affair with black slate roof tiles and thick columns by the door, where an ornate portico and roses stretched their way to embrace above the entrance. New windows were made to look renaissance and flanked by black shutters which never closed. Rather they were affixed to the wall as quite literal window dressing. It was a stout proud property and if dogs resembled their owners, then so too this house. It was the kind of place you imagined a former chief of the Paris police would live. An establishment home.

Between me and the rear garden, a rusting chain secured a tall iron gate with intricate fretwork. Dropping my rucksack, I removed a pair of brand-new bolt cutters, the price of forty Euros still prominent on one handle. They snapped two links like hoops of uncooked pasta, allowing access to the beautiful walled enclave, where more roses flowered, crying petals since the downpour. There were pinks and whites, yellows and dark reds, all in bloom and not a dead head among them. Even damp, they smelled somehow of childhood and happiness. Apart from Gabrielle, these were Pascal's pride and joy. By the rear doors was his favourite rose of all, *Bonaparte.* Its carnival of red, white and blue hues resembled banners strung along Les Champs-Élysées for state occasions. They marked Pascal down for the dedicated patriot he was, while above them an alarm box also flashed red and blue.

I knew for a fact that it was connected to nothing but the power source, Pascal having lamented more than once the crazy service charge demanded by his security company. The deterrent didn't work on me. Taking my lockpick from the bag, I set to work. Child's play. I was in and seated comfortably in a dark corner of his masculine navy lounge, moments before the chunky key turned in the front door.

There was a quiet pause while Pascal groaned, shaking his coat beneath the portico.

He hung it on the stand behind the door, and in an hour or two he would have to mop the puddle that resulted. Next, I heard him use the cloakroom, dispersing the water which had penetrated to his skin despite the bold claims of his raincoat maker, before heading upstairs for dry clothes. Leaning back in the comfortable chair, I pictured him up there cursing me.

When he returned, he did not notice me immediately. Entering the room he proceeded to the front windows, drawing his heavy damask drapes before turning to find me watching. Such was his experience he was not remotely fazed. 'Well? Do you intend to just stay there, or are you going to fetch us both a drink?'

He sat as I rose to open the rich mahogany cabinet where he kept his cognac, among his other trophies from the war on bootleggers, counterfeiters and smugglers. I poured his measure with twice the confidence of mine.

'You know they only use the finest grapes from Grande Champagne for this?' he said, as I passed him the glass. He raised it to me. 'Perhaps a little vineyard like your mother's?' It wasn't meant as a threat.

'So, what else did you learn?' I asked, sitting again, this time on his striped sofa from where the light framed him like a polished news anchor. Leaning back, he swirled his glass and watched as the legs of brandy coated the crystal. He took a large swig with a rasp. 'Magnifique,' he said, pointing his empty hand at me. 'You took a giant risk today, Berthier.'

'Not really. We both know the protocols.'

'So why do it?'

'I wanted to know how seriously they take the threat. Ten DGSE agents?'

He laughed. 'You're a wanted terrorist, man. Did you think they would send a couple of trainee gendarmes to pick you up? Right now, you're the number one target in all of France. Even Europol are on the lookout.'

'Why?'

Raising his glass, he motioned to the cabinet again then finished a double with his third mouthful. I shook my head and smiled, wondering how often he had sat like this inside the station or a car, some random darkened hotel room from where to extract a confession. Hanging on the wall behind him, was a black and white picture of his retirement presentation made by Mitterrand himself. A huge portrait, it was flanked by numerous commendations and service medals. While beside him, a gold Louis XIV table was adorned with an irregular assortment of family photographs and Pascal in uniform, like a miniature shrine to his former life. The room was at once both tasteful and cold, designed like the house from the pages of the establishment catalogue.

'Officially, you killed three tourists,' he said, as I passed him back his refilled glass. 'And then, of course, there is the small matter of assassinating your former boss – the most senior spy in France? For some reason, they don't take kindly to that kind of behaviour any longer. You're a one-man revolutionary, Berthier. That makes you extremely dangerous.'

'When did you know?'

'About you? When you asked about the body on the beach. There *was* no report on any website, obscure or otherwise. Only someone on the inside could have known about Baudelaire. I made some discreet enquiries which came back blank. That could only mean one thing in our line of work.'

'But you didn't say anything? Not to me or Gabrielle?'

Shaking his head, Pascal laughed and with his free hand pinched his slacks at the knee. Nationalism and loyalty were important to Pascal. His reaction at learning of my occupation was likely quiet satisfaction. Any man who fought for the republic, fought for Pascal. So much the better if they died. Now he didn't know what to make of my subversion.

He studied me, placing his glass on the table and bringing his roughened hands together. 'You don't know what you're mixed up in,' he said sternly, a warning rather than admonishment. Like Gabrielle, he had at his core, a seam of rarely mined compassion.

'Do you?'

Nodding, he stood and offered me another brandy, which I declined. He reached for the bottle, flicked the top with his thumb and poured, splashing a generous measure that resembled a large glass of wine more than cognac. 'You want to know why Bernard died?' Still with his back to me.

I was stunned.

How could he possibly know about Eric? Unless? Of course, *Leclerc*. The bureaucrat was unable to maintain his silence. I should have known his payment was just an apology. Pascal turned with both hands full. In the left, a fresh measure of XO, but now in the right he clutched his service issue revolver, a Beretta 92, designated for police use as the PAMAS G1. It took a classic Parabellum round as commonplace as cents in a fountain. He should have handed it back five years ago, but who would have checked? He was the Chief. He made the rules, not followed them. His hand was as steady as when he played a volley from the net. Iron straight. I was an unmissable target.

'Is that really necessary?'

'It's a precaution, Berthier. A wanted terrorist has broken into my home for what motive I cannot yet explain. Self-defence, that's all. Don't make me use it.'

A difficult conversation with Gabrielle would surely have followed. 'And don't think for a moment the idea of Gabi's sorrow would stop me,' he said, noting my sly smile. 'Like me, she is a patriot first and foremost.'

I pictured the glorious tattoo on the base of her spine: liberté, égalité, fraternité.

'Your cousin was a traitor,' Pascal said, still standing from where he had the textbook firing angle; from above, perfect proximity, aiming down: see *Diagram 4a, page 52 of the Police Guide to Firearms Usage in Close Quarters*, revised in 2016 following the tragic events at Charlie Hebdo the previous year. That night, *J'étais Charlie*.

'He was a journalist, and a damn good one at that. He was simply doing his job, digging dirt, that's all–'

Scoffing, Pascal took another swig while his eyes never left mine. He was a hard bastard who ran tougher men than me from the capital's streets for nearly thirty years. Each week almost without fail I had learned more about his politics and passions as we traded blows among the clouds of clay. He had the body and temperament of a man my own age. It was a fitness that, that night notwithstanding, would see him through a long and healthy life. His one and only weakness was arrogance. Just like the rest of us.

'Your cousin believed, mistakenly, that he had stumbled on some grand conspiracy at the very heart of government. I take it you read the files?'

I had. I read and memorised the most important points before I thinned them for the benefit of Leclerc: names, dates, and meetings; connections and communications; the rollcall of *Fraternité* contributors and patrons, public and mostly private. Then I took the brand-new laptop and hurled it into The Thames, depositing the flash drive in the one place they would never know to look. It was one I couldn't reveal even if they buried me in some sandy sarcophagus and poured water through muslin into my open throat.

'There is no conspiracy, Berthier. There is only the reclamation of France. What your cousin thought he found was nothing more than the normal politic. Wheels do not move unless they're greased.'

Greasing. Is that how he was describing it?

'Many things happen away from the spotlight of media consumption for good reason. The people don't always know what's good for them. Wouldn't you agree?' He smiled.

Democracy.

Such a simple word.

Gifted to us by the Greeks, who could have predicted that two millennia later it would have become the shield and spear of the elite? We had an aristocracy in all but name, just as they did in England and America. And now, thanks to Eric I had seen the evidence first-hand. The question was whether Pascal had seen it too.

'The people have the right to know who governs them, Pascal.'

He waved his gun. 'There is no question there. The people *elect* their leaders. The people always do, one way or another.'

For the first time, I saw the policeman. No longer the prospective in-law, the fatherly confidant missing since my teenage years. Not anymore was he the brother in arms, now he was just the arms, a simple dealer in patriotism and pride. This was the man Gabrielle both adored but also despised. And who, I now recognised, exhibited those self-same traits as me. Pascal was the very reason I may yet lose Gabrielle.

'Why?'

He shrugged. 'Why what?'

'Why would you sacrifice your principles for *them*?' I nodded my head in a kind of arc towards the piazza and the woods, where they would happily have gunned me down.

'You don't get it, do you? They are *my* principles, and they should be yours. They are the foundation of the republic. *Fraternité*, Berthier. It is in our vow to serve our country, first and foremost, to compromise our own beliefs for those of France. You are a believer too. I know you are. Gabi tells me so all the time.' His eyes narrowed, and the smile hardened as though the words were as much for his benefit as for mine.

Like many old men, his patience with moderation had grown thin. He now preferred excess in many things afforded to a man in his position: exercise, alcohol, proclamation and especially politics. His streak of liberal tolerance was frayed by insight and incident. He had scanned the same reports I had, studied the enemies we blindly hunted both without and now also within. But unlike me, he leaned towards an authoritarian solution. Perhaps I would too when I achieved his age. *If* I achieved his age.

'And what about *Liberté*? Which of our freedoms do you advocate we sacrifice on the altar of France?' I nearly spat but doing so would only sully the last remnants of our friendship. I liked Pascal enormously even despite his misguided nationalism. When this was over, I still planned to marry his daughter. If she would have me.

He laughed. 'You know as well as I do, that there is no such thing as freedom in a democracy, only concession. I have no desire to see a revolution on my watch. The people, Berthier, rarely know what's best for them. The job of government is to keep them safe. Beyond that, we must tell them only what they need to know to remain that way.' He glugged the last remnants of his drink and toyed with his glass, turning it this way and that. '*D'accord*, much fun as this has been, I am purely the bait for this expedition.' He tossed the crystal to me, which I caught instinctively. He reached into his pocket and removed his phone. 'And now, I really need to call in the fishermen to land my catch.'

As he squinted at the screen, I placed the glass on the floor.

'No sudden moves. I won't hesitate to fire.'

I rose despite his protestation, slipping my left hand towards my pocket.

'Stop there! I *will* shoot. Don't think I won't.' His grip on the revolver flexed, his thumb flicking the safety expertly, his finger tightening on the trigger. 'I mean it. Not another move.'

Ignoring him, I reached right inside the jacket.

'Berthier!'

He fired.

At the same precise moment as the click, I withdrew my hand and unfurled my fist. 'Nice to know where we stand.' I smiled and showed my palm, the six unused shells glistening like golden mealworms with copper heads. His spare magazine was also safe, buried inside my rucksack.

Pascal shook his head, continuing to raise the phone. 'Don't be a fool,' he said, resigned to his catch slipping through his oily grasp. 'Whatever you do next, wherever you go, remember we are on the same side, you and me. Fraternité, Berthier. *Fraternité.*'

FOURTEEN

Standing in the cold dank room, the blade reflected the light bouncing angled beams around the scarred moss-coloured walls, picking out cracks in the off-white tiles. Florescent tubes buzzed as though the wires were barely touching, or some inhibitor prevented the current from passing through unhindered. The resulting soft blue light flickered, creating a haze through which each movement was uncertain, the mirror throwing shifting shapes and reflecting more like a still puddle than solid glass. None of this was ideal since shaving with a cut-throat razor is awkward, even in the fullest sun.

The hairy vagabond look was blown.

For all his platitudes and urgings, Pascal would have sold me out the moment his latest 'maid' arrived to untie and service either him or the house. A high-quality rendering would immediately have circulated the media, accompanied by some vague mention of a sighting in the environs of Paris. There would be no explanation of their conviction that this vagrant was their wanted man, of course.

Shaping the rough damp beard into a goatee, I was at once no longer young nor old, but middle-aged and holding onto youth by fingernails. An architect perhaps, or car designer. A respectable middle-class occupant of an office in a corner from where I mastered my orbit with precision. To the few natural strands of grey, I added another peppering from a bottle until I was nudging fifty. It was a look I could grow into very easily.

Dressed in new designer jeans, their tags dispensed with by my teeth, I pulled my white shirt cuffs through the sleeves of a business jacket, put my phone and cash in the pockets and dumped everything else in the bathtub for trashing. I left the maid twenty Euros for her trouble. Outside, the storm had passed ushering a fresh new sun to thrill the tourists. A cooling breeze made walking bearable, blowing away the oppressive heat of previous days.

At the corner, there was a small supermarket where I purchased a pair of cheap sunglasses before making my way across the street to the Metro station and securing four new passport photos from a lone Photomaton booth. If I say so myself, I looked surprisingly good despite the scar whose sore red had faded to a dusky pink, like a misplaced lipliner ran up my cheek. Retracing my steps back beyond the shabby hotel, I found a café which was clean and uninspiring but for its young waitress whose pinched nose, sharp mouth and scraped hair were clues to Eastern European origins. She studied me awhile, unsure why someone of my ilk would patronise the place, concerned that any minute I may demand a statutory inspection of the kitchen. A quick smile and nod assured her I had nothing more sinister than breakfast planned, so she guided me to a table in the rear, back to the counter, eyes to the door. As well as satiating my hunger, the café served as a rendezvous point to meet my oldest service friend. Finding one who could be trusted was, by any modern gauge, as rare as locating rocking horse shit. I ordered coffee and awaited her arrival.

Barbara Solido came to our office a decade before on secondment from the Belgian Secret Service (VSSE). In her early twenties, she was the most fearless woman I had ever met, possessed of a naivety which would have killed lesser agents or seen them jettisoned for the ubiquity with which we are supposed to function. But Belgium likes her mavericks and Barbie used that rod of stubborn ignorance to skewer enemies, both metaphorically and sometimes physically too. We hunted down a gang of Albanian people smugglers, finally cornering them in a dilapidated former fishing warehouse on the quay at Menton. Given fair warning, they steadfast refused to surrender, so she ordered the place be torched, lit up like a Christmas tree while waiting for the minnows to emerge. Twelve of them came out fighting and were cut in two, four by Barbie's expert shot. The remaining sardines gave themselves up before the pool of blood drowned their resistance inside the tin.

The door swung open, banging hard against its stop. There was no elegance where the Belgian was concerned, only brutish force. Sitting down, she slid across her telephone which I immediately pushed back.

'You wouldn't be here if I didn't trust you implicitly.'

A smile flashed across her unmade almond face. 'It's a courtesy.'

'You look well.'

'You look like your elder brother.'

'I don't have an elder brother. I don't have any brother.' I thought of Eric.

'Your father then. Good looking in a middle-aged kind of way.'

She had not changed, this gargantuan with a delicate deadly touch. I had never thought of her as pretty since she spurned my amateurish advances, but striking described her perfectly. Orange hair fell to her shoulders where it curled like cinnamon sticks. Her eyes were mint-green and flanked her nose like sentries. Her mouth was so wide it looked strong enough to bite a rope in two, which she warned of by adopting bright red lips always. She kept a revolver in the back of her pants, and a knife in a garter around her thigh. A dark grey trouser suit trapped her, and a black shirt looked almost like a scapular, so parallel were her severe lapels.

'How is business?'

She studied me. 'We're overwhelmed, Bertie. What with all the fascists, I miss the Islamic State. At least they had the decency to hide. This new mob have no shame at all, flaunting their hatred in the streets. Do you know what the number one tattoo in Brussels was last year? The *swastika*. Can you believe it? After all we've been through on this continent. And don't get me started on those fuckers in clogs.'

I remembered, Barbie does not mince her words.

'Anyway. Enough of my good news, which angry husband gave you that?' she said, smiling and nodding at the scar, before beckoning over the astounded waitress who could scarce believe such confidence was possible in a woman. Barbie ordered a double espresso and calvados. It was just after eight-thirty in the morning. She shrugged. 'Awful journey.'

'It's not just grey hair, there are some grey cells now too.' I tapped my temple. 'No more jealous husbands for me, I'll be one soon, I hope.'

Her eyebrows steepled as she shook her head. 'I don't believe it. If I couldn't tame you, no one can.'

'You never tried.'

'I prefer my men wild.'

She retained all the flirtatious wit that first reeled me in, before she batted away my advances like a schoolmistress crushing a teenage heart.

'Someone tried to blow me up.'

She nodded. 'Figures. I guessed you didn't plant it yourself.'

I fell silent while the waitress returned in awe, placing the coffee gently and the large bowl glass even more so. I detected she was about to curtsy when Barbie touched her arm. 'Leave us awhile,' she said as though the girl was staff. And miraculously, the waitress did as commanded, slipping through the chain curtain from where I imagined she was spying on us, on her newfound heroine.

'McQueen is dead.'

Barbie whistled, then followed with another of her legion of expletives.

'It was maybe also meant for me, but they simply didn't care. Collateral damage.'

'Jesus, she was their poster child. What the fuck are you mixed up in?'

This woman needed no warning from me. She had given and received them all before. Death was her constant companion. An ally and adversary on any given day. So, I told her: I told her about Eric and his murder; about the files and their content; about the oligarchs who funded our politics; and about Pascal and his insinuations; about the things we did in the name of justice, or vengeance.

After a full five minutes, during which her pupils barely left me, not even to blink off the shock, she looked away. Looking back, she reached out a firm hand to mine. 'This is fucked up, Berthier, but I will do whatever I can to help. What do you need?'

Nodding, I gripped her back. 'I need to go to the home of dirty Russian money.'

The burgundy passport was hard and fresh, and issued in the name of Frank Cazenove, Barbie's idea of a joke. Apart from name, all other details – date and location of birth – were mine, but one year later, so as not to alert the systems but memorable enough for me. Placing it flat on the scanner, I held my breath and waited. Under the gaze of surly border staff, the two glass plates retracted and a digital green arrow directed me around to baggage reclaim where my half-empty suitcase would revolve forever uncollected by me.

Outside the terminal building, the thick air smelled of cars and buses. Diesel coaches belched prehistoric nitrous oxide, grumbling their apologies through gritted gears, the oily stench drifting down towards the pick-up point where blacked-out Mercedes taxis danced with hybrid Toyotas in a game of chicken. Which passenger would be left standing because their driver refused to park and pay the modest fee?

In bright sunlight, Barbie leaned on a bus shelter, blocking an advertisement for hair colourings so that her tousled ginger sat in the middle of a straight blonde bob giving her a halo like a Russian icon. I guessed she was worth it. She had arrived two hours ahead of me from Bruges, and even now preferred not to acknowledge Europe's most wanted. Instead, she sidled over to a silver BMW and popped the trunk, closing it again immediately as though checking it was shut.

All clear.

Making my way slowly through the ranks of confused tourists, I opened the rear door, while she eased into the driver's seat. 'Nice wheels.'

'It was the best that Enterprise could do. I wanted a Merc, of course.' She pushed a button on the dash, yanked the stubby leather lever back to *D* and pulled out without looking, oblivious to the driver whose angry horn lasted only until he claimed our vacated bay. Looking over my shoulder I watched the others swarm and curse their unfortunate timing.

Accelerating down the ramp, Barbie felt inside her pocket and handed me a Beretta over her shoulder, eyes smiling in the rear-view mirror as she did so.

'Where did you get this?'

'One of us isn't wanted by Interpol,' she laughed. 'It's amazing what they let you carry in a diplomatic bag. I even managed 250ml of shampoo.'

I looked at her hair, imagining the suds and water cascading through it.

'Stop it,' she said, her eyes narrowing.

'Watch the road.'

She smiled.

On the airport perimeter traffic was light. It was mid-afternoon in summer and the array of visitors preferred the tube or train into the centre of London, while we flashed past the sign that warned us of a charging zone twelve miles ahead and ultra-low emissions beyond that. Barbie accelerated again as though to burn off excess gas before it was forbidden to do so.

'I did some checking,' she said, changing lanes without indicating. 'Your father-in-law has some tasty history, you know. He ran security for the last G7, in Charlevoix.'

For a moment, I didn't hear her properly. The words, yes, but not the location. 'Charlevoix?'

'Exactly,' she said, '2018 at the Manoir Richelieu summit.'

'Quebec? Why would a French policeman be running security in Canada?'

Barbie shrugged, swerving around a UPS van and carving up an over-filled metallic brown family hatchback in the process. As if they hadn't enough bad fortune already.

'Are the indicators on this car working?'

'On and off,' she said, winking at me.

'Are you sure he wasn't just running point for Macron?'

Shaking her head, she raised her voice as we quickened to the next junction, a roundabout where our lanes fanned, only to collapse again on exit. No wonder the English were so angry all the time. 'Definitely not. He was appointed to the whole circus. And you know what they called that summit? They said it was the–'

'G-six plus one. I remember.'

Barbie nodded her head slowly. 'Exactly.'

Canada was a low point for the Group of Seven economic powerhouse nations. World leaders were torn asunder by their newest member whose erratic behaviour stunned even *his* close confidants. They expected the partisan showmanship and America-first philosophy. That was the entire basis of the reality-tv election campaign, after all. What they did not expect, and sent mighty shockwaves through the delicately balanced forum, was support for Russia's annexation of Crimea. The subsequent fallout from the American delegation took isolationism to the absolute extreme. Hence Quebec became known as the 'G6+1', six world leaders in solidarity against a dissident president whose response to challenge was to rip up every commitment on climate, multinationalism, and geopolitical unity. An infantile response to the challenges of the day, resulting for the first time since the second World War, in an American president finding himself in concert with the Russians. Only this time, the Germans stood alongside the French, English, Canadians and Japanese, on the other side from this most unholy axis. Business as normal it most certainly was not.

'You think it's coincidence?' Barbie asked as the traffic defeated her eager right foot and we began the inevitable slow crawl to the centre of the city.

'You know I don't believe in those.'

'Me neither.'

As we edged forwards my mind wandered to Eric and our last encounter, drinking Schnapps in a Bavarian Bier Keller not far from Les Parc des Princes before a six-nations rugby international.

'Look how far we've come,' Eric had roared to the assorted drunken Italians who had ventured north from Rome to Gaul like lambs to the slaughter. 'Here we are, Spics and Frogs, in the house of Fritz. Enemies only on the playing fields, no more the battlefields.' He spoke like a General rallying his troops to desert. 'We settle our disputes in here, or out there, but we do it like intelligent men, and not the fools who lead us!' he cried, riding his chair like Napoleon's horse. And which of us would disagree, and mount a defence of his own government? None from *Munich through Marseilles to Milan*, and certainly not on the eve of sporting war. Instead, we toasted Pavarotti and Paradis, Monica Bellucci and Bridget Bardot. Claudia Schiffer and Heidi Klum. Because, after all, what more did a man need than music, wine and the love of a beautiful woman? It is that which united and not divided us that mattered most of all.

'Why do you think he was there?' Barbie broke my train of thought.

'I don't know. There was no mention of him in Eric's files.'

'Was that meeting significant?'

'Can I borrow your phone?'

Barbie examined me in the mirror.

'I need to search the internet. I don't have a smartphone right now–'

She hesitated then handed hers over her shoulder. 'Don't use up all my data allowance,' she smiled, returning her eyes to the line of slow-moving traffic swapping lanes for no discernible reason. Looking to our left I watched the dull brown hatchback crawl past us, its Asian driver massaging his temple to relieve the strain or boredom.

I put my thumb on the phone screen. 'What's your code?'

She paused a beat. 'Thirteen zero five.'

I laughed. 'I don't believe in coincidences.'

'Don't flatter yourself,' she said, avoiding eye contact by searching for the unused indicator stalk. 'I had to pick a date that no one in the department could guess.'

The home screen revealed a picture that was unmistakably Barbie's father. Leaning on a blue Ford tractor by a country hedge, he looked at a girl in the seat holding onto the wheel. She was pulling one of the levers that raises the forks or changes gear or disconnects the plough. I wasn't an agricultural kind of guy, but the old man clearly was. He had sun-burnished rosy cheeks, a mass of reds and oranges from the neck up and sleeves down.

'Happy times,' Barbie said, as I looked up to find her watching me intently.

'Sorry, I won't explore any of your other photographs.'

'You'll only be disappointed if you do, selfies are not really my style.' She filled the mirror with an enormous grin. 'Use the *Viper* app for discreet browsing – it won't store or cache anything.'

I waited while the browser connected me to the internet, before searching everything to do with that G7 meeting, every conceivable search term: security, ministers, dignitaries, leaders, police, bodyguards, summit. But it was really photos I was looking for. There must have been a thousand or more, from frowning faces to boisterous banqueting halls. Until finally, there *it* was. On an obscure Japanese news site. It captured a scene from inside the lobby of a hotel, looking out.

In the foreground, was the silhouette of the unfortunate Nicole: dark leather skirt; thigh-length boots; a purse so small it barely concealed her service pistol; arms alert, ready to respond to any imminent threat, of which she will have perceived too many. To the right, but at least two metres ahead of her, was the assured figure of Christine, the scarlet woman. Her dress was the colour of Wellington's victorious armies. *Look at me*, it screamed, perhaps to distract attention from elsewhere, for nothing she ever did was by accident or chance. She was looking sideways. Directly towards *Pascal*. And there beyond his studied gaze, was the tiniest fragment of a face I had seen contorted beyond recognition. Baudelaire. So, that was where the whole thing started, whatever the *thing* yet proved to be.

'Blue lights,' Barbie said suddenly.

Looking through the gap between the seats, I saw them, and the reason for the interminable delay. Up ahead, a silver Audi sportscar was nose first into the concrete central reservation, its rear end all askew. Angled outwards a police car screened the embarrassed wreck, and a line of red and white cones funnelled traffic from the three sluggish lanes down to one. The driver was leaning against the barrier with his legs crossed, shielding his eyes from the sun, and speaking to the cop while both surveyed his heavily restyled front end.

'You think this asshole realises we've been sat in the delay he's caused for the past three kilometres?' Barbie moaned, looking at the mangle of steel and fabric roof. It seemed there was no one else involved and that he simply lost control.

'I think—'

With an unholy crack, the rear windshield fractured and then shattered, raining tiny shards of glass all over me. They spilled into my open-necked shirt, scratching my back as I began to move. Fragments showered in my hair. A sudden thump followed, and the back of the passenger seat burst open, its stuffing and springs erupting like angry clouds from the leather.

'What the fuck was that?' Barbie turned—

'Get out. Get out now!'

Dropping from view, I yanked the door handle and tumbled onto the tarmac while Barbie wrestled with the seatbelt that was meant to keep her safe. As she cursed and rolled, the side-window behind her disintegrated, exploding into a thousand glistening dancing diamonds. Screaming blue murder, she emerged head and hands first in a ball. Grabbing hold of her collar, I hauled us both to the meagre protection of the space between the open doors, for all the good it would do us. These things once made of steel were now mostly aluminium. Better for the planet. Not so good for soft flesh under sniper fire.

The brown hatchback rolled by, from where an old Asian lady in the back seat looked at us bemused, face pressed to her window apparently unconcerned that a man and woman were cowering by their car. As she watched, another shot rocked the rear of the BMW. The old lady didn't seem to care.

'Where the fuck is he?' Barbie screamed.

'He's behind us, southwest and high up is my guess.'

I flinched again from a sudden clunk of metal as a hole was punched in the rear wing, two centimetres above the filler cap. Ten lower and the fuel tank might have blown us both sky high. I had already survived one explosion. I had no desire to push my luck.

I couldn't help but laugh. This whole situation was surreal. There was no gunshot, no tell-tale flash from a rifle, no whiff of cordite, just the sudden impact and resulting clunk as another bullet pierced the tin, like a gigantic invisible hole punch. The only noise was the constant drone of petrol igniting and exploding inside a thousand pistons. The only smell, the stench of diesel fumes. And fear.

'We have to move, get around the other side and off the road,' Barbie yelled, as horns blared behind us. Incredibly, no one appeared to be able to see what was going on. Their only concern was that we'd stopped the flow of traffic. 'On three!'

I could barely hear her over the sound of my heart thumping in my chest.

Another round hit the tarmac a metre to my right.

'One, two–'

'Three!' Two shots struck the cabin as Barbie moved, obliterating the dashboard. Half a second earlier, and they would have passed straight through her head back to front. A third bullet narrowly missed my arm, exploding the rear light cluster as we hurtled around the trunk to the safety of the far side. The car jolted, and a sudden hiss greeted a tyre being shot out. The bastard had us pinned down. And the other drivers simply pulled around us like this happened every day in London. Perhaps it did.

Shielded from the gunman, we were two metres at most from the sanctuary of the barrier. We could have run and dived over it. That was until I realised, we were looking at the second or third floor of the offices and apartments directly ahead of us. There was even a roofline and chimney for fuck's sake. The drop beyond the concrete to the ground below must have been at least ten metres. Shit.

'That accident was no accident,' Barbie said.

'Which means the driver–'

There was an almighty crack as the front wing on the side closest to us dented, splintered and finally tore open. A hole the size of my fist appeared. Grabbing Barbie's arm, I threw open the passenger door for whatever meagre protection it offered, and pulled her to the rear, ducking low. There were two shooters. Either side. High and behind on the right. High and in front on the left. The nearside rear three-quarter of the car was about as safe as we were going to be. Which was no safety at all.

Out beyond the buildings alongside the carriageway, there was a new residential development converted from a former office block. Forty storeys high at least, it was wrapped with an enormous advertising banner with an appetising picture of the future homes to come. They started from as little as three quarters of a million for a studio apartment. Anyone who bought one might have found a few spent .50 calibre cases thrown in.

Because that's where the sniper on this side must have been. It was the only possible position.

The windshield shattered milliseconds before the passenger headrest exploded, yet still the other drivers peeled around us shaking their heads. Was no one ever going to stop? In a way, thank God they didn't. It was only their movement and the eddies and gusts of warm wind whipping between the buildings that were keeping us alive. Right then, we were playing chicken with bullets, and it wouldn't be long before one found us.

'We're pinned down,' Barbie said, ducking and pointing about two-thirds of the way up the same building I had already seen.

'Tell me something I didn't know.'

'So, what do you propose we do about it, genius?'

Turning, I spied an orange delivery truck. It was four cars behind us, angling out to pass our stricken motor. 'Six o'clock. There's our ride.'

Barbie smiled. 'Let's hope there's room in the cab for three.'

'Let's hope he lets us in.'

She flashed me the red-lipped smile. 'What say I do the asking?'

Another bullet ricocheted off the trunk with a clunk, before cracking into the concrete barrier halfway up. It left behind a blackened smudge like someone swatted a giant fly. Then the roll of cars sped up, and suddenly the gaps between them shrank. After a shiny SUV, the lorry moved towards us. The moment it obscured the rear shooter, Barbie risked crouching, before sprinting for the driver's door.

Another bullet whipped into the bodywork, right above my head with a shuddering clunk. It must have missed me by the thickness of a gnat's wing.

Next thing I saw, Barbie had leapt onto the sidestep of the truck, and was hammering on the window. A second later she was pulling on the door. This time there was a thwack and slap as the canvas beside her ripped apart. I took that as my cue to join her.

Running hard, I vaulted into the cab, slamming the door behind me. It was left-hand drive, and Barbie and I were now jammed together on the passenger seat, alongside our startled Eastern European driver. His excitement waned as I pressed against Barbie and away from the door and shooters beyond. Protocol dictated that with a civilian in the kill zone the shooting would stop.

It didn't.

The windscreen of the truck exploded. And two seconds later, the driver screamed like a strangled wolf. His right arm was leaking blood just below the shoulder blade where the bullet had nicked him. Twenty centimetres the other way it would have split his larynx. Twenty centimetres my way, it would have dissected Barbie's ducked head. *Again*. And the woman called me a cat.

'Vot the fuck?' the driver shrieked. 'Jezus Chrystus my arm, my *fucking* arm.'

'Move,' Barbie commanded. Yanking his seatbelt, she took hold of his shirt and pulled him roughly, sliding into the vacant seat and forcing the driver backwards into his bed-cum-cubby from where he continued screaming a mangle of multi-lingual curses. All bullet wounds are excruciating, even the slightest nick. No doubt his arm felt ablaze, worsening by the second as each individual pain receptor reacted in turn. With a little more luck, he might have passed out.

Once behind the wheel, Barbie wasted no time.

She pulled right from the funnel of slow-moving traffic into the closed lane and aimed directly for the cones. Behind them sat the police car and the cop. Facing away from us, he was completely unmoved by things he'd neither seen nor heard.

Swinging the truck right and left, Barbie crashed through the line of red and white witches' hats which disappeared beneath our wheels as another bullet ripped into us just below the windshield. An almighty crunching sound was followed by a jet of steam which blinded us but didn't faze Barbie. Instead, she accelerated, ramming the side of the police-car, pushing it back towards the accident 'victim' as the cop disappeared over the central barrier. From there he watched as his car was near flattened, smashing into the cute little Audi in a crunch of steaming metal and grinding gears. There was a whiff of fuel as the blue lights rotated a final time, before the bar supporting them wobbled sideways and crashed to the ground.

In seconds, we were brought to an almighty screeching stop. With the driver still screaming, Barbie leapt out of the cab, and I followed her into the queue of traffic shocked to stationary by the lunatic lorry and its crazy flame-haired driver. The road ahead was empty, but no-one was now moving. They were like metallic rabbits caught in the glare of the truck's mangled headlights and grille.

And there beside us was the little brown hatchback.

Barbie pulled her gun from her pants and hauled open the driver's door. She screamed at the occupants. 'Police, everybody out.'

They spilled, trembling and shrieking into the road: dad, his mother, the wife in her sari and two children, maybe eight or ten years old. Their colourful clothes blazed a flash of bright onto the dirty road-surface, where the boy started to cry as the girl squeezed his hand in hers.

'Thank you', I said pathetically, jumping in the back as Barbie stole the driver's seat. A stuffed bear grinned at me from the parcel shelf as though he knew our fate, so I tossed it out towards the children as we sped away. A second later, a bullet cracked into the passenger side-window, despite Barbie weaving manically between lanes. She slowed and swerved, accelerated hard and then braked as dramatically, throwing me side to side forward and back until finally the road dipped and we were clear of the shooting gallery, and Barbie was decelerating because there was a speed camera up ahead.

'How the fuck did they find us?' she said, slamming her hands on the wheel repeatedly.

I waited for calm to return. 'You mean me, how did they find *me*? I'm sorry. I've put you in terrible danger.'

She angled the rear-view mirror, so our eyes met. 'You know me, Bertie, I wouldn't have it any other way.'

FIFTEEN

Barbie toppled like she had been poleaxed, recoiling amid a barrage of cotton as her body hit the centre of the mattress. It was only early evening but already the day felt three weeks old. Adrenaline has that effect. For every minute it keeps you alive, it demands back ten-fold for recovery. She pulled a pillow across her face and gave a muffled guttural roar, before sitting up and blowing out hard. 'Tell me there's a mini bar.'

We had dumped the little car in a residential side-street as soon as the motorway became a major road, before joining a busload of private schoolkids for an hour and stopping more than moving until it dropped us near Park Lane. From there we found the first *affordable* hotel, but with its modest frontage and clean but sparse décor, it was still nearly three hundred a night for the smallest plainest double room.

Reaching beneath the desk, I pulled the cheap walnut veneer door to reveal a fridge concealing nothing more dangerous than still or sparkling water. I didn't have the heart or courage to take one out and hand it to her. 'We passed a pub on the corner, they'll sell beer, I'm sure.'

She leaned up on her elbows and studied me hard. 'I need something stronger than beer, Berthier. A damned-site stronger.'

'I tried to warn you this would be no picnic.'

She laughed. 'Screw you and your warnings. Let's go and get hammered somewhere before they catch up with us again tomorrow.' She said it with all the certainty of experience. 'I have no idea how they tracked you. But if they did it once, you can rest assured they'll do it again, however well you think you're hiding.'

'You want to freshen up before we go?'

'No. Everything tastes better when you're dirty. You would know that if you'd ever done an honest day's work your whole life.'

Sadly, I never had.

As well as hotel rooms, drinking in London also cost the earth. For a while I assumed the prices were like those in Paris, for the tourists - until I overheard a local paying the same. Leclerc's advance would be gone before I knew it. And long before any reunion with Gabrielle.

'Tell me about her,' Barbie said, raising her double shot of vodka and crashing it against my glass. The Belgian establishment had driven her to grain two decades too young.

'She's too good for me. Twenty-nine, super intelligent, mature beyond her years. You'd like her, I think. She knows her mind.'

'And yet, she fell for the charming spy, so not *that* smart?'

I thought about our last conversation, the disappointment in Gabrielle's soft eyes.

'Ah, you didn't tell her?'

'Another?'

Barbie downed her measure with a growl, banging the glass on the table. 'Bring the bottle, whatever's left of it.'

The bar was half-full. Mainly they were office clerks escaping early from the confines of corporate life with forced smiles and boredom written large across their empty faces. Two solitary Asian tourists splashed colour on the grey, sitting hunched with their backpacks and the thrill of warm beer while poring over an A-Z. Its myriad mazes through the city seemed to enthral them. Meanwhile, in the corner, an old local in threadbare tweed attended a half-drunk pint of dark ale wondering what had become of the place he used to call home. I sent him another pint, raising my beer as he looked up to find his benefactor. He nodded, affording me a modest gap-toothed smile, before a woman half his age approached, kissing him the way no daughter ever would. The sly old goat.

When I returned to the table, Barbie had her phone pressed hard against her ear, the other hand cupped over her mouth. I put the half-bottle between us, taking a pull of my reassuringly expensive beer. I heard nothing but a smattering of Flemish which was all double-Dutch to me. Whether she has swapped from French deliberately, I couldn't say.

After two or three minutes she hung up, taking the bottle and pouring to the point in her glass were the sides no longer parted. Where they began to lean in to trap the alcohol. 'You were seen.'

'Where?'

'Charles de Gaulle. They had an agent in border security. The facial recognition at passport control sent a follow and report alert. Apparently, you also failed to collect your checked-in luggage at Heathrow?' Her eyebrows steepled at the schoolboy error used as cover. 'I'm sorry, Berthier, I should have seen him.'

I didn't realise the technology had advanced so far so quickly. It was only eighteen months previously that the algorithms couldn't tell one Palestinian from another. But of course, all that software was written by white middle-class graduates. Was it any wonder they could spot an imposter disguised as one of their own?

'And you?'

She shook her head. 'All they know is that you had a handy driver.'

I thought about the agent protocol, re-running my arrival and exit from Heathrow in my mind. *Follow and report.* I did not approach the car until Barbie gave the all-clear. And she did not see them, or she would not have opened and closed the trunk. Which meant at best they might have a quickly taken smartphone image of the redhead from behind. Enough to send them scurrying away for known associates for sure, but not a hope for facial recognition – electronic or manual. The only two who knew the redhead's name were fellow liars, and one of those was dead. The others might have remembered her as a naïve strawberry blonde and slight. Not the towering, hardened agent sat simmering before me.

'They called in three assets and staged the crash,' she said, shaking her head.

Typical DGSE. We French are supposed to be the most finessed in Europe, but for all our exquisite DNA we also created the guillotine. Thankfully, the snipers had been concerned with killing me not Barbie. I doubted they even noticed her at all.

'They want you dead, Bertie. They don't care how, so long as it's soon.'

It was a confirmation I really didn't need. There was nothing so dangerous as an agent with a kill authority under a tight deadline. Protocol and planning became a hindrance quickly forgotten. If we were not more discreet, the collateral damage would make my tour of the Uzbin Valley look like a Sunday picnic.

'How many agents do they have here in London?'

I shrugged. 'At any one time there are a dozen in the UK at most. Three are permanently attached to the embassies, then one for each designated nuclear site. After that, it depends on TOPIs.'

'TOPI?'

'Sorry, it's a UK thing, *Target of Potential Interest.* MI6 provides a regular list of foreign residents with a grudge against France: NATO adversaries; Russians and Chinese with dubious origins; those opposed to the western democracies and our *rules-based governance*. You know how it goes these days.'

She laughed. 'Half the global population you mean?'

'I want you to leave, go back to Brussels. This isn't your fight.'

'It's already too one-sided for you?' She smiled, and eased the tension strung between us. 'Consider it a favour returned.'

When she was four weeks into her residence with us, Barbie tracked an FSB agent to his lover's apartment where the husband of a naval architect was a sucker for the Cossack's silver tongue. And when he wasn't sucking, he was passing on unknown inside information, like the locations and durations of his wife's latest projects. All given under the guise of safety from interruption. Such menial details were considered worthless by the husband but are gold dust in the palms of the effective agent. Each tiny insignificant piece is reported back to Moscow where the skilled cartographer stitches them together to form the landscape of European NATO operations. It was Barbie's misfortune to catch young Vladimir post-flagrante, with his hand very much on the grip of his pistol and not on his lover's warm body. He became my number eight. And Barbie's hair became enflamed for the first time.

'You don't owe me anything,' I assured her.

'Other than my life?'

'Pay me back some other time.'

She laughed. 'You're the very worst of us, you know that?' I raised my glass. Leaning in, she lowered her voice. 'Seriously, what can be so important that they would risk cover to shoot you dead on sight? The last time we had a kill order like that—'

'I know.'

She looked at me with doubt for the first time ever.

'Drink up or bring the bottle, there's more to this than even I understand.'

I looked around the bar now filling with office workers decanting from nearby blocks. Pretty soon they would crowd us in and make conversation as well as a rapid escape impossible.

Reaching into her pocket, Barbie removed a ten-pound note. She tossed it onto the bar as we eased slowly past, like two lovers taking our leave for quiet intimacy elsewhere. 'For the glass,' she said, tilting the rim towards the surprised barman.

Outside, the air was clammy. The sinking sun reflected from regency windows, striking shadows by formal ornate doorways, so that here and there the stucco walls were strafed in pink and red. In places it looked like blood stains that wouldn't wash out.

Back at the hotel, the room smelled vaguely of the forests

around the cabin, some cheap air-freshener sprayed to mask the slow decay. Barbie sat on the foot of the bed and motioned for me to sit on the single uncomfortable chair. A cheap upright seat with a curved wooden back, it had barely sufficient padding to qualify as cushioned. The label confirming European fire retardance standards stuck out from underneath. I wasn't surprised it passed. There was little enough material to light a match.

'Why do they want you dead?' Barbie asked, before I had removed my jacket, before I had settled, before I had even looked at her. She was also upright, but through her own discomfort from a studied perch aboard the soft wide bed.

I shrugged.

'Don't bullshit me now.'

'Revenge.'

She tossed the red hair. Smiled.

'Summary punishment,' I told her while she readjusted her jacket, flicking invisible flecks from just below the shoulder. Her eyes were everywhere but on me. She was an expert interrogator. The very best. And I was an expert in resistance. The very best.

'What did you do?' Her eyes finally settled on mine. Unblinking. Her lashes unmoved. They curled upwards with an inevitability of surrender. I tried to count them. 'What did you do, *Berthier*?'

When she first arrived in Paris, Barbie wore monstrous heels that clacked like a pair of Gestapo boots up our stairs and along the cheap vinyl flooring in our hallways. Her jackets were tucked at the waist and wide at the shoulder, her pants like a pair of iron drainpipes to hide any shape in her legs. She was a woman by admission rather than observation. She was an uncomfortable outsider in a man's world. Now she had us all in her feminine grip. The strength of ten men, the courage of a thousand and more intelligence than any.

'I killed her.'

She crossed her legs. Looked at the impression in the cotton.

'I killed her because she ordered the hit on Eric.'

Barbie was unmoved. If she was surprised or horrified, she did not show it.

'I had the evidence long before I was given access to Eric's files, before all,' I looked around the room, at the two of us, 'before all *this* blew up.'

'You had evidence?'

'Yes.'

She paused. 'What kind of evidence? An admission?'

'She commissioned an agent from DGSE to murder Eric.'

'And this *agent*,' she said, 'He confessed?'

'I heard them discussing the commission. He was reporting back success.'

She studied me in the way you might the loose vegetables in a grocery store, looking for bruises or the first signs of decay, ready to toss each piece rather than accept a flaw. Her eyes bored into mine to check for sanity. She knew beyond doubt that I was no psychopath when last we met.

'Jesus, Berthier, if every intelligence agent who murdered a journalist faced summary execution, there would be graves from Moscow to Michigan.'

Holding up my hands, I nodded. I know she's right. 'I thought–'

'You thought *what*? That a little revenge for the murder of your cousin would go unnoticed? You thought they wouldn't pin this one on you? That they would put it down to bad luck and timing? She was the most senior spy in all of France, for fuck's sake. All of *Europe*, even. Don't tell me you thought about this. One thing you were not doing, was thinking. You imbecile.'

She was right.

I had been angry.

I wanted vengeance for the only man I ever loved. I wanted Christine to pay, and him, Baudelaire, likewise. I wanted two guilty dead bodies in exchange for my cousin's innocent dust. 'I thought… I *believed* that he was murdered to stop him exposing some financial or gutter scandal, maybe to save a valuable agent's reputation, not killed to safeguard the nation I am sworn to defend. His was the most dishonourable murder. They made it personal, not me. And anyway, now we know it wasn't to protect their reputations. It wasn't even to protect France. It was to hide their filthy conspiracy. And now? I am going to blow it open. *Wide* open.'

Barbie began to laugh.

Her head shook as she rolled her eyes. 'Oh, Bertie. Bertie, *Bertie*. You are such a fool.' She stood and began unbuttoning.

I watched as she slipped effortlessly out of the sleeves, throwing her jacket at me. She pulled the gun from her waist and tossed it backwards towards the pillows, where it landed cushioned and swallowed by the bedding. She kicked off her shoes without looking, then stretched her trousers, before unzipping them at the side and sliding them down over firm thighs and taut calves. Her legs, like her face, were pale. Starkly pale. As though the sun had never deigned to touch them, or did so only once, bleaching them a pure and perfect white. Her toes, I noticed suddenly, were the same vibrant vermillion as her lips.

Her underwear was hidden beneath her blouse.

She smiled. 'I'm going to bed now,' she said, reaching for the bottom of her shirt and lifting it in one swift movement up and over her head, where it caught on her necklace and for a moment, she looked like Harry Houdini fighting to escape a straitjacket.

When she emerged, she watched me for a while. 'Well?' she said.

'Well, what?'

She turned and crawled across the bed, pulling back the covers. Only when she was safely wrapped inside, did she look at me again. 'Are you going to join me?'

I paused a beat.

I knew the drill.

We were old friends, not future lovers.

As I stood, she pulled the revolver. Flicked the safety. Raised the barrel and then lowered it again. 'One false move,' she said, 'and I will blow your balls to Brussels.'

Waking to the faint melody of *Les Misérables*, I looked around to find its source. It was coming from the bathroom. From a radio, or maybe from a phone. Monsieur Marius was lamenting that his friends would drink with him no more. I checked my watch. Eight o'clock. We had slept too long. At least, *I* had slept too long. Barbie was awake and from the steamy bedroom mirror had enjoyed a scalding shower. She emerged with a bath sheet wrapped around her body and another around her head to confirm as much.

'I need clothes,' she said, like a young wife pleading with a wealthy older husband.

'Not from where I'm sitting.'

Releasing her hair, she shook it so that I felt a fine mist of rain. 'I'm serious. My bag was in the trunk of the BMW.'

I baulked.

'Don't worry. All they'll know from that is that your accomplice is a size forty-four.'

'And 80D?'

She lashed me with the damp towel. 'Hurry up and take your shower,' she said, slipping back into her red underwear, the universal warning to stop. 'I'm hungry and then you're taking me to Harrods for a new wardrobe.'

Two hours later, we emerged into a busy Knightsbridge where those who now call London home preferred to dwell. Lurid supercars lined the street oblivious to local parking laws, their discreet Emirati number plates all that indicated their ownership. I knew from Eric that this stretch of London was now home to Arabs, Oligarchs and Chinese dissidents, their money more welcome than their politics. There was a certain sort of English snobbery which falsified welcome, a transparent charade maintained by all sides for the sake of civility.

With our clutch of dark green and gold bags and darkened glasses, we fitted right in as the doorman paved our way into the back of a black cab, closing the door to cleanse us from his mind. How those top-hatted former guardsmen must have regretted the occupation by age-old enemies. Yet still, it rarely showed behind the façade of gratitude and gaiety.

'Where to guv?' the cabbie asked eyeing Barbie, as well he might, now she sported a flattering summer dress and not the constraining business suit. The latter she left in the changing rooms since its ubiquity rendered it too conspicuous. Together with my own new attire, poor old Jules Martin was now practically penniless. So much for my wedding fund.

'Number six Kensington Gardens,' Barbie said to the pair of voluminous eyes in the rear-view mirror. 'The embassy.'

He nodded and maintained a discrete silence now that he imagined we were diplomats of some description. If we cared for the English language at all, it was not with the generosity to share it with him. He knew the type we were playing.

Yanking the wheel so that we span on our axis, he eschewed the main road preferring instead to weave the plethora of narrow side-streets flanked by lofty townhouses. Their golden brickwork and stunning white facades now hid a multitude of villains, as well as boutique hotels and offices for professionals of indeterminate expertise. On a corner, we passed a quaint English pub, *The Tea Clipper*, with an array of dazzling blooms around its midriff. Purples, indigos, magentas and blues resembled a colourful rope securing the building to its moorings. The sails of a tall ship billowed in its portrait sign.

Turning left, we skirted the park.

Despite mid-morning on an otherwise ordinary day, the paths were awash with runners and walkers, and nannies by the score relieving bored parents so they may regain their sanity by working. The city was alive with the happiness of friendship and freedom as we made our way to an appointment with those who would gladly quash that way of life.

Pulling up outside the embassy, we found ourselves among a small band of protestors. They were there to complain about Chechnya or Crimea, or some other crime against democracy. For they knew that any such demonstration on the streets of

Moscow would be met with rather more violence than of a pair of harmless English 'bobbies' in high-visibility vests. With our bags and Barbie's manner, one of the cops immediately escorted us to the gate and ushered us inside.

Without a hint of irony, the building was a grand Georgian affair in white. Not pure white, of course. Rather an ashen dirty pallor. A double-headed golden eagle ignored us from beside the portico. The ground floor windows were barred, and here and there drawn drapes prevented the views of London's freedoms leaking in. We climbed the stairs towards the door which opened to greet us.

An angry mute security guard as tall as a mountain nodded us inside. His revolver was as clear under his jacket as though he were wearing it on the outside, and a coiled wire snaked from beneath his stiff collar to his left ear. His thick face looked at me carrying the bags and sneered. I was the kind of cheap bodyguard who gave our profession a bad name. I glanced down at my handful of bags and shrugged, hoping to earn at least a modicum of sympathy. Disgusted, he simply turned away.

Inside the giant hallway with its chequered floor, sat a simple office desk with a short stocky woman behind it. She had a laptop, mouse and keyboard and a small notepad on which were listed the appointments for the day. Her black suit might have been a uniform, but it bore no official insignia. Once, she would have been a junior KGB or FSB grade officer, these days more likely she was a contractor drafted in to save the headcount budget. Even former communists are not immune from capital expenditure cuts.

She peered over red-framed glasses which teetered on the bridge of her angry nose. 'Mrs Bordovsky, I presume?' she said, dismissively.

Barbie responded in perfect Russian.

'Take a seat.' Our unwilling hostess invited us to sit on a wooden bench along the hallway, but not so comfortably that we could not be hauled out and ejected by the brutish bear at a moment's notice. He had eyes only for me. Not so much as a glance at my impeccable employer. A dozen squares from the doorway, we were twice as many again from the foot of a marble staircase which curved towards the inner sanctum of ex-Soviet intentions in the formerly 'great' Britain.

Presently, a clatter of footsteps descended from the heavens, followed by a young diplomat in his late twenties or early thirties. Average height, dark hair, square jawline and chiselled cheeks, he was as Russian as his bright enamel lapel pin. His gaze swept me and fell on Barbie, from where it would leave only by necessity and not through choice.

'Mrs Bordovsky?' he said, laced with hope.

'Please, *Luisa*,' Barbie stood and stroked his arm as he reached ground level. '*Lulu* to my friends.' She gave a little laugh which our new host found charming. He didn't notice me at all.

'I'm Lebedev. Delighted to meet you. Please, come this way,' he said, pausing as I rose to follow my mistress up the stairs.

'He's harmless,' Barbie said, taking the young man by an arm. 'He hears nothing, and everything.' She laughed so that her frame jiggled. Poor Lebedev would never sleep again.

At the top of the second flight, he guided Barbie down a corridor flanked by pictures of the great ancestors of the Russian state. Lenin loomed large over Gorbachev whose narrow guilt frame reflected the disappointment of perestroika. Alexander smiled as the beautiful redhead passed, while Stalin dreamt only of the Gulags. We were directed through a door to a modest oak-panelled anteroom, a secretarial booth in which sat one of many embassy moles whose only job was to spy on their diplomats and report any anti-Russian activities back to Moscow. Little more than a cubicle, it is where I was invited to wait.

The secretary eyed me knowingly as our paymasters disappeared behind a solid oak door. She was a blonde eastern European with a hardness to her features that blighted and blessed all her type. She would age well but frown indefinitely. When she laughed, she would captivate a crowd, but when she scorned her blue eyes would as good as strike you dead.

'He will want coffee. You too?' she asked.

'*Spasibo.*'

She studied me. 'You're not Russian.'

I shook my head. 'Chechen.'

Leaning back in her chair, she smiled. 'You want a vodka rather than a coffee?'

'Both. Thank you.'

'Come, you can help carry them.' She nodded towards the pile of bags. 'You have practice, after all.' Rising, she sashayed through the doorway casting backwards to ensure I noticed. Her smile was all meant for now.

I followed her at a safe distance and surveyed my surroundings. It felt like Mother Russia laid an egg for Christopher Wren to hatch. Even Fabergé could not hide the opulence of the English architecture. Marble spawned from every orifice. Each extrusion more fantastical than the last. Looking up, I saw the cornices swamped the security cameras which must have been as good as useless up there. We crossed the second-floor lobby and followed a short corridor to a kitchen which contained just the bare necessities of city life.

'What will your boss have?'

I thought about Barbie. She drank calvados mainly. 'Coffee with cognac.'

'Typical oligarch's wife,' the secretary said. Left alone, I believe she would have spat in the cup before pouring. 'How did she end up with you?'

I shrugged. She nodded. We had all set aside our pride and principles for money.

'I keep a Stolichnaya in my office. Or there is Smirnoff in here.' She opened a head-height cupboard which was stocked for the apocalypse. 'The procurement guys insist on buying from a local supplier who is clearly a recovering alcoholic.' She laughed. 'You're the strong silent type?'

'Is there another type of chaperone?'

She busied herself with tiny cups and saucers, a cafetiere and a brand of Columbian coffee that smelled too rich. I know there are producers who perfume their packaging and I suspected that this was one. The real smell of coffee is not the bean, but the essence of the Amazonian Forest in which its forefathers were planted.

'Take this,' she said, handing me the tray. It appeared she would carry nothing, instead she would walk ahead and distract my gaze from the labyrinth hazards of thresholds and risers waiting to trip me and spill my cover.

Back in the room, she poured two coffees, opened a deep drawer and removed first a bottle of Napoleon brandy and then the vodka. She added a single measure of the former to the first cup and double of the latter to the second. 'It might loosen his tongue,' she smiled. 'I presume she's here for the dirt on her old man.'

Knocking, I opened the door to the main office for my new friend. Inside, Barbie had the diplomat entranced. She was sitting beside him at his desk while he showed her something on his computer screen. She ignored me completely, smiling at the secretary with the kind of condescension for which oligarch's wives are famed. Barbie had missed a dramatic vocation.

Closing the door, the secretary scoffed. 'She is cute enough, I suppose. Former hooker?'

I smiled.

'And that's why you leave her well alone, I guess.' She poured us both a vodka and coffee, with the emphasis on the vodka. 'Have you been home recently?'

'Such a thing is not possible for me.'

'Of course. I fear you would no longer recognise it, anyway. No shortage of work for a man with your… *qualifications*.'

'And you? You have been here in London for a while?'

She nodded. 'Before this, Paris.' She gestured disgustedly towards the closed door. 'He is a climber. Where he goes, I go. Not fast enough for him.'

I raised my eyebrows.

She smiled. 'No. Don't think he hasn't tried. He is a trier.' She laughed, a dirty guttural laugh. 'He likes that I have friends in Lubyanka Square, that's all.'

There was a coldness to the woman that I recognised. She hadn't asked for or offered a name. She had spent more time in Lubyanka than any friend she'd ever met or imagined.

'Where next?'

She pondered this a while. 'He wants New York. What Tatar doesn't? Can you imagine his mother back home? The little boy from the banks of the Volga living it up on fifth avenue?'

'You don't like him?'

'I don't like anybody, but the hired help.'

'Thank you, I think.'

'I finish at four.'

Before I could respond, the heavy door swung open to the sound of comradely laughter. Barbie emerged first, the diplomat's hands now more confidently on her back.

'Oh Pietr, you are a star,' Barbie said. And then she looked at me. 'Come–' she began, about to use a name that she suddenly feared we did not agree and might reveal us both. 'I have a hair appointment. You can take these home,' she gestured to the bags and then turned back to her quarry. 'And I shall look forward immensely to seeing you again. Soon, Pietr, I hope.'

Lebedev blushed, deliberately avoiding his secretary's fixed stare. 'Please, Anya, would you see Mrs Bordovsky out,' he said without looking at her, nodding instead to Barbie and aiming to fulfil her request as soon as was decent, ideally sooner.

Anya looked back to me. I shrugged.

At the front doorway where she left us, she wished Barbie a begrudging pleasant day and turning, whispered her number and reminded me she finished at four.

A black cab pulled up at the gate as we left, which meant our destination would be reported back, so the one Barbie gave was far from where we were staying, and our conversation was brief and perfunctory. Barbie dished out a list of instructions for a house she did not own to satisfy a husband she did not have, and which she thoroughly enjoyed, winking at me from her comfortable seat. While I perched silently on the 'jump' chair. Eventually, we arrived at the Connaught Hotel where once again

I was left to pay the fare and carry the bags.

SIXTEEN

At just after five in the afternoon, forty minutes later than agreed, she arrived. The champagne which had been chilling since our appointment sat in an ice bucket next to my right arm. Rising to kiss her on both cheeks, I plucked the bottle by the neck and filled her glass roughly so that it fizzed and almost spilled. I could not look too skilled in the art of seduction. Not for that encounter, anyway. She offered no apology for lateness, and nor did I expect one. She had honoured me with her presence, and that, she needed me to understand, was a great deal more than any man deserved.

A short black summer dress wrapped her, tucked at the waist and circled by a belt of solid gold. A matching chain hung around her neck, dangling a slither of amber which she expected me to admire. I was a hired gun, after all. Brutal, simple, a man of work not words. This is what attracted her, if she was not there to elicit the same from me as I desired from her. Information. Her honest make-up said the motivation was far more physical than philosophical.

'How long have you been here?'

'Fifty minutes,' I lied.

She liked this very much, raising her glass to me. 'And who babysits today?'

I shrugged. My days of safeguarding Barbara Solido were long since gone. Now it was me who was mainly babysat.

'I hate them, you know,' she said, as though this needed some other confirmation. 'They live here or Paris or Amsterdam and claim loyalty to a cause they long ago abandoned. They're no more Russian than the dolls we peddle to the tourists with *Made in China* stamped on their asses. When was the last time your boss went back home?'

I didn't bother to answer. I had a feeling that most of her questions would be rhetorical. My words needed to be carefully rationed to ensure that each received the appropriate attention.

'They are afraid of him, that's the truth of it. Like they were of Stalin before him. And why? Because it's not their money, that's why. The wealth belongs to the people, not to these gangsters. You know what they come to us for, all of them: *where should we live? where is safe for us? who can we pay to keep our secrets? how do we minimise our taxes?* You know that's what your gangster's moll was doing at the embassy, with Lebedev, right? Asking all those types of questions. You know what she means? She means, how can we hide *our* money. But it's not hers. It's yours and mine.' She paused from the lecture. 'What is your name, by the way?'

I had the feeling she only wanted to know, so that she could use it to hector me more precisely. 'Josef.'

'That's a good name for a Chechen.'

I nodded. 'And will he?'

'Will he what?'

'Your boss, will he help her?'

Laughing, Anya gestured to the bottle and waved her glass at me. I was thinking of pacing myself, but it seemed I wouldn't have to. I had only had one mouthful to her full measure already. 'Of course, you care only because she pays your wages.'

'No, I care because it's good to know where your boss stands on such matters.'

'He's an asshole, I told you that already. He will help her.' She didn't tell me whether he would report it afterwards, and that's all I really needed to know. That was all I was really doing there. Because what the likes of Pietr Lebedev told and to whom was, somehow, at the very centre of the grand conspiracy of Eric's making. *Follow the money, Bertie–* 'You were a soldier?' she asked, suddenly.

I nodded.

'Not like them, then. You fought for a cause not just for yourself.'

'I'm alive because I fought for both.'

She laughed. 'How many kills?'

'Dozens,' I told her, because there was no point lying about things that might as well be true as false.

'Life is cheap.'

I knew then that the only way I would elicit what I needed was in passion – in flagrante or a fight, either could easily be to the death. There is a certain type of person for whom adrenaline is more than just a drug. It is their elixir; the substance on which they have come to rely for pleasure, for pain, for perseverance; for the continuation of their life with or without meaning. They cannot succeed or fail. They survive. Blameless. Anya had 'kill or be killed' emblazoned above the headboard of the bed in which she had done both. Easy come, easy go.

'What do you want from me?'

Studying me, she tapped the rim of her glass with a scarlet nail. 'Aren't you bored of all this?' She cast around the hotel bar in which we sat. It was dark and moody, and mainly empty but for business types on fractured liquid lunches that would last all evening too. Olives were scattered like confetti on low kidney-shaped tables, the décor screaming decadence. Leopard print and valour abounded. Black wooden legs outnumbered trouserED ones. There was a menu without prices for cocktails without volume. If Tinder were a bar, this would have been it.

'Bored of London?'

'Of this life. Of *us*.'

'I didn't want to be a bodyguard. I wanted to join the GRU.' She did not care for my confession. She had no interest in men with failed ambition, but the ease and speed with which she inhabited then occupied talk of Lubyanka might also have been bait. It was possible my new-found friend was doing a little fishing or recruiting of her own.

'Why didn't you?'

'I told you. I am Chechen by birth.'

'It's the GRU, not the Nazi party. We aren't looking for Aryans, more's the pity.'

I shrugged. 'I am only to be trusted with a trigger, apparently.'

'Poor little Josef. The motherland makes orphans of us all. Pour me another. I want to finish the bottle, then you can take me to the room *I trust* that you have booked?'

◆ ◆ ◆

Lying in the bedroom in the blackest darkness, things began to make more sense. Pascal was at pains to direct me from a grand conspiracy, and he may yet have been proven right, nothing more than an honest broker between a service and its former spy. But if he was wrong, then he and I were both about to watch the whole of French Intelligence blow sky-high–

At the soft clicking of the latch, I reached under the pillow.

The door eased, and a silhouette was framed by the dusky hallway light. There was no attempt to illuminate the room and the door closed as quietly as it opened, but enough for me to release the metal and slide my hand back to pull the covers.

'How was your day?' she asked, as she undressed.

'Productive. How was your night?'

'Illuminating.' She kicked off her heels and slipped between the sheets, sighing. 'What did you learn?'

'The secretary is an informant. She'd like me to watch you closely, and better still the movements of your unknown oligarch husband. He is currently a mystery to them. You?'

'Just hints and suggestions. He asked about contributions to the cause, but he was at pains to be vague. Of course, he will discuss the details with *my husband.*'

I laughed. The very idea that somewhere there was a man to whom Barbara Solido would be subservient was beyond my comprehension. In another life, perhaps. Not this one. 'It's a patriot fund,' I said.

'For whom, the embassy staff?'

'Not for whom, for what. They're raising money from emigrants to fund pro-Russian activities in-country. That's where your husband's *contribution* will go. The embassy will collect the cash and–'

Barbie rolled over, turning on the bedside lamp before sitting upright. 'The GRU will spend it?'

'Exactly.'

She turned to look at me as I leaned on my elbows. 'Jesus, Berthier, you know what this means? Every new exile, every migrant, they're paying into a secret service levy, totally off the books. Completely without a paper-trail–'

'What does it matter? Is it any different to a tax? Who do you think funds your salary, and mine?' It reminded me, I hadn't checked whether human resources at Le Troisième continued their regular weekly deposit into my account, despite my new status. Such administrative oversight would be par for the course.

'For sure,' Barbie continued, 'but think about the sums involved. How much would an expat expect to pay? One percent of wealth? Five percent? *Ten*? What could they do with that amount of money?'

'What are they *already* doing with it?'

She paused. 'Destabilisation. It's perfect. All run in-country, under local control. No reporting, no movement of international funds to track. No bank transfers. Handled in cash?'

'Or Bitcoin or some other currency we'll never see.'

'Brilliant. And when we're planning our annual intelligence spend, we're doing it based on a fraction of our adversary's known budget. Because we can't see their budget. Because it's hidden right under our fucking noses.'

We both nodded, the only movement in the silence between breaths.

Eventually, Barbie lay back, lowering like a marionette in a puppeteer's soft hands.

She folded her arms across her chest. 'What next?'

'I don't know.'

'You think Eric knew?'

I did. I thought that was why he was dead. He had been about to break the story.

'Even if he did,' Barbie continued, a singular train of thought exploring the same terrain I had scoured relentlessly since returning to the room, 'Why would your own people kill him? He would have done them an enormous service, right? Berthier, right?'

I said nothing.

And waited.

She sat bolt upright again. 'Holy fuck!' Turning to look at me, she was shaking.

'Yes,' I said. 'Exactly'.

SEVENTEEN

Thankfully, my half-hearted protestations went ignored and my new partner was now a thousand miles ahead of me, awaiting my arrival. Her contacts had located Pascal. Business or pleasure we could not confirm, but where and when we could. Such was the sacred trust we placed in the documentation of those who frequent our airlines knowingly.

Aboard my own plane was Max Haaland, a Dutch engineer whose acquaintance required nothing more than a bottle of peroxide, but whose egress to the United States had demanded the delicate operation in my airplane's bathroom. New fingertips, courtesy of the Belgian secret service, were already sticky with my sweat when they rested upon the scanner.

'What's your business in the United States of America?'

The big Latino face was as unwelcoming as the tone, a first line of defence against those Europeans who might still arrive to colonise.

'Visiting friends and distant family, some sightseeing too. I have no business here.'

There was the usual pause designed for me to fill it. 'Length of stay?'

I shrugged. 'A week or two at most. It all depends on the weather.'

It was the middle of July. I might have melted into a sidewalk and never returned home again. His stubby fingers flicked the passport back and forth while we waited to confirm its authenticity and absence of any record which would divert me to the nearest return flight. Reluctantly, the pages were closed, and another would-be migrant was allowed to swell the ranks of unwanted visitors.

I collected my case from the carousel this time, before hailing a cab.

The early evening sunlight sliced through the buildings, lacerating locals who even then stuck mainly to the shadows. In and out of the light we waded, easing left and right amid the waves of yellow which preceded and pursued us through the city. Offices and homes cocooned us at ground zero, where we were nothing more than ants amid the giant stems.

A sudden swerve and I was deposited on the sidewalk inside one of the many shadows which obliterated the street. The upper floors of the hotel narrowed to a needle, which together with a shorter twin, almost masked the Empire State. There was no reception desk, but rather a square hole in a grey wall from which a smiling black face appeared. A part-time doorman, greeter, receptionist, or bellhop. The lobby was no bigger than a modest lounge, home to the hole and a single elevator. The Ritz Carlton it was not. But then, neither did our budget stretch since Barbie's London shopping spree. From my dwindling resources I paid for the booking in dollar bills in advance. Should anything happen to us, I would rather leave no debts.

News of Pascal was all too sketchy, but we did have one thing on our side. The man was as inflexible as an ancient oak in a howling gale. So many times before he had visited the sleepless city, each time booking the *Conran Hotel* about which he had frequently waxed lyrical to Gabrielle, imploring her to stay in one of their sumptuous executive suites with their commanding views of the city. I hoped and prayed the leopard retained his spots.

By contrast, our own bedroom was sparse but ample, and bereft of any evidence of the Belgian save for a small overnight bag placed delicately on the stand reserved for such things. I thought about opening it, but feared it may be booby-trapped, and besides what was there to know about this woman that I did not already? If she had brought a gun, she would have taken it wherever she went. If I wanted my own, I would have to scour the streets and buy one. That might have been necessary, but I hoped we could avoid such dramas.

I opened the minibar for a coke. That's where I found her orders:

P is registered to attend 'The Global Defence and Security Summit'. Details online. Starts tomorrow. Meet me near there as soon as you receive the note.

PS. The minibar bill is on you.

I left the coke and made my way back down to the would-be concierge, who was only too happy to search the internet on my behalf and locate the conference, before hailing me a cab for a few folded bills pressed into his sweaty palm.

Two blocks from my destination, I decanted to reconnoitre the terrain for I imagined security would be tighter there than anywhere; New York needed no reminding of its scars.

There was just one thing that troubled me. *Why now?* Pascal was one of the main men in charge during the Friday 13th Atrocities. He had brutal first-hand experience of terrorism and carried his own deep mental scars accordingly. But his expertise on policing had surely been superseded by events? However much our oldest ally still admired its Gallic benefactor, it was impossible to conceive how my former future father-in-law had anything to offer a security fraternity whose depth of knowledge and budget dwarfed our own. But of course, I was a mere foot soldier. And the machinations of the fools rarely made sense to liars.

At the corner of 33rd and 9th, I exited the cab to slip into the treacle of Manhattan. It was midday, and the triangles of sun that bleached the sidewalks also overwhelmed them, leaving only sporadic awnings for shelter. Stopping in the shade of a jewellery store, I scanned the scene behind me in its window. A couple of blocks from my destination, movement was brisk. This was no lazy shopping district. Even so, on a far corner above my left shoulder I saw her, like a match alight in the shadows. Unmissable. Turning back to the sidewalk I signalled my intent. She walked swiftly the other away.

At a chic diner on the next block, she was already in their window like a striking objet d'Art in a gallery case, all creams and golds and topped with scarlet. This is why they never saw her coming. Because they were all too dazzled by her approach.

'You're late,' she said as I slid in opposite her, before beckoning a waiter. 'I expected you last night. What happened?'

'Last minute change of flight. Can't be too careful in this line of work.'

A broad grin flashed across her pale face. 'But not so careful about your sugar intake?'

Smiling, I relayed my order to the handsome young waiter who had eyes only for my companion.

'He's there now?'

She shook her head. 'Today is some sort of technical set-up and run through. He goes on stage tomorrow afternoon at four. Will he rehearse?'

I thought about Pascal's diligence; a more meticulous man I could not imagine. But nor could I picture one more certain in his own beliefs. 'He will need no rehearsal.'

Barbie raised her eyebrows, while the waiter placed a coffee before me, along with a slice of homemade pecan pie. It had been another ten hours since I had eaten.

'How much do you think he knows?'

I studied Barbie's fresh face. How could the stresses of our occupation leave so little trace? I shrugged. 'Is he a pawn or powerbroker? I don't see his connection to Russia, but he is a resolute patriot. He would have been first in the queue to volunteer to serve the republic in any endeavour, that's for sure.'

'Weren't you one yourself once?' She took my fork and levered more than a mouthful from my plate, laughing as nuts and pastry escaped the plump lips, showering her dress.

I thought about Helmand again. There were simply too many to avenge. 'Listen, my allegiance was only ever to the flag, not those who wrap themselves inside her to cloak their aims.' It sounded bold enough, but I was more wracked with doubt than ever. What was I fighting for? What were any of us? To preserve the status quo or to vanquish it?

'So, what's the plan?' she asked, summoning the eager waiter for another napkin and a coffee top-up. 'We snatch him off the street and then what? You have some place in mind for an interrogation?' She smiled sarcastically as the coffee arrived and was poured. The slow river of black gave me thinking time.

'You tail him from the hall tomorrow. I wait inside his hotel room.'

She raised those ginger eyebrows.

'What?'

'You don't want to know who he is meeting here? You think he will give up his secrets to his prodigal son-in-law? Berthier, I had you pegged for a liar not a fool.'

I closed my eyes. She was right. *Merde*.

'We need to tail him. We need access to the event. At least, *I* need access to the event. You, he will recognise, but not me. With luck, maybe I can… *befriend* him.' She smiled and winked.

'No, it's too dangerous. He'll make you in a heartbeat.'

Barbie laughed. 'Thank you for the vote of confidence.'

I studied her again. Would he? Make her? Or was he, like the remainder of us monstrous gallic males, blind to his own arrogance and stupidity. 'What's your cover?'

'I'm a reporter. You know the drill.'

I knew the drill. If you wanted to ask questions, assume the role of journalist. If you wanted to take pictures, assume the guise of photographer. The world of fictional spy-craft is ever more complex, while those of us who inhabited that world for real swore by a single motto: KISS – Keep it Simple, Stupid.

'I have accreditation from the VRT.'

Such was the benefit of a state-owned broadcaster. 'And how do we know he is meeting anyone of value? What if he is here purely as an expert in his field?'

Barbie shook her red mane which carried her argument for her. 'You said it yourself, Berthier, this man was sent to bring you in. He lectured you in his own lounge. He may no longer be connected to the intricacies of the service, but nor is he some innocent clerk fulfilling orders. Not of man of his reputation. Of course, maybe he is here purely for the conference–'

'I don't like it.'

She smiled. 'What don't you like?'

'You, in the lions' den, alone–'

'Sexist.'

I could have claimed chivalry, but she knew me too well. 'Listen, Barbie. It's not that I don't trust you–'

'It's just that you trust yourself more?'

Even a liar must occasionally concede the truth. Pascal knew more than he had revealed, of that I was certain. And he would rather have died than reveal any more to me. My Belgian conscience was right. She had the greater chance of success, for I had chosen the wrong side.

Barbie took my hand. 'Cheer up. Let's do some sightseeing, then you can buy me dinner and agree *our* plan.'

That night, I left the comfort of the soft warm bed, taking the cold hard stairs to the ground floor. Reluctantly, I had agreed for Barbie to attend the conference alone. But for then, and the next few hours at least, I remained master of my own destiny. Heaving the great glass door open, the clammy claw of the city gripped me. It was wet. Not raining, but water hung angry in the air. Just a short walk from the doorway to the end of the street, my shirt was already clinging like a new child at the breast. The air smelled stale, like the end of a long day in cramped quarters.

It was eighteen blocks to the Conran and despite its global promise, the city mainly slept. A distant siren bleated more than wailed as I stepped around a body on the sidewalk wrapped in a blanket and cardboard, dead to the world. A solitary police car crawled the centre lane disinterestedly, and the clank and rattle of garbage trucks masked the snoring commuters oblivious to the fate of all those beneath their beds. Only lovers and liars were ever alert in a city after dark.

Just beyond the corner of 8th and 36th I saw her.

Unmistakable.

She had her back to me, but I would have recognised that profile anywhere at any time. Day or night. She leaned on the wall, cigarette in hand, bathed in the soft light of a club which defied sleep. A sleazy jazz bar or speak-easy. A solitary doorway through which she could have slipped unhindered, for what mortal could deny such a goddess.

I sank back into the shadows and watched.

She pressed a phone to her ear, and I instinctively reached for my pocket, but there was no tell-tale vibration. Nothing. Her call went unanswered. She watched the screen, waiting, stepping foot to foot. She shivered but not from cold. Then turned to study the street. A lazy cab slowed but a shake of her hair depressed its accelerator, and it sped unhappily away. Her outline was lit green by an overhead traffic light, and this was my signal to cross, but at the moment of decision the light changed, and that flash of red stopped me where I stood. She turned back to the doorway as two men spilled out. The first was young and vigorous. And handsome. She nodded to him and in the shadow maybe also smiled.

The second man was Pascal.

'I knew I couldn't trust you.'

Barbie's breath was hot on my neck where I detected she would rather have been holding a cold steel blade. 'Who are they?'

'It's her.'

There was an angry pause while I knew, without turning, that my accomplice appraised her competition for my attention.

'Then why is she here?'

That I didn't know. Maybe to accompany her father, maybe because she needed a break after the trauma of recent events, maybe because she loved this city more than our own, maybe because

'Is she here to flush you out?' Barbie pulled gently at my collar.

Maybe. *Maybe.*

'And the young guy?'

I shook my head.

'Come on. We need to get you back to bed before you do something I regret.'

I could not shake the image. Conscious or asleep, Gabrielle stalked me. Her sylph-like figure wandered through my dreams and out again; a waspish silhouette beyond touch, beyond imagination. I tried and failed to picture her face caught in the spotlight of the open doorway. But each new turn of her head shrouded her beauty in a mist of unattainability. I longed to see her. To hold her. To listen to her minor complaints and irritations with the life of a busy assistant in a city of a million fools. I yearned for her truth, as we liars always do.

She should not have been there.

There was no earthly reason why she would have accompanied Pascal. He was a lion. He needed no taming from anyone, let alone the angel he adored so feverishly. Why would he have brought her? Regret? Apology? Or, to expose the man who stole her heart as nothing more than monster.

While Barbie claimed otherwise, I could sense it troubled her as much as me. Whatever my supposed indifference to Gabrielle's presence, my colleague wasn't buying it, and who could blame her? We should have aborted and regrouped, but neither of us won awards for patience. Impatience on the other hand, was usually rewarded with an early grave.

For the second time, I slipped out of the covers.

In the solace of the bathroom, I connected my phone to the hotel Wi-Fi via VPN.

I tapped out a silent message, hovering over the 'arrow' to send it.

Before I saw sense, it was gone. Along with any hope of anonymity or surprise.

Now we would see how much trust remained between lovers. And the following day, we would know whether there was any future for us. Any semblance of life ahead for me at all.

EIGHTEEN

Pascal rose from his seat like a Roman emperor at the Coliseum, a gently waved hand quieting the applause from an audience left in no doubt about his credentials from an introduction that had painted him a saviour of France. But then, Americans had long since stopped caring about truth. Pascal was a chief of police who trailed and caught terrorists, not the man who restored a republic, whatever he may have been about to claim. In the curved arc of the concert hall, his would be no soaring solo to charm the birds. A carrion call, perhaps.

In a typical sharp grey suit and thin black tie, he nodded approvingly. Slowly, deliberately, he reached forward and bent the microphone stalk. '*Mes amis*,' he began, before smiling. 'My friends – English is better, yes?'

The echo of applause dissolved into a smattering of laughter. 'Ladies and gentlemen, our two countries, the oldest of allies, are at a crossroads. One that requires no further illumination from me. The evidence surrounds us every day. The threat to our liberties and the liberal values which define our respective states have never been so great.' He paused to watch the nods of agreement and despondency. 'No quicker do we act to re-assert our way of life, than the forces massed against us react and evolve. It is a case – what would you Americans call it – of "pinning *Jell-O* to the wall"? Yes?'

More muted laughter.

'But this is no joking matter.' He dropped an octave, thrust both hands to the side of the podium, leaned in, drew breath, scanned the front rows for possible insurgents. 'This my friends, is a matter of life and death. *Our* way of life, or the death of it.' He paused, grew to his full height. There may have been a collection of notes hidden out of view, but if there were, he was not using them. This was Pascal the orator, the collector of wayward minds, the navigator of troubled waters, the safe and secure harbour in a storm of anxiety. I pictured him before the wide-eyed raw recruits in Place Louis Lépin, rousing them from their liberty to liberal fanaticism.

'In November 2015, we lost 130 innocent French civilians. It was an act of pure terror. It left a deep scar on our capital. A scar not unlike your own. And while our pain and the scars linger, the stain on our freedoms must not. My friends, those innocent men, women and children did not die at the hands of terrorists, whatever our media may claim. They were killed in cold blood by murderers. Brutal, bloody murderers who cannot stand our way of life. They died at the hands of fascists. Yes, that's what they were. Not the nihilists the media would have you believe, nor some radicals exhorted to wage a holy war against an empire. *Fascists.* As sure as those whose scourge blighted my continent to be rescued by yours. I call them fascists, because that is their goal – a total and utter destruction of all our liberal values. Our freedoms. This is what they crave. The wanton annihilation of a way of life. *Our* way of life!'

Suddenly, they were all listening intently. He wasn't the first to demonise jihadists, he was likely the first to classify them as the Fourth Reich.

'They say that when evil comes,' he continued, 'it comes dressed in the clothes of patriotism. It comes, they say, as *nationalism*. The state versus the individual. A government versus its citizens. Today, nothing could be further from the truth. Today, the state is the citizen and the citizen the state. And our enemy comes not from within, nor even from forces without. It comes from forces operating not in the shadows, but in *broad daylight*. Forces operating with complete impunity!' He reached into his jacket pocket and removed a cell phone. He waved it violently like he hated it. 'Forces who seduce and corrupt us in plain sight. Forces we embrace because we believe in free speech, but which only emboldens our adversaries...'

I tuned out to scan the audience. I knew where this path led, already. From freedoms to falsehoods. Our way of life must be secured, he would no doubt claim, but only by removing the very essence of our liberal values. More surveillance, more controls, more regulation, more monitoring, and all to safeguard and enshrine free speech.

From my seat with the production team in the shadows, I could see mainly the backs and sides of audience heads. Old heads, but not necessarily any the wiser for it. They possessed, by and large, white faces. Including two I knew intimately. They were sat no more than two metres apart and both had their gazes trained on Pascal. I turned to find the monitor for the inevitable webcast, watching as the camera tracked the crowd. It stopped on Gabrielle. Naturally. She was half the age of those around her, and the most beautiful by far. She sat entranced by her father, but surely not his theme. Nonetheless, the soft brown eyes overflowed with love, blind to the bile he spewed.

The camera panned the front row from Gabrielle to Barbie, where it paused again, predictably. Hers was the only other face under fifty, after all. But her gaze didn't linger for love. Barbie was alert and willing the speaker to catch her eye. Which he would, inevitably. Because not only was the woman a master of manipulation, she was also pushing at an open door. A chasm created by Pascal's supreme arrogance. I was a fool to think he'd make her. She could have him enthralled and entranced at will. Ironically, the only obstacle in her way was my own fiancée.

A thunder of applause accompanied the camera sweeping back around to the speaker. His work was done. The touchpaper was alight again, not that it ever truly dies. Our fear means it's never less than a glowing ember, ever ready to be sparked into a rampant blaze whenever it suits our politicians: to misdirect us; to cover up some scandal or other; to justify our security budgets; or simply and mostly to maintain the status quo. A raft of raised hands followed the applause, questions which Pascal was nothing less than delighted to address. Prime among them was Barbie's. It was to her that he turned first. Of course, he did.

'Are you available for private consultations on this matter?' she asked.

He smiled. And were it not for the two hundred eager faces, I swear he would also have licked his lips. 'Why don't you catch up with me afterwards?' he said, staying with the questioner longer than needed. 'I'm always happy to entertain *offers*.'

There was a frisson attached to his final word, over which

he paused indelicately, followed by a satisfied murmur among the predominantly male audience for whom Pascal confirmed their preconceptions about us French. I looked to Gabrielle, who bristled. Her back stiffened and, sub-consciously or otherwise, she shook her head. She may yet prove our undoing.

There were other raised hands, but none which warranted my continued attention. The air was rank with patriotism and pride, xenophobia lurking eagerly in the shadows of the auditorium. So too, did security guards. A small battalion in black suits with earpieces and holsters were stationed in the quiet recesses around the walls. Whether they could operate the guns slung beneath their shoulders I could not say. Sometimes these people were drafted in for effect, other times for their capability. Today, I suspected it was the usual mix of both. I was relieved not to have seen the liberal or the Norse, nor their fierce dark-haired leader. It did not mean they were not there, but the ease with which I was able to slip into the production crew, and from there to pay my way backstage, suggested the usual local custom prevailed; security farmed out to the lowest local bidder and not one of the government's understaffed agencies.

The technician on the sound desk turned Pascal's microphone off as another round of applause greeted his triumphant departure from the stage. 'Seen everything you needed to see?'

I handed him another hundred dollars. 'Sufficient for our plans.'

He thought I was a competitor who might shortly call upon his services for an event of my own. Or maybe he didn't care either way but was grateful for the cash in an industry renowned for its casual disregard for labour.

I slipped out of the production booth and away through the

bowels of the building, into a narrow corridor which ran the length of the conference hall for use by caterers and crew, several of whom I dodged and weaved around in my haste to exit before the crowd. I had promised my Belgian accomplice that I was not there. It would have been unwise to give away my lie so soon.

A set of double doors were marked 'Fire Exit' and by my calculations they would deliver me to a plaza at the rear of the venue. I waited for a lull in nearby activity, the rising applause of the next speaker being introduced, then pushed the bar and eased my way outside.

Into impossibly bright blinding sunshine.

And right behind the Norse.

He was seated on a low brick wall, no more than ten metres ahead of me, smoking. He turned as the doors clanged closed like a dinner gong behind me. *Shit.*

I looked left. Dead end. High wall. Too high. A rusting fire-escape. Three metres off the ground. Way beyond my reach.

Right had potential. It needed to have, since it was impossible to run straight through the monstrosity who was too quickly off his ass, and weaving towards me while reaching into his jacket–

I went.

Out towards the plaza I thought was there.

He yelled. At me, at colleagues, who knew? There was no time to figure it out. Bolting through a narrow archway into what I imagined was the plaza, I realised with crushing fury I was at completely the wrong end and side of the building. *Idiot.* Why was it always so damn easy in the movies? Because they had a script. While all I had was improvisation. And prayers to a god I had long since lost faith in.

Instead of the wide piazza with its helpful crowd, I was stuck running through an alley. Narrow, shallow, a mix of different darkness of shade. The exhibition hall was on the right, the back of coffee shops, restaurants and independent stores were to my left. There were a dozen garbage trolleys, heaps of bagged up trash. Sprinting and weaving, I heard the first shot ricochet off the nearest cart with a metallic ping. *Shit.* It was quite literally a shooting gallery. And without a weapon of my own I couldn't dive left or right for cover and hit back. Another shot from the silenced revolver sliced through the bags up ahead, throwing up dust and feathers from a discarded duvet. I hurdled them and sprinted like crazy for the safety of a crowd. *Any* crowd.

It didn't come.

The alley spilled me into another courtyard exactly like the one I had just escaped. Only this time there were four solid red-brick walls. A half-dozen windows: waist-height, wood framed, and with their blinds or drapes drawn. One solitary door. Closed. Another shot sliced through the air nearby, clipping the wall ahead and coughing up concrete dust. *Shit. Shit. Shit.*

I ran left. Picked up pace. Arms across the face, hands inside my sleeves. And I dived.

Towards the closest window, as another shot bit into the frame above my head.

A colossal crash followed, quickly joined by the screams of those whose table I had landed on in a shower of glass and part-rotten oak. Thank budget cuts for a lack of maintenance. The guy to my left was sprawled on his toppled chair, wearing what looked like a spaghetti suit. A woman to my right was rocking back in her seat and yelling. She started to rise.

As did I.

But not before a livid waiter came out from behind a counter which ran the length of the establishment. An Italian bistro for sure. At least he was carrying a baseball bat and not a gun. Scrabbling to my feet I offered my hands in apology, but he swung anyway with a string of expletives in his native tongue. He didn't ask for explanations. But then, what would I have said? Was there some plausible justification for my mode of entry? 'Hey, sorry but the door was closed...' I swayed my hips to dodge him, as he swung again like he meant to plant me firmly in the bleachers. Other diners further into the front of the restaurant were also getting to their feet. That wasn't good–

Behind me, the two spilled diners were also regaining their composure. Equally, not good. But behind *them*, the window was empty. The Norse had gone. Presumably tracking around the block to await me at the door. He knew he couldn't shoot me in a restaurant – although, this was America. It probably wouldn't have been as unexpected as my entrance. My mind was made up.

Turning, I ran back towards the window, sprang off the upturned table and crashed back into the courtyard amid more screams of panic and dismay. Barrel-rolling to my feet, I felt my bloodied wrists which were the only injuries I'd suffered. Cuts and bruises I could live with. A bullet in the back, not so much.

Thankfully, the Norse appeared to have gone.

At least from view. If he was loitering in the passageway, a clever double-bluff, I was as good as dead. He wasn't, so I tracked through the alley as casually as a man with a blood-stained jacket could, before stripping it off, wiping down my arms and dispensing with the bloody garment in the nearest garbage cart. Back in the yard behind the concert hall, there was now a clear exit out onto a busy city street. I hurried through the opening vacated by my pursuer, took a quick look back towards the restaurant and turned away. Straight into the liberal.

He shoved a discreet revolver into my kidney.

'Let's take a walk,' he said, quietly into my ear. 'You know I wouldn't hesitate.'

I did. His colleagues had established a pretty persuasive case to want me dead no matter the collateral or political damage. And with the barrel pressed into my side, the sound of a deadened gunshot would have been no worse than the myriad crashes and bangs from the construction sites which peppered that part of town. He hustled me awkwardly down the busy street and into the rear of a waiting silver sedan. So, Pascal *was* bait. And now I had no way of alerting Barbie that she too was swimming directly into their net.

The liberal shoved me across the bench seat as the Norse entered from the other side, trapping me. Two guns. One for each kidney, for added reassurance.

No surprise who was driving. Same black suit. Same satisfied smile which beamed at me from the mirror. No eyes. Just plump lips and impeccable tigerish teeth.

'You're a difficult man to pursue, Berthier. But not impossible.'

'Evidently.'

She turned her gaze back to the road. 'You're as predictable as the rest of your ilk.'

I would have cursed her if it wasn't true. My ingress to the conference should have been the first clue. I was as arrogant as the man they brought here to lure me, as foolish as any liar has ever been. On the upside, I was still alive. 'You have no idea what you're doing, or for whom.'

She laughed as she pulled away from the sidewalk and into

the steady stream of cabs and tourists. Some slowing, some speeding, dancing through the streets like beetles. 'Really, Berthier? A lecture from you on ethics? I expected better.'

'You're not fighting for the side you think you are.'

'We're not *fighting* for anyone. We're simply upholding the law.'

I shook my head. It's no use arguing with a fundamentalist. They can't see sense in front of their face, and those three were the very worst types of militants; devotees to a cause, they refused to question orders. They were where I was before my damascene conversion. I hoped for their sakes it didn't take the murder of a family member to open their eyes.

My assumption that we would leave the city for some hideaway safe house was wrong. We were heading back towards the financial district, along Madison Avenue, parallel to Central Park. To the heliport perhaps and rendition to one of our lonely former colonies where they would grill me through sackcloth before a lingering death. Or maybe to the consulate to be despatched more quickly, now that we knew such a fate earned nothing worse than rancid tabloid headlines and the mildest international ire.

Leaning across the Norse, I could just make out the back of the gargantuan Trump Tower, a colossal edifice to bankruptcy, dripping in sunlit gold.

'Hey,' the big man prodded me with his revolver. 'It's not a sight-seeing tour.'

The rest of the buildings flashed by as we accelerated to and from the relentless battery of stoplights. At each intersection, the barrels squeezed me tighter for the brief period while the car was stationary. They were unlikely to shoot unless I made a move, for fear of killing each other. If I went right and over the Norse, he could have shot me in the stomach. If I went left and over the liberal, I had until my body hit the street. Wherever that car was headed, then, Agent Berthier of the third French intelligence service was along for the full fare.

NINETEEN

Pushing thoughts of Barbara Solido from my mind, I followed the liberal from the car and into a cold concrete car park at the bottom of a long and winding ramp. Ours was one of only three sedans, parked amid dozens of empty bays in the cheap glow of fizzing neon.

So, this was the end.

Against the wall in the corner of some unnamed basement with the stench of stale piss. So much for the glorious *Sundance Kid* fantasy finale. But when you had lived and worked among the rats, perhaps you should not have been surprised to die in the sewer.

'To the elevator,' the woman said. 'And, Berthier, don't even think about it. In this space, no one will hear you scream.' Even though I had two guns trained on me already, she slotted in behind and pushed another tiny revolver into the small of my back. Taking an arm each, the liberal and the Norse hauled me to the elevator, where the Norse released me for the three seconds necessary to thump the call button. Not long enough. Not when the reaction time to put a bullet through my spine was two hundred and ten milliseconds on average. And I had no doubt the woman was far from average. You didn't make team lead at DGSE at her age by being average.

The car arrived with a jocular 'ping', clearly unaware of my predicament. Even so, I couldn't disguise a smile.

'Something amuses you, Berthier?' she asked, prodding me forward into the silvery void. In the reflection I saw her face. It was sharp, chiselled, as stern as it was athletic, devoid of any empathy, as only a woman controlling three men and many more besides could be. She didn't turn me around. Just left me staring at myself, and her. With eyes that didn't blink or shift, I swore she had nothing but the greatest contempt for me.

'I'm satisfied, that's all.'

She scoffed. 'Satisfied?'

'Your scams will be exposed with or without me, I've seen to that.'

She shook her head. 'There are no scams. No conspiracies. Other than those in that deluded mind of yours. The rest of us are doing our job, keeping a nation safe. I used to like the scents from your office, but all we smell over there now is bullshit. It's over, you know. Le Troisième is over.'

She might well have been right. They had been trying long enough to close us down. We all want our guardians dead at some point in our lives. They had been prepared to kill me several times over, so there was no doubt in my mind they feared exposure. Else they would have tried much harder to bring me in.

'How could you do it?' she almost spat. 'How could you kill her?'

'You'll understand one day.'

She jammed the barrel tighter until it stung. 'I won't. Not ever. Nicole was everything that you and your type will never be–'

'Nicole? You think *I* killed Nicole? What, and nearly killed me in the process–'

'I watched you.' The liberal spoke.

'We've all seen the tapes,' the Norse joined in. I wondered if his rasp reflected his health. I had outrun him twice already.

'You've seen fuck all. Whatever you think you saw, let me assure you, you didn't see me kill your colleague–'

'Friend, Berthier. She was our *friend*.'

That was bullshit. None of us had friends in the service.

I was about to argue as much when we slid to a halt and the doors opened.

Spinning me, they shoved me out before the doors closed behind me, and into a long corridor like that of a cheap motel. But here, all the walls and doors were grey. So too the cheap carpet, a mottled pattern of other greys within the nylon. Even the recessed lights burned drearily. There was no hotelier or developer in the world who would inflict this on a client. I had seen warships with more lustre. But this was a colour reference I knew only too well: Government Drab.

At the far end of the lifeless tube, a mountainous security guard opened a door which looked tiny in his presence. He beckoned me on and in, and–

I couldn't believe my eyes. 'You're dead.'

Closing the door and directing me to the only chair, beside a barren laminate desk, she moved around to lean against the wall. Against a waist-height two-way mirror that confirmed ownership of this building. 'Only if we both are,' she said, smiling. Here again, that bright lipstick, the red dress. A hazard warning in heels.

It was possible. We were destined for the same hell, after all. 'I watched your head explode.'

'You watched *a* head explode but thankfully not this one.'

I saw it all again, reviewing every final second of her treasonous life: the doorway, the movement, the darkness, the grey shape, her silhouette, the round head in my telescopic sight, *exploding*. Frame by frame it flicked through my mind like a stop-motion movie. It was possible it was not her.

'But I spoke to you.'

She smiled. 'You did. That much is true.'

And now it all made sense.

She knew about Paul before the call. He'd been the bait to flush out anyone Eric had spoken to. They probably hadn't expected me to kill him. Confront him perhaps. I wanted six weeks, I needed them. I had to be sure. They must have warned him. He must have known. Maybe the guy was sloppier than his reputation. Maybe he was high on the glow of his recent liaison. Maybe after six weeks, they all relaxed in the belief that Eric's secrets travelled with him to the grave. They had found nothing. They had searched everywhere. They must have seen his diary, skipped over the reason for his medical appointment in Grenoble. They must have figured no one was coming.

Then I came.

I signalled my intent.

And from the moment they found Baudelaire's body, Christine had been waiting. In the beautiful apartment or elsewhere.

I had called her to come to the door.

I never heard the phone ring.

Never saw her answer.

'Who was she?'

Christine paused. 'A lookalike, chosen from a modelling agency. Paid handsomely to live in my apartment and open the door whenever instructed. She thought we were on the trail of an infamous art-thief, found the whole thing most exciting.'

'It was a suicide mission. You killed her.'

Christine shook her head. 'On the contrary, Berthier,' she said, circling the back of my chair and leaning on the cold grey table, 'I rather think *you* killed her.'

Defence of the nation is no excuse for the murder of an innocent catalogue model. As it wasn't for the ill-fated photographer aboard the *Rainbow Warrior*.

'And anyway,' she continued like some conjuror revealing the mystery of her tricks, 'I never expected you to murder *me*. Confront me perhaps–'

'So, you sent your stand-in to meet me? What did you think would happen? That I would be fooled in the darkness? That I would challenge some imposter over the cold-blooded murder of my cousin?'

'There were two agents behind the door. They were going to arrest you. Better still, *Jean*,' she used my name to taunt me, like she knew every single one of my secrets and would drop them like breadcrumbs on my route from that chair to an electric one, 'they were going to kill you as you attacked a half-dressed woman in her doorway. Attempted rape is the most abhorrent crime.'

'And Nicole?'

Christine sighed deeply and inspected her polished nails. Why do I imagine she felt no such remorse about condemning a second woman to a premature death, only for the time it had taken to find me? 'You honestly don't know?'

I didn't.

Until six minutes beforehand Christine was resting on a steel bed beneath the hospital. Now, I was expecting Nicole to come bounding in as her accomplice. Perhaps it was she who tracked me the whole of Europe.

'It was meant for you,' Christine said. Her stare pierced me like a warrior's spear.

'Then why plant the bomb so close to her?'

'We didn't. Your sommelier, or rather *our* sommelier, left the ice bucket directly beside *you*, away from her, away from… *everyone*.' Pausing, for the first time I detected a flicker of emotion in the steel eyes. 'Trust Nicole to go and claim it.'

'But you detonated it, anyway?'

'No!' she barked. 'You know the drill. Tactical decisions are made in the field not from behind a desk.'

I thought about Leclerc and all those *tactical* decisions he had avoided to satisfy just such ambivalent governance.

'Nicole was unfortunate collateral damage but framing you for murder gave us everything we needed. We knew you'd go to ground. We knew you'd unearth every old contact, and we'd see how much you knew. But it turns out you didn't know *anything*,' she spat this accusation as a failure. 'Not until you went to the house, and then Oxford. The girl in the hotel remembered very well. How fortunate to find a student of Somerville in the bar. But then you always were a lucky bastard. Didn't they used to say you had nine lives?'

'What did you do to her?'

Christine looked at me astonished. 'The girl? Why nothing.

We're not monsters, whatever you or your cousin may have believed.'

'I meant Agnes. What did you do to *Agnes*?' I pictured the pretty little sandstone cottage near the church, its purple wisteria weeping for the brilliant professor of linguistics. Agnes's warm lace and florals were an anathema to the cold angular woman who sat before me. There was nothing fragrant about Christine.

'She was our only loose end,' she said without emotion. 'A shame because she was a true believer in the cause. Independence from the ludicrous machinations that are slowly killing our constitution, eroding our very freedoms. She would have martyred herself for us, I'm sure.'

'Except you never gave her the choice.'

'No, Berthier, *you* never gave her the choice.'

I was angry because it was true.

Agents too often leave behind us a trail of destruction. I should have warned Agnes, I should have protected her. I should have been more careful. 'She didn't know anything–'

Frowning, Christine said, 'Know anything? What does that matter. She knew *Eric*, she kept his secrets, she passed them to you, and saw your face. You know this game well enough.'

I did.

I said a little silent prayer for me as much as Agnes.

'Why?' It was all I wanted to understand. The end was inevitable, now. At the hands of the woman who had commissioned Eric's death. And who would shortly send me to join him. Closure before sleep was the only satisfaction I could cling to. I was just so damn tired.

'The problem with your type, is that you don't see the

bigger picture.' And so began the justification, the explanation. The words rehearsed if not for me, then for her curious grandchildren, her own deathbed confession. 'We're under siege, Jean. We have been for decades since the end of the Cold War. Pah, some *end*. And yet, they believed it. All those hapless politicians with their liberal naïvety. They believed *them*. No more Iron Curtain. "it's the end of history" they cried, "Look, the West has won". But now that rusty drape is drawn back, what does it reveal? Nothing has changed. *Nothing*. The same old enemy in bright new clothes. Couture communism. Now they come in Armani suits, but with the same basic aims. Disrupt, disarm, disable. Destabilise our way of life. Spoil the rules-based international order. Play us off against one another. Corrupt our politicians and democracies.

'And how are we supposed to protect ourselves? Now that every bastion of our defences lies buried in bureaucratic red tape, if not in Paris at the palace, then in some nondescript office in Brussels or Strasbourg, or *Maastricht*. We're no longer architects of our own republic. Do you understand that? We don't make our laws, control our borders, we can't even determine our own foreign policy. That's fine, for the politicians to determine. But our *security*? You really want that to be subservient to a council of unelected representatives? You imagine there is safety in pooling our resources? In exposing our operations to the Germans, or the Poles or Lithuanians. The Latvians, maybe? We are short on resources; you should know that better than anyone. But, to surrender decisions about defence and security to the eastern Europeans, for Christ's sake... So, if the Russian aims and ours happen to coincide–'

'Can you hear yourself? You're taking Russian money to

further the interests of France? Are you serious? You honestly believe that our aims can ever align?'

Christine shook her head. 'I knew you wouldn't understand.'

'Try me.'

Slipping from her perch, she circled the room, standing, striding, angling for poses which supported her unsupportable stance. Facing the mirror, she began to persuade herself, again: 'Take these *Gilet Jaunes.* Who do you think is funding them, organising them, directing them? You think this kind of movement happens by chance? An accident of social media and circumstance?'

'Yes. Is that not how movements of the people *always* begin?'

'Christ, Berthier, don't be so naïve. There are dark forces in the shadows that you could not begin to conceive. A red hand behind so many of these 'spontaneous' actions. The people have been set against one another by state actors – Russian, Chinese, North Korean. You know this, man. Who do you think you have been fighting this past decade?'

'So, expose it. Confront it. Deal with it.'

'Who would believe us? We no longer control the message. It's too late for that. Don't you understand? These people are subverting our values from within our very walls. They don't want to challenge our democracy, but to undermine it. They expect us to react by clamping down, restricting freedoms, removing liberties to preserve the status quo. They agitate for change to weaken our resolve.'

'So how does taking their money possibly help?'

'We control some of the groups they fund. They have no idea we divert the resources into activities that support the aims of France–'

'*Your* aims.'

Christine shook her head once more. 'They are aligned.'

They were not. These people were insane. They had convinced themselves of a French purity which could only be preserved outside the rule of law. 'It's a slush fund.'

'Yes.' Christine nodded, confidently. 'Yes, it is. You want me to apologise for that? Their *investment* is a lifeline. It's the difference between withdrawal and surrender. The politicians deny us the resources we need, yet demand greater security than ever–'

'What about the rest of it?'

'What about it?'

'What happens to the funds you don't control? Where are they directed?'

Christine turned and slid backwards to the wall, folding her arms and crossing her feet. She leaned like a scarlet flamingo offered the opportunity to use both legs but clinging to the habit of balancing on only one. Such precariousness defined her position uniquely. 'We know where most of the money is going. We prevent any catastrophic damage, but in any war–'

'You have to lose some battles.'

She said nothing. This was how they justified their crimes. Churchill uses Coventry, Roosevelt, Pearl Harbour. We turn two blind eyes to the assassination of former dissidents, and the exponential growth of the far right. All fair game.

'How do you think the British pulled off their coup?' Christine asked, smiling like a dog that knows it is about to curtail the wayward Tom's last remaining life. 'Upping defence spending, cyber-developments, tackling the Chinese, their own *Space Command*, for fuck's sake. How do you think all that was funded? In the teeth of a global economic crash–'

The word crash was accompanied by another, from somewhere outside.

Christine started, then barked at the guard outside the door before turning to me. 'Leave this room, and it's the last move you'll ever make. I mean it.' With that, she pulled the handle and disappeared towards the source of all the noise.

I looked at the mirror. There was no-one the other side. No-one Christine would have let overhear such a confession. Instead, all I saw was the face of a murderer. The cold charred face of a calculated killer. The scar was fading, part-hidden by the beard. Likewise, the lips which had acquired a taste for cruelty. And what of the eyes, Berthier? Dared you look yourself in the eye?

I had set out to kill Christine.

Instead, two innocent women were dead.

My fault. All *my* fault.

Whatever they taught me, whatever they tried to ingrain, human life mattered. We only ever took those whose actions warranted retribution. It may have been summary, but it was still justice. Christine now had a second sentence coming. Only this time, I wanted to look into her cold grey eyes as the life bled out and her murderous soul departed to await our reunion–

Leaping up, I hammered on the door. 'Hey. Let me out. I need the bathroom.'

Muffled movement. 'Wha'd you say?'

'I said, I *need* the bathroom.'

Quiet laughter. Then quieter still. 'Shit on the floor. We'll use your corpse to clean it later.'

He was awake, then. A little noise would surely bring him in.

Lifting the chair, I hurled it at the mirror, waiting for the crash. It bounced off with barely a metallic whimper. Ok. So, that was how it was going to be. I looked around. Nothing. One desk, one chair, both government issue; functional, practical, only of use for the singular purpose dictated by the procurement team. Great.

The walls were bare and tapping them revealed they were also thick. Solid. Not the kind I could have kicked through into the next room. Likewise, the floor. Concrete or as good as if my heel didn't lie. I lifted the chair, put it on the desk. Assessed the ceiling. Also, solid. It would give with a sledgehammer I didn't have, and the chair legs would bend before the fabric of the building relented its firm embrace.

The door, then.

Removing the chair, I laid the desk on its side halfway across the room facing my exit route. A makeshift barricade. Then I carried the chair to the door, lifted it and began to scrape the metal legs down the back of the veneer and around the lock. It wasn't perfect, but it was a sound as close to the removal of hinges or the levering of a grate as I could muster. An air vent, maybe? I was banking on the fact the goon outside was hired help, that he hadn't been inside the room, that it was above his paygrade or security clearance. Christine's last command was likely still ringing in his ears.

I stopped and waited. No response. Nothing.

The edge of the chair was just slim enough to run down the slot between the door and the frame. I rubbed it up and down hard a dozen times, then scraped the leg down the door again. Better. Sounded maybe like the hinges were loosening. Like maybe I found a way to somehow unscrew them–

Thumping. 'Hey, what's going on in there?'

Back to the doorframe, more of the same. Fifteen seconds worth.

More thumping. 'Hey, I said what's going on in there.'

Same again from me. Ten seconds, this time. Then I left the chair behind the door, darted around behind the desk and waited.

Either he would come, or he wouldn't.

He thumped again. Said something, I couldn't hear. Eight seconds passed. Twelve. Before I finally heard the lock, and then the door handle turning. Probably, he would ease in and check the room. See the desk. I would know how far he was advancing by the rubbing of the chair legs on the cheap nylon. Until he was inside. Then it was a case of hit and hope. Either way, it sure beat waiting for Christine to return–

I heard the chair move. A centimetre, maybe two. Not enough to squeeze his fat head around the door. He knew for certain I wasn't armed with a gun, but it didn't render me harmless. Two more centimetres. No doubt he was checking the mirror but that wouldn't tell him what he needed to know. He might have seen the upturned desk. He was about two metres tall, after all. He wouldn't see me, though. Pure physics saw to that.

Three more centimetres. It was another ten at least to create the space for his gigantic frame. Five more. Slowly. Could he possibly squeeze through–

The door flew open with a crash.

Ok JB, I had to think quickly. Doorway to the desk. Three metres? I held my breath. Three, four, five... He must have been halfway–

Now!

I launched. Grabbing the underneath of the desk by its frame and ducking my head, I wielded the table-top like a shield in my left-hand hurtling forward. If he was still outside the room, I would slam into the doorframe and likely earn a bullet to the stomach for my trouble. He wasn't.

Connecting with his torso, I felt the soft flesh at the same time as he yelped a startled 'oof'. He stumbled backwards. Tight hand poised, I dropped the desk and threw the biggest punch of my life towards where I prayed his head would be. It wasn't. Instead, glancing off his chin my fist connected with the side of his throat, but it was enough to hurt like hell and jolt him painfully off guard.

I jabbed again at his Adam's Apple with my left fist, then followed-up again with the right almost toppling over the desk which was now balanced like a blade between us. He clutched his neck as I leapt and barrelled him outside the door.

He ended up flat on his back, scrabbling for his sidearm. I headbutted him. Smashed his nose. Reaching down behind me I felt around for his gun and missed it. He riled and writhed, put a hand under my chin and forced my head back. It wasn't enough. I whipped backwards, leaping to the balls of my feet and stamped on his left knee as he tried to roll. *Crunch*. Then as he grabbed his broken knee with both hands, I stepped back and aimed a colossal kick towards his groin. It only half-landed. But well enough to send him into spasms of roaring agony.

He rolled away clutching at his balls, unsure whereabouts on his body to hold for a mercy that would not come: his knee, his chin, his larynx, his groin–

Dropping onto his prostrate back, I levered his revolver from his waistband and crashed the butt on the top of his spine. One giant sigh and he slumped. Possibly dead. At least he was now pain free.

The airless corridor was silent again, our fracas appearing to have alerted no-one.

The dozen grey doors – same height, same handle, same thickness as the one that now gaped open on my former cell – remained resolutely closed. What chance the other rooms were also occupied by captive agents? I couldn't hang around to find out.

Dancing along the corridor, I listened intently for any sounds of movement while studying the gun in my hand. Glock 19. I opened the magazine. Fifteen rounds. Some economy was therefore required. Each door remained closed. Perhaps on American soil, use of the ugly place at the back of our consulate was limited to special cases? Maybe I should have been flattered.

Beside the elevator was a fire-door, with a slim window of wired glass – even rendition required someone to sign-off on the 'Health and Safety Policy'. It opened onto a simple industrial staircase with a metal rail and perforated aluminium steps. Leaning in, I risked a glance both up and down. Nothing. There were maybe three more floors upwards, more than ten below me. I should have gone down. Every fibre of my being screamed at me to head towards the ground. That's when I heard it again. No doubting it this time. An explosion somewhere above my head. Not for the first time that day, then, my mind was made up for me.

Easing forward, I kept my eyes fixed on the stairs above. No one climbing could hit me without coming into my peripheral vision and I backed my own reaction times. Up one flight of steps, I heard it again. Much closer this time. Maybe a single shot. Followed by another. Up another flight, there was silence. I wished I knew the layout of the building. Were all the other floors like the one I'd just vacated?

My back slid uncomfortably around the concrete walls, sticking hard with sweat. I might have jettisoned my jacket, but I was still burning up even down to my t-shirt. Adrenaline, and pain fuelled me and pushed me on.

There it was again. As clear as a bell, this time. A double tap. The unmistakable signature of a professional calling card. And it had come from the floor on which I'd just arrived.

Ducking next to the door, I took an angled look through the glass. It was nothing like the scene I'd left behind.

This floor was unfinished. There was a carpet of polished concrete, and huge swathes of translucent plastic hanging at intervals like the entry to a gigantic butcher's shop. A thick black chord snaked across the floor to a bag – no, a *body*, slumped. Blood pooled at his or her feet. It was difficult to tell a sex without exposing myself, and as I tried, a figure darted across my field of view, behind one of the billowing sheets. This figure, however, was instantly recognizable. At least, from the neck up.

She squatted down at the corpse and felt around for a pulse. I pulled the door and whispered her name.

She turned, revolver poised, so I slid mine out across the floor. 'It's me.'

'Come out with your hands raised.' She scanned me up and down. 'Anyone behind you?'

Shaking my head, I retrieved the gun. 'How the hell did you get up here?'

'Never mind that, what the *fuck* were you doing at the

conference? Berthier, I specifically told you to–'

'Enough. I'm sorry. You were right. But it doesn't matter now.'

She let go the limp wrist and stood. 'What doesn't?'

I looked at the body. It was the liberal.

'Berthier, why doesn't it matter?'

'We need to get out of here. I've left another like him downstairs. So, how did you get up here?'

Barbie nodded back over her shoulder, beyond the PVC drapes.

'And no one else came up the way I did?'

She aimed a kick towards the corpse. 'He came up via the elevator, on his own. And he didn't play fair with introductions.'

'No Christine?'

Barbie started. 'What?'

'It's – she's–'

Something behind me stirred into life. *Shit*. The elevator. It was maybe four floors away at most and coming our way. And coming our way too quickly.

Barbie moved before I did, through the first and second curtain, darting for wherever she came in. We scooted low, beneath a half-made plasterboard wall and around the central core to the solid rear of the stairwell. There was another door there, but it was locked and judging by the make-shift signage, went nowhere but the roof.

Crouching, Barbie gestured towards the perimeter. It was a phalanx of oxidised steel awaiting glass. Grid upon grid like a giant tennis net. 'There's an equipment elevator and a chute for waste,' she said almost in a whisper. I moved towards it, but she stopped me. 'The controls are up here or on the ground. Once you're inside, you're at the whim of the operator.'

'So, we can't use it?'

She smiled. 'I didn't say that.' She took a phone from her pocket, set a timer and slid it far across the floor, sending it back into the void of concrete, plastic and wires. It stopped against a power-chord. 'When the alarm goes, make for that external elevator and set it going down. Take it–'

'But you said–'

She waved her gun. 'I'll shoot the mechanism up here.'

'And if there's someone on the ground?'

She shrugged. 'Shoot them if they don't shoot you first.'

'And how exactly will you get down?'

She smiled. 'For once, you imbecilic Frenchman, why don't you just follow orders and leave the rest to me.'

I didn't like it. I had seen the movies. A cage on the outside of a construction site was no place to be. Leaving a comrade behind just made it a thousand times worse.

She gripped my shoulder. '*Agreed?*'

I nodded solemnly, just as the elevator's muted ping announced the arrival of our next obstacle. One set of footsteps emerged and stopped. Then another. Barbie checked her watch, held up five fingers and folded them; four, three, two, one–

The phone vibrated. Just audible. Probably not to our new guests.

But then it burst into life.

La Marseillaise. What else?

Barbie shoved me hard, spinning to watch the phone.

I went, no second invitation needed, taking the most direct route, under and around the plastic, ducking, weaving, but keeping the core between me and any threat, always assuming, of course, that the angry Belgian didn't shoot me in the back for disobeying instructions. I reached the patchwork wall before a volley of shots and shouting. I thought about stopping, looking back, returning to help–

Then I reached up for the control box of the makeshift elevator. The cart was little more than a square bucket, lightly guarded by scaffold poles, but strong enough to haul up a cement mixer, so good enough for me. There were two arrows on the panel. Hitting down, I leapt aboard as somewhere above my head a tired electric motor whirred reluctantly into life.

Looking out, I must have been eight floors up, at least. Maybe even ten. There was a good chance the stairwell I'd just climbed dropped below ground level. There was a good chance too that someone would exit the building before I was even halfway down. There was a gunfight near the roof which had rendered two lifeless bodies already. No matter the clandestine world in which we walked, where instant death was commonplace, such a commotion always drew a crowd, and usually they were armed.

The cage was slow. Painfully so. Its jittery descent reminded me of my mother's sole trip to the capital, where her acute vertigo left us stuttering down the steps of the Eiffel Tower, an obstacle to those behind, a barrier to those below. There was simply no speed and no means to create any either, unless of course I cut the cable and allowed gravity to take its course–

Two more shots. Different guns.

Come on Barbie. Whatever your plan, get it done and get out safe. The idea of another body on my watch–

The building opposite was another tower like my own but taller, a glistening cube pulled skywards to a point. A revolving door opened at its foot and a pair of smart executive suits exited pursued by junior colleagues. They didn't even lift their gaze towards the noise, sauntering away towards a four-lane street of traffic. Madison Avenue? Maybe. They were offices for sure, amid the usual gamut of advertisements and coffee shops to satiate commuters.

Our building, meanwhile, was one of the few still under construction. A giant crane climbed limpet-like to my left. To my right, a flexible orange chute slipped down alongside the rusty framework which held my juddery ride in place. I turned around. Dark privacy glass enveloped each floor. If any of the offices were occupied, their current view was obscured by eighty-five kilos of former French secret service agent. A more conspicuous location I could not have chosen. Slung thirty metres above ground, moving like a sloth, visible for kilometres in every conceivable direction – I began to laugh. How couldn't you? Strung out there like a target dangling at the end of a range. What was my alternative? *Jump*?

Another shot rang out above my head. A single tap this time. Close quarters and muffled by the plastic and distance. Even so, with the soft eddying wind buffeting the car, a gunshot was a gunshot. Unmistakable. Yet still, the world below me revolved unmoved.

No more than four floors up, the scene below bgan to solidify. The elevator slowed, the buildings tensed, the concrete earth began to take on shape. Regimental patterns appeared in the sidewalk, a broken bond of anthracite like some colourless yellow brick road. A gaggle of office workers crossed the street and passed beneath my feet, oblivious to my fate. I thought about attracting them and then discounted it. It was bad enough that my actions had curtailed at least two innocent lives already, lest I martyr half a dozen unsuspecting administrators for the cause. One looked up but stared right through me before they turned the corner to the main street and out of sight. Another tap. This time it ricocheted so likely missed its target.

I was three metres from safety when I heard the faint yell or scream.

A woman's voice.

It was swallowed by the traffic, dissipating as another more guttural cry came closer, pursued by the sound of tearing cloth. A sudden slap rocked the elevator as the orange chute billowed and twisted like a cobra ready to strike. Below me, it coughed up the curled-up corpse of my grey-suited, redhaired saviour. She hit the ground with an unholy thwack.

Leaping over my captor's rails I landed beside the battered body as the head began to rise. 'Fuck. I thought you were dead.'

Levering herself up on her elbows, she smiled. 'What, and let the French boy scout have all the fun?'

Easing her up, I threaded my arm around her and hauled her to her feet. 'Can you walk?'

She shrugged me off. 'Even if both my legs were broken, I could still outrun you, Berthier.' She dragged against me, stiffened up straight as a rod and brushed down her suit. 'I think the ankle's sprained. But I'd rather not see a doctor right now. I'll wait until I'm safely back in Bruges.'

'Come on, we need to get out of here and regroup.'

She stared at me. 'No shit genius. I can see why they want a man of your prodigious insight dead.'

TWENTY

Over her shoulder, the twenty-four-hour news channel soldiered on presenting happenstance as circumstance. There was no mention of a gunfight at the consulate in the centre of the city; no bodies; no manhunt; just a relentless rollcall of social media re-presented as fact. PR dressed up as journalism and slotted between the flavoured editorial.

'That's it?'

I shrugged. What more was there to say? 'That's all I know.'

'Why didn't she kill you?' Barbie slid off the bed and contemplated the minibar.

'She was going to, I'm sure of it. But you know what these narcissists are like. Couldn't resist one final opportunity to hector me with propaganda. These people really believe this shit. They're convinced by their righteousness. It's like a religion to them–'

'We have to move, Berthier.'

'And you thought *I* was Captain Obvious?'

From the tiny bar she removed only a sparkling mineral water which she opened before tossing the cap towards the trash. It missed.

Sipping, she studied me like a tamer might their lion. Ever vigilant, she remembered that domestication is but temporary, a simple veil that wraps each wild and wayward beast. I'd let her down, I knew I had. Barbara Solido was now embroiled in some catastrophic international outrage from which there was no return. Certainly not to the hunt for homebred terrorists on the boulevards of Brussels. Now neither of us knew how long we had. We were not yet popcorn for the people, but for all I knew we might be stars among the city's hoteliers and hospitality brigades.

Perched on the bed, facing the television, she asked quietly, 'How high does it go?'

I picked up the remote and flicked through every other available news channel, from Fox to Al Jazeera. We weren't even a whisper on the wind. 'High enough to mean a trip to the Belgian consulate is off the agenda.'

She turned sharply. 'I'm serious, Berthier.'

'So am I.'

'Then where?'

I kicked off the bed and re-opened the minibar myself. 'We have to break it. We have to go public, to the press–'

She scoffed. 'And how exactly do you propose we do that?'

The whisky was cheap and the cognac even cheaper. I took a weak beer and pulled the ring. 'What was Eric's motivation? What first interested him?'

She looked up from the screen.

'I mean, why was my cousin investigating this new movement,

this *Fraternité*? What's their connection to the service? Someone must have tipped him off. Someone must have known something.'

'Known what exactly?'

Think Berthier, think. 'Does this television have internet access?'

Seizing the remote, Barbie fingered it. She pressed to summon the search bar and waited, watching me closely. 'Well?'

'Keep it vague. Search French political parties and then take it from there. Go plenty of wrong ways before you go the right one.'

She smiled while she selected the letters on screen, the most ponderous way to hunt imaginable. 'Wow, you really don't trust anyone, do you my old friend?'

'Just because you're paranoid, doesn't mean they're not out to get you–'

She searched on the left, the right, Macron, Le Penn, the old guard and the new. And the guard who were once new challengers full of hope but have since been subsumed into the status quo to become what they all supposedly despised. She read avidly, while I reclined and closed my eyes. 'Why do I imagine you're not political?' she said, wistfully. Maybe a thought that escaped into sound before it could be squashed. It had echoes of Gabrielle's constant lament.

'Why bother? Nothing ever changes. Like Orwell wrote, the two wealthy classes squabble over power, while the little people are left to pay the price and pick up pieces if they're lucky. When voting changes anything, they'll stop us doing it.'

She went quiet for a while.

'Here,' she said, nudging me back to vertical.

On the giant flat screen was an image of a tanned middle-aged man with gold-rimmed glasses and greased back hair. His shirt was white and his jacket a rich navy blue. Good looking, he was the type to summer in Monaco and winter in Val-d'Isère. The gawdy golden watch that wrapped his wrist must have been worth the whole of my apartment block.

'Who is he?'

Turning, Barbie raised her eyebrows. 'You don't know? Christ, you lead a sheltered life, Berthier.'

'I find it's best to keep my mind clear for the task in hand. So?'

'That's Laurent Delfont, the man who founded Fraternité, and the owner of *Mediacors*. He's–'

'Holy shit.'

Barbie stared at me.

'He's Gabrielle's *boss*.'

I didn't want for this. For five years, it was my priority to manage two universes and to keep both orbits solitary in the most unholy work-life balance: two jobs, two full and very different lives. Such compartmentalisation was meant to protect my treasures, but also perhaps mainly to protect me – from life, from loss and from the all-consuming self-pity that trades on grief. I cannot deny selfishness. Only the most unwavering narcissist could ever do my line of work.

Suddenly, however, those worlds had collided.

'This feels like the worst plan in the history of making plans.' Barbie looked at me from beneath a newly acquired fringe. The hair had shed its blood-orange and now wept a dark satanic black. Atop her pale face she looked unforgivably non-conformist, far too conspicuous to represent a risk.

I, on the other hand, had added a good twenty years, greying away my former colourful life. Art mirroring its future. To any casual observer we were father and daughter, uncle and niece, husband and mistress, sharing coffee. And in a city of a billion lonely claustrophobes, even the casual observer sees little, obsessed instead by the wretchedness of their cell phone fantasy life.

'Anyway, what makes you think she'll listen, let alone agree?' Barbie paused while the waiter delivered us a welcome breakfast. *Eggs Americain.* An omelette in anything but name. 'What if she simply turns you in? Have you considered that?'

Of course, I had. It's all I had thought about. 'You don't know her.'

Barbie shook her new head. 'No, Berthier. It's you *she* doesn't know.'

'I trust her.'

'She trusted the old *you*. And look where that left you both.' She speared a giant slice of tomato with her fork, before lacerating it with her knife. 'I don't like this idea at all.'

Outside the window, the world passed by untroubled. Commuters, dawdlers, a million lazy tourists. The ignorant in pursuit of the unimaginable, waiting to scale the Empire State for a view that would tell them nothing they did not already know. While beneath their feet, it fell to volunteers like Barbie to preserve their veil of peace. It was but a veneer never thinner than it felt that day.

'If something should happen to me–' I took Barbie's raised hand and lay it flat upon the table. 'If I don't come back, you need to know the location of the flash drive. Then it will be up to you to decide–'

Pulling her hand away, she wrapped it hard into a fist. I feared she was going to brain me with it. 'You, you – you are a *fool*, Berthier. As gigantic an ass as your leviathan boss. But if you insist on this course of action, then I will not stand in your way.' She rested the hand back upon the table. 'But nor will I fulfil your lofty ambitions. It's not my job to floor the French establishment.'

I thought about protesting. But she was right.

I didn't set out to bring down my own service, to collapse the empire from within. And maybe if Christine had stayed dead, that would have been enough for me. It was only summary justice I craved. Eyes for eyes. Teeth for teeth. 'You should go. There was no CCTV in the stairwells or on the top floor. They have nothing on you, for now.'

She scoffed.

'It's true. Go before it's too late.'

Her hand unfurled and she clutched my wrist. 'You are an idiot, Berthier. But even you are not so foolish as to believe I would run from a fight. From this fight, especially.' A wicked smile cracked those ruby lips. 'We're Thelma and Louise now.'

Deep oak panelling adorned the walls and from the ceiling, a collection of toys and objets d'art swung in the gentle breeze of the air conditioning. There was a Pan-Am plane, a football helmet, a boxing glove, all signed by ghosts and dancing in a macabre waltz, kissing and twirling like apparitions. In the gloom, Gabrielle sat opposite Pascal, clutching a goblet of red wine which she had barely tasted. Twice already she had looked right through me. The wealthy old bachelor alone with his steak, his lasciviousness not restricted to his meal. Just another lecher frequenting *The Four Ace Club* where women like Gabrielle were mainly serving men like the man I was playing. Maybe too, like the man I really was.

She wore a leather blouson buttoned high, despite the heat, but her hair was down and trailed around her collar like a new mink. She had always doted on Pascal, but now there were demons too. Her eyes deserted him too often for devotion.

It took an hour of conversation before she finally excused herself for the bathroom and, as soon as her back was fully turned, I slipped quietly from my seat and followed.

She climbed the wide stairs eschewing the golden handrail for her cell phone, while I embraced each step with uncertainty sure not to look in her direction. At the summit, she rounded the bend, and I sprang four steps in a stride to catch her. I needed her at the door before it closed.

Reaching out, I gripped her shoulder as she entered the bathroom, sliding my hand up across her mouth and bundling her inside. She elbowed me hard in the ribs. Harder than I had been punched by adversaries. And even when she finally saw me in the mirror above the sink, she didn't think twice about repeating the dose. At least the second time, I was prepared.

'You bastard. What the fuck are you doing here?'

'Gabrielle—'

'Don't you "Gabrielle" me.' She looked me up and down with disgust. 'I swear to God if they don't kill you, I will.'

I feared she really meant it. 'Gabrielle, hear me out. Please. Doesn't the condemned man deserve that at least? To air his confession?'

She grimaced. 'No. You don't deserve your penance or

whatever forgiveness you crave. You're nothing but a two-bit murderer. I hope they make you swing.'

She motioned to leave, pushing me aside.

'Your boss is responsible for Eric's death.'

She stopped. Shaking her head, she turned. Her eyes were closed and only opened to scorn me further. 'Berthier, you need help. Serious help–'

'Your boss is funded by the secret service. His new party, his newspapers, his satellite broadcasts. Who knows what else.'

Laughing, she turned away and watched me from the mirror. She reached into her purse and removed a lipstick. 'Berthier, you're insane. Papa told me everything. You killed your boss because you think your boss killed Eric. And now she's dead, you're coming after *my* boss too?'

Fuck.

'My boss isn't dead–'

'But you murdered her, in her doorway. Two hours after fucking me and drugging me. Or is that all in my imagination? I swear I didn't want to believe him, but it didn't take me long to find your bag. Jesus Christ, *under our spare bed*? What sort of psychopath are you?'

'She's not dead.'

Gabrielle shook her head.

'I killed someone else that night. It was a woman sent to her death, the same way she sent Eric to his death–'

'Can you even hear yourself? What happened to you? How many other times did you leave me naked in my own bed to commit murder? Did you have your hands around my neck stained by the strangulation of – of *another woman*? Do you discriminate? Or are we all just bodies to you?' Her eyes bored into me as she recoloured her lips, puckering and smacking like she had made peace with her hatred of me. Like I was no longer fit to breathe her air, as if I ever was.

'I know my apology counts for nothing, but I'm truly sorry I ever lied to you. But you must believe me now–'

Dropping the lipstick, she turned and slapped me across the face so hard my glasses flew off. I gripped her flailing hand.

'Let go of me, before I scream this place down–'

'Gabrielle, listen to me for one minute and then I'll be gone from your life for good.'

She winced.

'Eric was investigating *Fraternité*. They're funded by Russian money at the direction of elements within my organisation. My 'boss' was overseeing the whole thing. I don't know how much of this your media magnate knows, but Eric was killed by my people because of it. That's the truth, I swear to God.'

She shook her head violently again.

'All I need to prove it, is access to his office. Just the–'

She pulled away, pushed her hand hard into my chest. 'Oh no. No, no, *no*–'

'The access code. Gabrielle, it's all I need to clear my name. To clear *Eric's* name.'

TWENTY-ONE

Dusk hung like a filthy mood, draining all life from the city. The pink glow of satisfaction was gone, stained by the corruption which leeched from the Paris streets and sidewalks. The last of the day shift had leaked away from the giant glass monolith and now the reluctant nightshift was arriving to vent its liberal spleen upon an expectant centre-ground.

Inside, fresh light gave me the knowledge I craved: two desks; one lackadaisical security guard; a bank of elevators hidden from view and accessed via swipe card. To the left, an enormous screen hurtled through the day's events in silence, while to the right black leather sofas awaited guests who were at least another twelve hours away. The rear fire exit was inaccessible, so my only entry point was the glass revolving door which sucked in the city's dirty air and spat it back out dirtier. So much for the element of surprise.

As I watched from the uncomfortable bench on the opposite side of the cobbled piazza, however, providence played her helpful hand once again.

Leaping from my seat, I sprinted across the corner of the square before he had a chance to change his aim. He looked at me astonished, gripping his brakes for dear life as I stepped into his path.

'What the f–'

'How much?'

His eyes narrowed. 'Excuse me?'

'For the bike, the jacket, the helmet, the take-out. Name your price.'

Angling backwards awkwardly, he swore again. 'Fuck off you old lunatic.'

I stepped across, gripping the handlebars. 'A thousand euros?'

He stopped. Couldn't believe I was serious. So, I took out a roll of notes and peeling two off, I thrust them into his unwilling hand. 'I'm no more lunatic than you.' I glanced back towards the office building. 'But the deal expires in ten seconds.'

For a moment he thought about it. The bike he would replace for a hundred Euros maximum, but losing the branded jacket and cap would most likely earn a fine. He might have missed a day or two of work as well, until the new ones arrived. Or maybe this was all the incentive he needed to kick his filthy habit and join a union.

'Fifteen hundred?' He asked with all the confidence of a confessional sinner.

'Nine hundred. For wasting my time.' The night shift was dwindling to a trickle.

'Ok, ok. A thousand.'

The exchange completed, I scooted across towards the road proper, cycling in a fast unsteady loop around to the building.

Throwing the bike against a huge glass window, I hammered on the door until the security guards looked up and beckoned me to use the revolving entry. Clutching the bag of food and fighting angrily with the strap of my helmet, I hurried inside.

'Sorry, sorry, *sorry*. I got held up... they must be going mad upstairs, right?'

The guard sized me up and down. 'Who?'

'The guys on the finance desk or something. Floor eight. They tore my boss off a strip and now he's giving me hell.' Looking apologetic, I shrugged. 'You want to run upstairs with it. Last time they nearly swung for me–'

He motioned to pick up a telephone.

'And I'm on a warning too. This could be my last delivery.' I hopped from one foot to the other and swore under my breath.

Holding the receiver, he studied me, before dropping it slowly back into its cradle. 'Fuck them. Arrogant little shits. Take the elevator and take your time. Maybe spit in their food for good measure.' He smiled as he pressed the button which opened the small glass gate. 'First two elevators only. The third goes all the way up to God.'

I nodded. 'You're a lifesaver, my friend.'

He laughed. 'We're the gig economy, right. If we don't look out for one another, who will?'

I hustled through to the second elevator, well out of sight and called it, before doing the same with the third. I imagined this one to have some kind of security card like the penthouse in a glitzy hotel, but it didn't. The second car arrived, and I held its doors while I waited for my ride so I could time their departures to coincide. The third car arrived as a straggler for the nightshift entered the fray. His long hair was swept back with sweat, and he was puffing like a well stoked steam engine. He paid me scant attention. 'Top floor?' I asked quietly.

He shook his head. 'If only.' He nodded towards the box. 'Alright for some, eh?'

I smiled. 'How the other half live.' Before nodding my goodbyes and darting for the third car as the doors hissed their welcome.

The express elevator had only four floors, starting at the twenty-first. Pressure-powered, it fired me skyward with a near-silent whoosh of mammoth acceleration. It gave me only moments to check for cameras, none, and then dispense with the delivery gear. I had no need for pretence once the doors opened. If there was additional security at this rarefied level, the use of a disguise wouldn't wash any cleaner than whatever claims I might have imagined. I was banking that a peddler of supposed truth would be unable to resist the opportunity to grill a convicted liar. Then there was the matter of our mutual bond.

There was no abrupt halt and but for the near-silent operation of the doors I would not have known we were stationary again. So quiet was our stop, I double-checked that we were not suspended between floors. But if there was an oblivion into which I was stepping, it was wrapped in the trappings of opulence.

Exiting the car, I was at once surrounded. Not by the shuffle and clank of security, but by glass - a short squat lobby with an elaborate floor-mounted vase in one corner from which a golden plant erupted and tumbled like Midas' touch had alighted on a small fountain. To my right came a quiet hiss as a wall retreated into a doorway without a single touch upon the keypad, while what lay immediately in front of me was hidden by my own reflection.

'Come on in.'

He was sat behind a chair angled for a view of downtown Paris, with our tower lit up like a Christmas tree and the sun escaping while she still could. His office spanned the entire floor, while the desk - high and black and wide - created an effective barrier to foreign influence. An angled lamp was off, and there was no computer, no paraphernalia of station, or any kind, in fact. Just a pile of the following day's headlines. His own and everyone else's. A television buried in a wall of books relayed real-time events that took place in the seconds while the signal was beamed into orbit and back again. Three voluptuous yellow sofas encircled an enormous glass coffee table, and it was to one of these that the rising titan directed me.

'Take a seat,' he commanded. 'Care for a drink?'

I didn't. He clearly did. Crossing to a walnut art deco cabinet, he retrieved a decanter of cognac and a cut-glass crystal goblet. In a stride and single action, he reminded me of Pascal. But unlike our former Chief of Police, Delfont kept his hands where I could see them, free of the shirtsleeves. With the stone-washed jeans and loafers, I would have painted him more lothario than leviathan. I wondered why Gabrielle had never talked about the man.

'I've been expecting you, Monsieur Berthier.'

'You have?'

He smiled. 'I fear, though, that I am not the arch villain you were hoping for.' Sinking back into the plump cushions, he crossed one leg atop the other like he had a new book or film to promote on a primetime chat show. 'Salut.' He raised his glass to me.

'Are you responsible for the death of my cousin?'

Pausing, he leaned towards the table and placed his glass upon it, before spreading his hands and nodding slowly. 'I'm afraid, I rather think I may have been.' He sensed my hackles raising. 'But not in the way that you believe. Are you sure you don't want that drink?'

'How are you responsible?'

He took a deep breath, and I watched as his shoulders sagged. 'As you know already, your cousin was working for me. Your *fiancée* introduced us, and Eric was one of the very few journalists I trusted most implicitly–'

'Bullshit. You had him digging dirt for your filthy gossip columns.'

He smiled. 'As a cover, yes, that much is true. But if you think I would employ someone of Eric Bernard's talent and entrust them only with a shovel, you are very much mistaken. Your cousin was an extremely talented and intelligent journalist, Monsieur Berthier, that's why Gabrielle brought him to me.' I flinched at the mention of her name. 'He was working on something much bigger than the tittle-tattle for which he was being paid. It is that something that I believe has brought you here tonight. *Yes*?'

I studied the man's face. I knew from Wikipedia he was just fifty-five years of age, but he showed little of it. Some exacting healthcare regimes no doubt. In the gym at five a.m. and regular exfoliation. These types seemed capable of summoning time that few of us could afford. I knew also that whatever he was telling me, he most assuredly believed. It didn't mean a single word of it was true–

'How much do you know?' He retrieved the glass and swigged

generously.

'Your new political party. I think I know where you're getting your money. That's what Eric discovered. That's why you had him killed.'

He shook his head.

'You're taking money from the secret service. I've seen the files and joined the dots. What I don't know is how much you know or care from where those funds originate.'

Draining his glass, he turned it in his hand. 'I'm going to get another cognac,' he said languidly. 'I think you should have one too.'

'Fine.'

Watching him, I saw his pockets were empty. No cell phone on which to summon a brigade of henchmen. No concealed weapon. Not that I expected a man in his position to bear arms. A man like Delfont wouldn't bother with the kennel of hounds and stop to bark himself. Still with his back to me, he said, 'You know how we used to make our money? In the good old days?'

'Advertising.' I was neither businessman nor fool.

'Correct. Advertising. When I started in this company, the largest single department – bigger than any editorial team – was our advertising sales division. There were hundreds of them. The first four floors of this very building dedicated to nothing but selling ad space. To whom and for what, we really didn't care. All that mattered was their budgets. Alcohol, tobacco, parfumiers, car companies, banks, all fair game. It was like the news only ever existed to generate more sales. I'm not a journalist, I'm an accountant. But even I could see the folly of allowing sales to drive the news agenda.'

'So, you put a stop to it?'

He laughed aloud as he poured. 'I didn't need to. The internet beat me to it.'

'What do you mean?'

Returning, he handed me my glass before sliding back into his comfortable seat. 'When I inherited the predecessor of this firm from my late father in 2007, I was also bequeathed the dawn of the new media age. The 'social network' revolution. You might remember it? At first, of course, we ignored it as a fad like all the others. But what you can't ignore, what *none of us* can ever ignore, is the most basic of economics. Cash.

'Pretty soon, we started to haemorrhage money as all those traditional advertising revenues dried up. Gone almost in an instant. Here one morning and evaporated the next. And it was easy to see why. Who wanted to spend a hundred thousand Euros reaching millions of the wrong people, when you could spend a tenth of the cost and reach *exactly* the right ones? No board in their right mind could resist the appeal. Only it wasn't just advertisers who grasped the potential of this bold new era, was it?'

I sniffed the cognac. It had the aroma of a century in oak. 'It wasn't?'

'*Coca-Cola* and *McDonald's* aren't the only ones in the persuasion business, Berthier. Surely a man of your talents and *network* understands that?'

He was right. The use of social engineering to reach and influence was once the stock in trade of our business. Befriending an adversary, winning over an uncertain ally, turning a current or former Soviet. Now, like so much else, such missions were entrusted to the data engineers. Algorithms were waging and winning wars in the grey zone before the meagre foot-soldier was alert in his bunk.

'So, what was a man in my position and with my responsibilities to do? Watch an empire whither on the vine? Jettison the staff and wish them all the best? Or join the revolution and take a little share of that pie back from the new guard in favour of the old?' He smiled knowingly and tilted his glass, studying the warm brown cognac as though it was liquid gold.

'What did you do?'

'Social media. I turned my advertising sales team into *social media experts*. I set them selling a new channel to old brands and selling brand new advertisers into age old ideas – like frequency and scale, and total dominance of a media landscape. Don't just target your prospective buyer, chase and harry them around the internet until eventually they concede just to make you go away! You know, Mediacors is now the world's *largest* advertising sales agents, and barely a cent of it ends up in my actual pages.' He nodded towards the pile of newspapers on his desk and winced.

'And what exactly does all of this apparent success have to do with the funding of your politics? And more to the point, what does it have to do with the murder of *Eric Christophe Montcalm Bernard*?'

'Everything, Berthier. *Absolutely* everything. Because, as your late and much-missed cousin found, the source of so much of our advertising revenues was neither for who nor what was claimed.'

TWENTY-TWO

It was dark. And the darkness was my best friend, since I was prepared for her final warm embrace. Beneath the trees the shadows swayed, dancing in the soft gale which haunted this hillside. A sharp scrabbling to my left startled me, but the guilty rodent bore me no malice. Assessing me, she sniffed the air before turning her nose and scuttling hastily away. Just another rat waiting for a scrap of humanity on which to gorge.

Ahead, the castle's keep lay motionless.

A solitary glow ebbed from an upstairs window, but it was the sliver of gold leaking from the floor below which gave her location away. She would be sat in the corner of the room as always, hand never far from a trigger. God help the visitor she did not recognise, but tonight I feared it was familiarity that may hasten my demise.

I waited until the moon dipped gracefully behind a thick bank of cloud before I made good the short distance between the treeline and the walls. Even then, the crunch of soft soles on gravel sounded like the deafening rattle of a machine gun. I hoped that image was no omen. When last I visited, she only owned an ancient pistol.

Pressed into a dark corner of the building I awaited any tell-tale signs that my movement had awoken the silent sentries, but their mute surveillance continued, staring blankly out towards the trees and the vista of blurred lights from the drowsy town below. The silence terrified me. In the city, it was the constant hum that reminded me I was still alive. On the hushed hillside, I might already be dead without knowing it.

Creeping sideways along the rough concrete wall, I felt its sharp fascia scraping at my hands and face. I figured there was maybe half a metre of margin where the cameras were blind, a slim black corridor through which I ghosted until I reached the door. I closed my eyes and visualised the code, strafing my fingers quickly down and across the keypad, trying to remember whether there was some innocuous siren which signalled visitors as I hit the lit green button. I waited for its shrill announcement, but there was nothing more than a quiet click to greet my entry.

Silently and swiftly, I slipped inside.

Ahead of me the hallway split in two. The kitchen and dining areas on the right, the living quarters on the left, and between the pair a giant wooden staircase encased by glass ascended to the stratosphere. Up there, a minor planet emitted the glow visible from outside, and which inside bounced unnaturally on the polished anthracite walls. Everything was so precise, so clinical, as though it might have been slid into place by robots rather than any artisan.

I turned towards the vast open lounge and, stealing myself,

prepared for one final interrogation.

She sat in the semi-darkness with her back to me in a giant modern chair; black leather, wooden arms, with a motorised mechanism by which she could be righted without effort. The kind of thing one might find in a psychiatrist's office. A comforting throwback to her days as a Professor of Philosophy perhaps. A vocation from which she had been retired for a quarter of a century, but which kept her mind as sharp as the render which coated her ugly outer walls and as slippery as those within. Her other senses, alas, were fading like the world whose passing she begrudged.

'Isabella? It's me, *Berthier*.'

'Well don't just stand in the doorway, man. Come here where I can see you properly.' She wrested a book from a shaking hand and laid it peacefully upon a quaint side table. She was the archetypal matriarch, from whom Pascal inherited his faith and Gabrielle her passion. There was nothing about which *Mamie* had no opinion and no battle into which she would not gladly despatch her unearthly wisdom.

I eased around to see her face, as stern as ever, framed behind thick glasses she could barely see through, and aged equally by fortune and forbearance. Her hair, like so many of her generation, retained an unnatural lustre, coiffured twice a week on a budget that would deprive Gabrielle of any inheritance. She wore a smart blue dress and sported a soft cashmere shawl around her neck and shoulders. She sized me up and down. 'You're a mess.'

Shrugging, I held up my hands. 'I've been busy.'

'Making a mess as well as being one?'

She watched me like a hungry hawk as I reached inside my

dark blouson, her eyes darting to the drawer beneath the table. Like mother, like son. Pulling out my hand, I unfurled my fingers from around a tiny voice recorder no bigger than the old girl's lipstick.

'And what is that?'

'It's the only chance I have to save my love for your granddaughter.'

Her lips curled into an uncomfortable grimace. 'And to save your skin?'

'Trust me Isabella, right now, I don't even know which skin is mine.' It was true. I had been through a dozen different iterations in a little over three weeks. Right then, I needed a mirror to remind me who I was. 'What matters is that the woman I adore no longer trusts the man she used to love. *This is my only chance to bring her peace of mind. To prove she was not wrong to love me.*' I offered the contraption which she at first ignored.

'Like I said, to save your skin.' A grating whirring sound announced Isabella's decision to stand, and the chair raised her to the maximum of her delicate potential. At nearly ninety, the years had claimed back the height which youth bestowed. 'Bring it here and let me see it.'

I hesitated.

'Well?'

'Before I play this recording to you, you should know that it implicates your son. I have no fight with Pascal, but I fear he has a fight with me, and maybe also with the republic you mourn–'

'Let me be the judge of that.'

I thumbed the button and turned the volume to maximum.

TWENTY-THREE

She looked towards the doorway. She tossed the machine back, asked me to turn it off, knowing only too well what followed. The remaining admissions of a mogul which implicated the very people she revered: the very people she was once married to; whom her son was and is one of; and in whose number even I was until very recently included. The French establishment, our establishment, was complicit in the death of my cousin. And Mamie's son, the man I once longed to be my father-in-law, was prime among the guilty.

'What do you expect me to do?' She backed into her chair again and allowed the electrics to return her to her previous comfort. 'It's a long time since I carried any sway with my son or his former employers.'

'I don't care about Pascal or even justice. I want – I *need* only for Gabrielle to know the truth. She listens to you. She adores you. You can make her believe I am not the villain she thinks I am.'

Mamie scoffed, wafting her hand like she meant to dismiss me. 'Pah, aren't we all villains, depending on your point of view?'

She was right. I didn't even really know why I was there. It was nothing more than a last desperate roll of the dice in the hope of salvaging something beautiful from a wretched ugly business. I was resigned to my fate. But there was no reason Gabrielle should not benefit from my reclaimed reputation.

'Why do you care, anyway?'

I looked up.

'Why does it matter to you who controls and funds our way of life? Vengeance I understand, but you're no crusader, Berthier. No gallant knight would have chosen your way of life. Did you never stop to ask yourself how many of the other deaths at your own hands were warranted? How many justified and by whom? Isn't that what all this is *really* about? Your awakening? Your remorse?'

She was right. Of course, she was right. Every trigger pulled, every timer primed, every cold hard body left mute or mutilated was a repugnant stain on our values. *Values?* Who was I kidding. I had been an agent of the status quo not the state. But wait a second–

'How did *you* know my real vocation?'

She shook her head. 'What do you mean?'

'You asked me *how many other deaths.* Those were your exact words, but how could you know about those, unless–' I turned at the sound of the safety catch being removed. *Pascal.*

'Sorry to break up the confessional, but I'm afraid it's time to bring an end to this unholy charade. Berthier, you have been a fool. I am sorry about your cousin, but you know yourself this is a game of sacrifice. We all must surrender to the greater good.' Cloaked from head to toe in shadow, he didn't smile, while his revolver beamed like a maniac about to pounce. He waved it sideways. 'Over by the wall, hands where I can see them.'

'I am unarmed. I didn't come to kill anybody.'

'Other than the republic?'

I smiled. He still believed it. 'I'm afraid my republic is already dead.'

'You were given every chance to save it.' He paused. '*Maman*, I think it's time for you to retire for the evening, while Berthier and I discuss his… *future*.'

Isabella whirred into life once again, before nodding sorrowfully. Her eyes avoided mine as she ghosted behind her son, but I detected a regret that she would no longer be able to berate me with her conservative views on life. We enjoyed bating one another while Gabrielle played umpire.

'It's a shame it had to come to this,' Pascal said as Mamie took the stairs. 'You were a good man, Berthier. They tell me you were also a good agent, among our very best.'

'And yet here we are?'

He nodded. 'You had help. In London and again in New York.'

So, despite it all, they still didn't know. So much for all the infallible facial recognition. That was the result of pensioning off the human intelligence in favour of anti-social college kids from darkened bedrooms. There were no eyes to review the camera footage and recognise the darling of the VST. 'She's dead.'

Pascal shook his head. 'I don't think so. You've left a trail of bodies, but hers was not among them.'

'She was shot in New York and died later in my arms. She'll wash up along the Hudson soon enough. Thanks to you and your bloody band of murderers.'

Waving the gun, Pascal directed me further into the room, away from the door and in front of the enormous glass wall that afforded Isabella her god-like view beyond the trees to Fontainebleau. 'You expect me to believe that?'

'I don't care what you believe. You've long since lost touch with reality. This dream you're pursuing of a *new* France–'

'There is nothing new in our aims.'

'And your use of a media tycoon to manipulate the masses? I suppose there is nothing new in your targeted use of propaganda either, brainwashing the uninitiated into believing your warped view of the world? Tell me how that sits with your patriotism.'

'We're not the first to use technology to help enlighten the proletariat–'

'Oh, spare me the sermon. You and your cronies are shovelling dirty money into buying up media space and funding a political campaign to launder it, furthering your own warped aims in the process. That's about the long and short of it. Isn't that right?'

Pascal laughed.

'Well now Delfont knows the truth. That's what Eric was doing. Digging into your filthy little plot on Delfont's behalf. And since I delivered the man the remaining evidence, he has everything he needs to expose you all. Your murderous little cabal at the heart of our secret service–'

Laughing even harder, Pascal waved his gun, a bead of sweat glinting on the breach. 'Oh Berthier. You really are a bigger fool than I credited. You think Delfont will expose us and undermine his entire campaign when he sits on the threshold of power? And risk his own neck in the process? Of course he won't. He values his life a great deal more than you, my former friend, appear to value yours. And anyway, what is there to expose?'

'You're shovelling donations into *Fraternité* by spending

millions on campaigns that set the political agenda. But what's the source of *your* money? Russia. You're bankrolled by the Kremlin You're taking *Russian* money and using it to further your own aims.'

'And what if we are? We were once on the same side before, weren't we? Didn't your own father serve alongside the Cossacks? Sometimes your enemy's enemy can be your best friend, you know.'

I backed towards the glass.

'You know your problem, Berthier? You're an *idealist*. You and your cousin both. The naïvety of your righteousness blinds you to the reality around you. If you want to get things done, to really succeed, there is no option but to bend and break the rules. That's how we achieve progress. That's how *I* achieved progress. Not through endless layers of bureaucracy and argument. *Action*, Berthier. That's what gets results. It always has and always will.'

'The end justifies the means.'

'Exactly! Now, I think it's time I took you in.' He clicked the safety off and back on for effect, like he'd seen in some cheap movie. 'Turn around and place your hands behind your back. I'm going to cuff you. And don't think I won't put a bullet in your spine. What with you breaking into my mother's property and threatening her.' A broad smile flashed across his cheeks. Ever the policeman.

But before I could move, Pascal's eyes were drawn to the bright red dot which traversed his face and then settled stationary over his blackened heart.

'Sorry. I lied about her being dead.'

TWENTY-FOUR

Wrapped in a thick black coat, she moved sedately through the park, a cup in one hand, her mobile in the other. Her thumb flicked the screen across a diet of bulletins that were neither new nor news but remained the accepted propaganda of the hour. There was a grace to her I had not observed before. Gliding more than walking, she avoided the knot of winter tourists by simply keeping going, expecting them to clear her path, which of course they did. And not with hesitance or scorn, but simply because she was there. Because her progress demanded submission just like it always had. Here and there they looked away. Here and there a glance became a look and lingered far too long.

Perhaps the passing of time or my new independent status had lent me new powers of surveillance, opened eyes that were formerly half-blind. Or was it that recent events had blessed me with an unexpected ignorance, ripped down that veil of certainty through which I viewed the world? In any case, she no longer resembled the woman I thought I knew.

Among the rank and file, she descended the stairs to the walkway beside the river, her back to the fast-flowing water swollen by autumn's rain. The deluge had released the pungent odour of the Seine, that singular stale reminder of the mystery lurking beneath the brown surface and reflecting our capital's incestuous sins. Today the sun shone, but a cruel wind reminded me that there were harsher times ahead. It was already mid-afternoon and in an hour our star would slink away, afraid to heat the city after dark. Paris was colder than ever it had been.

I followed her along the riverbank towards the office where her shift started later these days, her responsibilities diminished because of me. No longer was she welcome in the beating heart of the organisation. No more was she the alpha female with her finger on the pulse.

After half a kilometre, she climbed towards the Pont de Bir-Hakeim.

Now was undoubtedly my best opportunity.

Waiting until she was almost out of sight, I darted up the stairs between the crowd, hidden by their winter fur and scarfs, careful not to create a disturbance that would draw their ire and cause a scene. The bridge was the most beautiful in town and its rows of formal colonnades helped to mask my approach. Above, the Metro train rattled ever onwards, hauling lazy tourists away from lunch. Ahead, the rows of amateur photographers posed to remember their visit to our infamous city of love.

Was this its most romantic setting? I didn't have time to stop and contemplate such dreams despite the heart-warming waft of roasting chestnuts from the brigade of sellers.

She was but fifty metres ahead, negotiating the thin crowd by chance and habit. Until halfway across the bridge when she stopped suddenly. Ghosting to the iron railings, she lifted the coffee to her lips and gazed at the great iron pyramid that defined our home. Even in winter, its legs swarmed with visiting ants hurrying in the cold to claim the summit.

'I wondered when you'd come. I know you've followed me before.'

'And yet you never changed your routine?'

She sighed. 'Some things are inevitable, no matter how we avoid them.' Her eyes didn't leave the tower.

Sliding closer I pressed my hand to her back from which she did not flinch.

'Did you enjoy your work?'

It was a strange question and one I could not answer easily. 'I always thought I was on the right side. I was satisfied with that.'

'And now?'

'Now I know there are no sides but mine. In future, I will let my conscious be my only guide.'

She turned sharply and I caught a whiff of the scent I knew so well. Florals, lavender, and lingering memories I would have a lifetime to bury. 'That's it? That's all you have to say, after everything you've done?'

'Would you have me apologise?'

'Yes! Of course. You ruined everything. And for what? For revenge? Only a fool does not recognise revenge is a cancer. Another death doesn't erase the past, doesn't resurrect the dead. Look at what it's done to you. Look at what it's done to *us*, Berthier. You've sentenced us all.'

She was right. I was now an outlaw. The innocent Nicole was dead. Pascal was in the custody of his former friends where he would languish unsentenced for the remainder of time since his was the sole recorded confession. Mamie would now live out her life without the presence of her loyal son. Only the fat bureaucrat had escaped unharmed, his reputation soaring thanks to me. And as for Gabrielle–

'Well, what's next? Do you have a plan?'

I did.

Lifting the hem of her coat, I slipped the syringe into her thigh, watching as surprise became acceptance, her eyes rolling back and her limp body falling into my arms. Lowering her gently down against the railings, I sat beside her and let her still head rest on mine. My arm around her shoulders, we were simply two lovers escaping from the tedium of time.

I would wait until the thinning crowds dispersed and then she would join the other sins beneath the Seine. No matter what she felt about revenge, victims deserved their justice and sometimes it fell not to the courts but liars to deliver it.

TWENTY-FIVE

Leclerc winced and for the first time I detected an ogrish satisfaction despite his claimed regret. He kicked at the battered briefcase by his feet, sliding it toward me. 'It's a grim business, Berthier. The very grimmest.' Glancing at his watch, he summoned the waiter. 'Did she say anything before she died?'

'She was sorry they gave you the job.'

He scoffed. 'No ID or mobile, I trust?'

What did the fool take me for? 'Just a written confession and a love-letter to a certain Remy Leclerc. It's pretty graphic too–'

'Alright, alright.' He raised a hand. 'You made your point. You're a professional. We'll wait until she washes up and claim another suicide.'

I thought about the pathologist passing his whispered prognosis for a second time, while Leclerc ordered for us both – two plain omelettes, two small salads, two even smaller beers – before waving the disgruntled waiter away again. 'Your other villain isn't very forthcoming. They've given him a proper going over at *Tourelles*. He claims it was a small cabal of fanatics. Refuses to give up any other names.'

'And you believe him?'

Leclerc shrugged. 'Who knows what to believe any more–'

'Foucault?'

His giant eyes near exploded, before he roared with laughter. 'Christ, he doesn't have the wit. Not unless some lobbyist advised it. He'd rather take my children than responsibility. No, the old man is clean. Don't think I didn't check. I've been keeping tabs on him since the day I met Marie. As corrupt as they come, but Frank's no traitor. More's the pity.'

I believed him.

'And anyway. He values his daughter's happiness too much.'

'You make her happy?' I thought about the way Pascal still doted on Gabrielle.

'Fuck off. Just because you no longer work for me, don't think I can't have you arrested, or worse. There are plenty of volunteers only a telephone call away.'

'But right now, only one of us is carrying a gun.'

He hesitated. 'Anyway, our former chief of police will likely follow Christine to the morgue–'

'No!'

Looking up, Leclerc's eyebrows steepled.

'I mean, you can't. I don't believe him and even if I did, I might yet need him.'

'*Need him?*'

'This isn't over, Leclerc. You said so yourself, we can still make use of the funds. We could make use of him in time too. *I* could make use of him. Whoever signed this off is still at large–'

Leclerc nodded. If he had a gram of intelligence beneath those kilos of flesh he would know the name of Pascal's daughter, and maybe then connect the dots. 'Tell me', he said lazily, as though this was no more than mere conversation, 'was that recording of his confession the only version in existence?' Even the awkwardness of his question betrayed its origins. He was never cut out for interrogation.

'If you mean, did I secrete a copy, what do you think?'

The waiter brought our beers, and I raised mine, waiting. Begrudgingly Leclerc nodded his irritated acceptance. 'A Mexican standoff, then.'

It was my insurance. The only reason I was still alive. One copy, along with Eric's evidence, was vested with the reluctant representative of the VST, and the other inside the safe of a coffee shop near avenue George V, with instructions for distribution in the event I failed to collect my usual order to my normal schedule. But the bureaucrat much preferred me alive in any event. He hadn't had someone off the books in whom he could place his complete trust before. Finally, he could start to do some dirty work of his own, without fear or favour. Except, of course, that he didn't own me and never would. I owned him. And he knew it. All the time I lived and breathed there was a noose around his neck linked inextricably to mine. The recording would bring him down inside the house. Impossible to claim ignorance. My continued existence was the surest guarantee of his prior knowledge. The perfect paradox.

'What next for you then?'

He echoed Christine before she died, but I had no such drastic plan for Leclerc. 'You tell me?'

'We're looking east again, of course. But you can't take all the credit for that.'

I couldn't. Russia no longer hid her iron aims inside a velvet glove. Their war had moved from media to murder, reigning a ferocious fire on former neighbours in the name of vanity. One man's monstrous agenda. A man who former colleagues of Leclerc across this very city where we sat had emboldened, turning a blind eye for the sake of security and washing dirty money through their books as efficiently as any mafia laundering operation. How many innocent lives had been bought by the oligarchs? It pained me even now to think of it.

'Isn't he doing a good enough job of killing his own?'

Leclerc paused. Fiddled with his enormous lapels. Looked towards the plasterwork in the café where we dined and lowered his shoulders and his voice despite the scarcity of other diners. 'We need to sew a little more discord and disruption, Berthier. Pull some triggers, point some fingers–'

'And you don't care who points at whom.'

'Quite. There's a list, of course. Viable targets. Some not as well as they might appear. Some a little clumsier than usual. And some more melancholy too–'

He said no more, nor did he need to.

Murder is a shameless habit at Le Troisième.

'I shall need a name for you, mind,' he said, taking a satisfying pull of his beer. 'And perhaps in time some colleagues. A little private service I… *we* can call our own.'

His ego knew no bounds since he inherited the top floor. And perhaps now a fool was back in charge we could finally undo the complex web of deceit spun by his predecessor. Maybe the world was a safer place when incompetence was the worst of our flaws.

The food arrived and Leclerc speared his with relish.

He stopped his fork in mid-flight.

'Le *Quatrième!*' He began to laugh before stuffing his face. Grinning through a mouthful he repeated again. 'Le Quatrième, eh, Berthier?'

The End

ACKNOWLEDGEMENT

I should like to thank my wife and family for the forebearance, tolerance and support, as I combine my working life with my aspiration of becoming a full-time author. I should also like to thank anyone who purchased, borrowed or even stole this book. If you enjoyed it, please tell your friends. If you didn't, please tell me. You'll find me on social media. But be warned, I know some very interesting people, Berthier prime among them...

ABOUT THE AUTHOR

Stephen J. Prior

Stephen Prior has worked in communications for more than thirty years. His clients include many of the world's leading defence and security companies, as well as government and  military agencies. He combines his time between London and southwest England, where he lives with with his wife and their dog.

	AM	PM	Eve
Sun		Beach	
Mon			
Tue		[snorkelling trip] 4×50	
Wed	Ruby call		
Thu	← Boat rental →		
Fri		Venice 4×85	
Sat			
Sun			

~~events @ skylon at~~

~~Stay~~ event @ skylon @
at

Printed in Dunstable, United Kingdom

evolve ~~events coffe~~ collection. com